Also by Vica Miller

SHORT STORIES

The Room
Charlie's Angel
Aunt Lucy

POETRY

Big Little World (Collection)

Ladno Books titles may be purchased for educational, business, or sales promotional use. For information, please email promo@ladno.com

FIRST EDITION

Library of Congress Cataloguing-in-Publication Data has been applied for.

Publication Date:	May 14, 2014, from Ladno Books

All rights reserved.	© Victoria Miller 2012
Cover photo:	© Ruslan Lobanov, 2008
Cover design:	TM/R Design
Back cover & interior design:	Yelena Ebel

ISBN-10:	0-9913834-0-0
ISBN-13:	978-0-9913834-0-5

Vica Miller

Inga's Zigzags

a novel

Ladno Books

Посвящается моей маме.

For my Mom.

"The question isn't who is going to let me; it's who is going to stop me."

Ayn Rand, *The Fountainhead*

· 1 ·

Perhaps I should have never returned to Russia. My life would have been a straighter road, with fewer bumps and turns. Yet the most thrilling adventures lie hidden around the corner about to be turned. Or so I thought.

It was June when I left New York City. June 22, 1997, to be precise, a week after I had signed my divorce papers, a month after I'd received my MBA. I couldn't wait to board the plane to Moscow, to escape the scorching heat of the city, to be suspended in air-conditioned anonymity that would shield me from the recurring thought that my thirst for Russia – a thirst fueled by my aggravation with business school – had killed my marriage to Mark.

Wobbling on the gray carpet towards the airplane, surrounded by overweight tourists, bronzed businessmen, and flashy young Russians, I felt I was leaving behind a decade wasted on trying to belong in the land of the dollar, to have a degree from a prestigious school, to comprehend the surface emotions of American men. In the end, on that fading summer day of my ninth year in New York, I found myself a double single – *divorced with no boyfriend* – with a pile of student loans and a dried-up bank account.

Back then, I didn't know that I represented a whole class of people itching with ambitious plans for their former homelands. My only claim to fame was a year-long contract with a recently opened Obundy Moscow office, where I'd be a consultant from New York with an MBA and flawless English, not a poor Russian immigrant living in Yorktown walk-up. My best friend Kristina, another St. Petersburg transplant, advised me against going to Russia. She'd always said that New York supplied everything a person could ever dream of. But Kristina was happily married, trying to conceive. We lived on different planets.

When we had first met, for the whole first year of our life in New York, Kristina and I would walk up and down Broadway, peeking into the comforts of family brunches at cozy restaurants, so unattainable to us, or picking out the strangest character on the street – from a man in drag to a woman with dreads, entangled and unwashed, that almost reached her knees – marveling that no such characters existed in St. Petersburg. Looking around and talking about love, we'd walk from Washington Square Park all the way up to 72nd Street and Broadway, trying on New York life as if to see if it would fit, as if we still believed that our sojourn to the U.S. was only temporary. Kristina still made mistakes when she wrote in English, despite her own decade in the city and her sociology degree from Hunter College; despite her being married to an American.

I stepped on the plane and instantly became Russian, as if dipped into a pool filled with my former countrymen, pushing back the thought that a journey started on the anniversary of the Nazi invasion of Russia was bound to be a disaster. New York was fading, frozen in a glass box, its Manhattan voices muted, images blurred, problems forgotten.

Aeroflot's Nordic beauties greeted me with sparkling smiles, proudly wearing crisp red-and-white uniforms, bearing no resemblance to their stern and indifferent colleagues of just a few years earlier. As I inched towards my seat, a couple of young Russians ahead of me, Kate Moss-slim and dressed in Prada, turned back and rolled eyes at their former countrywomen walking in the other aisle, clearly residents of Brighton Beach, draped in leopard skin and see-through tunics. As I watched them struggling to stow their bags and briefcases before others did, I felt connected to both groups of Russians, even though I didn't represent or belong to either. Or, at least, didn't feel that I did.

"Just look at this one, for instance," a man's husky voice behind me said in English. "Excellent example of what Moscow has to offer – gorgeous, tall, slender, with big eyes and tight boobs. I noticed her in the lounge."

Another man answered, "And I hear they're all an easy lay. That's the best part."

I turned around.

"You have your facts wrong," I said, hoping they could feel the needles darting from my eyes. "Only whores and the most desperate single mothers will sleep with overweight aging men like you, so don't get your hopes too high. And I'm not from Moscow."

The men, their hair gray, both in dark-blue blazers that didn't hide their weight issues, looked at me as if they were fish thrown ashore, gasping for air. The fat-cheeked one behind me turned the color of beets. "*Suki*," I muttered as I turned away – loud enough for them to hear but not understand. *Fuckers.*

My blood boiling, I wondered if anyone else had heard their remarks or if I was the only one left to feel insulted for the female population of Moscow. I landed in my seat, the men hidden by the rows ahead of me, and opened the *New York Times,* my hands shaking.

The front page had a tale about yet another wildly successful enterprise launched in Moscow: a chain of exclusive health clubs, with a six-month waiting list to join, not to mention a $36,000 annual fee. Apparently, things had changed over there. I'd read a flood of such stories while sweating over my MBA at NYU's Stern. This enterprise, however, had not only been started by someone my own age, but by a woman, which made me itch even more. I, too, wanted to live on the last frontier of the Wild East, and make things happen, instead of slaving in a New York cubicle, spending hours on market research and analysis, comparing profit margins and revenues of companies I didn't care about, all the while treated like a borderline idiot due to my accent. I wanted a Cinderella tale; my immigration story had worn me out.

For years, I'd been trying on America like a new skin, yet I didn't belong anywhere. As if sitting on two chairs, I was afraid to fall in between Russia and the U.S., into nothingness, where neither country would claim me as its own. Nine years in New York had left me haunted by "What if?" *What if* the real me had been left in Russia? I'd stopped sleeping at night.

The captain's voice – breaking, in Russian, into my

reverie – told us to prepare for departure. We lifted off, and, watching Jones Beach and Far Rockaway shrink into thin lines, I knew I was running away. I was tired of New York, with its neurotic men looking for their perfect matches before they turned fifty, all the while comparing their year-end bonuses and real estate decisions. I missed the dirty Russian sense of humor, un-translatable into "American." I missed the way men flirted in Russia without being offensive or crass, the warmth of intimate conversations with friends, and drinking into the wee hours to the sound of someone's guitar. And I wanted to speak my native tongue, without foreign words getting stuck inside my brain. But at that moment, I wanted to be still and quiet, to swim in the evasive nothingness of the nine-hour flight. It was the first time I'd be allowed to do nothing about being in between.

Only once the 747 had broken through the clouds and reached cruising altitude did I push my seat back and try to sleep, my efforts rendered futile by the screams of an infant two rows behind me. I turned the pages of the issue of *Poise* magazine the woman on the right had lent me. As I knew from seeing the cover, the center spread was devoted to Airplanes, the band of a man from St. Petersburg who'd been the beginning of the end of my marriage: Anton. I smiled and turned off the lights, and almost immediately, the infant behind me stopped his howling. I thought how nice it would be to find myself in Anton's bed again. He was the best lover I'd ever had – and I'd had a few. But mostly I yearned to be understood without having to translate my emotions from English into Russian, which had always been the case with my ex-husband.

As I succumbed to sleep, I dreamed of Anton's hands gliding over my breasts as if I were his guitar. But I was soon awakened by a thud. The slim lady on my left had dropped a stack of papers. She leaned forward, hurriedly collecting the pages scattered on the floor. I turned on the light above my seat to help her look. She was in her mid-forties, dressed in black – as if in mourning – with a long, pale face and tree bark-colored hair held by a massive hairclip. A few locks fell over her forehead as she tried to reach under the seat across the aisle. I picked up a few pages and handed them to her.

"Thank you," she said. "I'm going to adopt a little girl." I couldn't tell if she'd been speaking to me or to everyone who looked on. Once all the papers were back on her lap, she pulled out a photograph and held it under my reading light. I saw a small, round face framed by white curls and giant blue eyes lingering in sadness – a true child of St. Petersburg.

"Tanya is an orphan," the woman confided. "Nobody wants her but me. Yet they keep asking for additional paperwork and proof of income. Why are they making it so hard? I'm the only chance she'll ever have."

"I wish you luck," I told her.

"It's my fifth visit," she said. "I think my luck ran out a while back."

We sat quietly for a few minutes watching as *Fried Green Tomatoes* played on the screens in front of us.

"Why are you going to Russia?" she asked me.

"It's my home." Or was it? My mother had died a year after I arrived in New York; my father remarried six years later; and Mark, my American husband, couldn't handle the pendulum of my "Russian" moods – from complete melancholy and nostalgia bordering on depression to the throbbing exhilaration of living in New York, the coolest city in the world. Where was my home?

"Your English is very good. I can hardly detect an accent," she said. *Why did they always have to talk about accents?*

"You're too kind. I have an accent, all right." Then I paused, stunned by a thought that I found to be quite original. "But my emotional accent is even stronger..."

She gave me a strange look.

"You see, I think that the soul of every relocated person has an accent. Even though I've considered myself a New Yorker for a while now, my Russian sensibility takes over rather often, sometimes when I least expect it, and then I feel completely lost, out of place. Worst of all, I feel that *nobody* understands me in those moments. Nobody."

She kept looking at me with a concerned expression.

"It's actually a great thing, to have double the feelings. But sometimes it gets really hard." I paused, surveying the clouds beneath us, the sun crawling towards the horizon. "It might affect your future daughter, too. But then, I came to New York when I was 20, and she's only two. So maybe she'll become a nice all-American girl and you'll have nothing to worry about."

I didn't know why I felt compelled to present that diatribe to my neighbor. But it's always easier to pour out your true feelings to a stranger: they're like a safe deposit box the key to which will be lost forever once you step off the plane.

She looked out the window, too, shuffling the papers on her lap, then turned back to me, her lips stretching into a half smile, her mouth sagging on the left, as if afraid she might have made a mistake by wanting a child from Russia. What if they all turned into such strange characters as the woman next to her, with her heavy *emotional accent*?

"Sorry. I'm sort of moving back to Russia after a long time in the U.S., and it makes me very nervous," I explained.

"It's okay," she said. "I often feel like nobody understands me either, and I only speak one language and have lived my whole life in the small town where I was born." She bit her lips to hold back tears, and I cursed myself for starting the subject. "Chatham, New Jersey. Have you heard of it?"

I did: the hometown of my ex-husband – a small one, indeed.

"No, I haven't."

"It's a nice little place. Not many attractions, but the Christmas Fair is great. The main square gets so festive, lights everywhere, the carousel right in the middle, church bells ringing – like a fairytale. We're all really proud of it."

I struggled not to roll my eyes. The Christmas Fair. Did I "know about it"? I'd gone to it three years in a row. It was always followed by the same half-dozen parties, where I had to pay respects to all the friends of Mark's parents, always feeling like a black sheep – *the Russian wife! In a black mini-dress!* Having to talk to people I didn't know (all dressed in variations of checkered green and red, from blouses to ties, as if competing for "The Most Ridiculous Christmas Outfit" award), always answering the same idiotic questions: *So how do you like it here? You're in business school? How admirable! Very impressive for a person who just got here.*

Strange that I hadn't encountered the woman sitting

next to me at one of those parties.

"Sounds great," I said.

"I hope Anna will see it one day," she said, biting her lip. "My daughter."

"I'm sure she will."

The woman fetched an apple from her red leather bag and bit into it as if trying to scare the Russian authorities that kept her from becoming a mother.

"Are you from Moscow?" she asked.

"St. Petersburg. But I have lots of friends in Moscow." I had two: Dmitry Vernik, an old friend from high school who was picking me up at the airport, and Sanjay Ameshvari, a friend from New York who'd agreed to let me stay at his Moscow apartment for a few weeks until I found my own. "But, if you don't mind, I really need to get some sleep," I said, hopefully not too tersely. The woman shrugged and continued eating her apple.

I turned off the reading light, put on my headphones and closed my eyes, the latest Russian pop music flowing into my ears – Zemfira, Shura and Linda. I hadn't even asked my seatmate's name. Never mind. I was on my way to a country where small talk didn't exist, and I couldn't wait to get there.

· 2 ·

Moscow's Sheremetyevo airport greeted me with glowing billboards, a renovated ceiling with blinding lights, and porters in uniforms swooshing by. All new. Heavy-set Russian men puffed on cigarettes under a "No Smoking" sign. The usual. Curvaceous, middle-aged women in tight jeans teetered on stilettos towards the luggage belts, and gray-faced border patrol guards followed them with flat eyes. The familiar whirlpool of Soviet leftovers and Western innovations was pulling me in. The ads for credit cards from Citibank, 18% mortgages from Dialogue Bank, sushi at Radisson-Slavyanskaya hotel. Who, exactly, were these ads for? The Russians who didn't have credit, had no idea what "mortgage" meant, and had never tried sushi, or the visitors who didn't speak Russian and, even if they did, would think the financial offers ludicrous? Maybe they were for people like me – in-between ads for in-between people.

I was lucky I didn't have to fight for a cab. Dmitry Vernik towered above the greeters, holding white lilies, my favorite flowers. At first, I didn't recognize him. I had somehow foolishly expected the Dmitry I'd last seen eight years ago – tall and skinny, with nervous hands and a shy smile on his round face, framed by unruly curls the color of wheat. New wrinkles had appeared under his pale blue eyes, and more weight padded his midsection. His gaze had become more self-assured, and the smile had a touch of condescension. It hadn't been that way when he first tried to kiss me, a dozen years ago, in the school cafeteria. That fleeting attraction, unreturned and long forgotten, made me feel at home. I smiled back as he cut through the crowd.

He walked with the swagger of a man who had it all. There was a new softness, almost a delay, in the way he moved, as if he was too important to be in a rush, observing the airport crowd from his private plane, cruising above the frantic human movements below. A black market trader turned marketing executive, he exuded satisfaction and earnestness of an overachiever. For me, he'd always be the kid I met twenty years ago, when I didn't have to wear a bra and he didn't have to shave. We had always been friends. Then, when we turned 20, I traveled to New York as part of a newly-instituted student exchange program, and he moved to Moscow to study business. We both wanted to try new things when the chance had presented itself – and had both gotten stuck in metropolises that weren't home. We hadn't seen each other in eight years; letters, photos and international phones calls, at $1.50 a minute, had kept our friendship alive.

"Inga Belova! Just look at you!" He hugged me with such force that I almost tripped. "You cut your hair! And where'd you get the tan?"

"Look at *you*!" I said.

Decked out in a dark-gray suit, he beamed with pride, his new paunch held in by a black leather belt with a small silver buckle, visible under the jacket, the last button of which was properly unfastened. We walked to a shiny dark-green BMW, too clean-looking for Moscow. Dmitry dangled the car keys and smiled at me.

"Last year you sent a picture of a different one, no?" I said.

"Good eye, Belova. Yes – that's a new one. Gotta keep up with the times," he said, opening the door for me. "It's either a Bimmer, a Mers, or no respect."

I couldn't hold back a smile. He'd always kept up

with the times, first trading Soviet pins and fur hats for T-shirts from American tourists, a decade later moving into a marketing position at one of the U.S. firms in Moscow. A seamless transition.

He drove us through a newly-built parking lot, past yellow guard poles and ticketing machines, and flew toward Leningradsky Prospect and the center of Moscow.

"Are you staying with that journalist friend of yours – what's-his-face?" Dmitry asked. "I saw him the other night. He lives somewhere in the center."

"Sanjay. He is on Sivtsev Vrazhek, near Tverskoy Boulevard."

"Has he published anything recently?"

"Something in *Newsweek*, I think."

"Looks like things didn't go that well for him in New York," Dmitry said with his usual cynicism. "If they did, he'd be stationed here as a foreign correspondent, not a freelancer, right?"

"You know it's easier for them to start careers overseas and return back with impressive-sounding titles. *After* that, they get stationed as correspondents."

"Maybe."

He stomped on the gas pedal; I grabbed the door handle. At least one other thing hadn't changed in Moscow: in no other city on Earth did people drive with such suicidal zeal.

It was a sparkling June morning. The sun painted the first strips of hazy yellow across the pavement. The trees stepped out of their silhouettes along Leningradsky Prospect; the road glittered. Mercedes and BMWs flew by, putting to shame dusty Ladas and Moskviches crawling in the right lane. New billboards offered kitchen appliances and furniture from top Italian suppliers, jewelry and shoes from boutiques on Tverskaya. Yet the buildings behind and around those billboards looked just as old and run-down as before, and the morning pedestrians presented a tired gray mass featuring babushkas, with their worn-out *avos'kas* – all-purpose shopping bags. Would I fit with this mix of new wealth spread against the fading panorama of the Soviet past?

"Obundy didn't get you an apartment, being a global agency and all?"

"I told them I'd find one myself. Didn't want to live alone right away."

"I still can't believe you got divorced," muttered Dmitry. "Why did you leave Mark?"

I looked at him sideways. "If you need to know, I left him because he wasn't Russian enough."

Dmitry looked at me as if doubting my mental health.

"How could he have been, born and raised in New Jersey?" he said.

"I don't know, but he could have tried."

"You're insane, Belova," Dmitry said, lighting a cigarette even though he was driving. "But you're *it*: smart, beautiful, the *crème de la crème*. And don't forget: long legs, perky boobs – the whole shebang. And they love this combo even more here in Mother Russia, so you'll do great."

"I hope so," I said. "I got really tired of New York. You know how men pick you up in a bar? It's always the same: *Oh, you are from Russia. Your English is so good!*

– So is yours.

– How do you like it here?

– How do you like it here?

– I live here.

– So do I.

Seriously, getting away from that is already worth the trip."

"Then why don't you move back for good? Not just for a year – forever. It made sense to be in New York in 1990; at least they had food there, unlike us. But now Moscow is the place to be! And you know it, Belova – *that's* why you're here. There is so much money and so many idiots. We could move mountains together. But you need more than a year for that. And what's so special about New York? You can travel half the world on the money you spend on rent there."

"Thanks for letting me know." I rolled down the window

and put my hand out, the wind caressing my palm. "I did want to start my own company, but not in New York. Too crowded. Everything you think of – someone is already doing it. You know, I sent a proposal to McLadley to open a rep office in Moscow. They never answered. That was supposed to be my reason for returning to Russia, but they never answered. So, Obundy saved my ass."

"Still not bad. You can always start a company after your contract is over, right? I'd love to work with you, my dear – you know it. Remember, we shared a desk in high school. That's a bond for life, if you know what I mean." He waved his hand in the air as if tying a knot and winked at me.

We laughed as if we were back in our teens, when everything was possible and ahead of us – love, adventures, success, recognition. Dmitry held the steering wheel with one hand, wiping tears away with another. I laughed until I had a coughing fit. He tapped me on my back and then put his hand on my knee as if to keep from falling over. I removed it. After all, Dmitry was a married man. We crossed the bridge from Leningradsky Prospect towards the Belorusskaya metro and entered the city center.

The car pulled into a quiet backyard. We unloaded my bags at the entrance to the Soviet-style skyscraper, the kind in which Politburo members would once have lived: large windows, high ceilings, solid metal door guarding the lobby. I rang the buzzer, waited, and rang again. Nothing. Dmitry and I sat down on my suitcases by the entrance and waited. I was too tired to worry whether I'd have to look for another place to stay.

"How is your dad doing?" Dmitry asked.

"He's good. I think. We don't talk much. In the last letter, he congratulated me on graduating from NYU and wished me good luck in business – no mention of love. I guess he still resents me for divorcing Mark."

"You're overthinking it. Your dad has always been supportive of you. He just wants you to conquer the world and is being polite about the rest." Dmitry lit another cigarette.

"Maybe. I'm going to St. Pete in a couple of weeks. I really miss it." I turned to face Dmitry. "Don't you?"

"I do, and I don't. Everything that's important in my life is right here, in the capital. No nostalgia for this guy."

"Good for you."

Nostalgia was my constant companion. And I really missed my mother.

A half-hour later, Sanjay appeared in the archway, a notebook under his arm.

"Thanks for being home on time, dear!"

Sanjay looked at me, dark circles pronounced under his

brown Indian eyes. He'd emailed that he had to attend a VIP event for Bosco di Ciliegi the night before my arrival, so I took no offense at this grim greeting. He'd probably spent the night shacked up with some strange woman he'd met in a bar, whom he'd lubricated with enough Stoli to float whatever was left of the Russian Navy, and had rushed home (almost) in time to greet me. His breath reeked of yesterday's coffee, cigarettes, and metabolized vodka. Welcome to Moscow!

Sanjay's three-room apartment was light and spacious. A blossoming tree outside cast curvy shades on the yellow walls of his living room – now my bedroom. Birds chirped in the yard, fighting for bread. I opened the window. A row of babushkas occupied a bench at the entrance below, feeding the birds and gossiping. It felt like home.

"You look tired," I told Sanjay as he walked into the kitchen and turned on the radio.

"You do, too," he said without looking at me before walking into his room, as if preoccupied with something. He returned with black socks in one hand and a notepad in another.

"Want to grab something to eat?"

"Let me take a shower first."

Afterwards, I put on a pair of designer jeans and a white tailored shirt with an open collar, hoping that New York "business casual" would translate into Russian. Sanjay also changed into a white shirt and a dark gray corduroy jacket that clashed with his baggy, beige-linen pants, an issue of *Poise* magazine in his hands. He could have taken some lessons in style from Dmitry.

We decided to walk to the restaurant. It was warm and quiet – that magic time before the sun was about to start its descent, the air still and transparent, soft wind whispering inside the tree crowns. As we walked along the shady boulevard, I couldn't help comparing Moscow to Manhattan. Couples kissed on the benches, neither teenagers nor exhibitionists, just lovers celebrating summer. Young women, slender and big-eyed, strolled hand in hand, yet they weren't lesbians. New Russians, those with recently-made (mostly illegal) fortunes, rushed by with cell phones – still rare gadgets on the streets of Moscow – jammed to their ears. I almost felt at home, the balmy evening reminding me of many such strolls I had taken along the Neva in St. Petersburg, when the evening air was full of possibilities, the sun refusing to descend as if commanding the summer to never end, installing the reign of the White Nights for June and July, with no room for darkness.

We approached the renovated Church of Christ the Savior, with the ever-present babushkas feeding bread-crumbs to fat pigeons, as if determined to exterminate their hunger forever. The Church reminded me of a plump bride, sitting on the river's edge and waiting for her fiancé to appear with flowers from the station. Some people did bring flowers. As I watched them, I remembered black-and-white images from old documentaries: the church ravaged to the ground, an open-air pool built in its place, swimmers splashing. Then my country had found temporary sanity in 1987, and a decade later the church had been resurrected, its renovation the main present for Moscow's 850th birthday.

We kept quiet, as if obeying the stillness surrounding us, and crossed the square into *pereulki*, curved side streets left untouched by urban development and city noise. Quiet and dreamy, lined with trees and two-story houses, they always felt like old St. Petersburg to me, with their names so tangible in their noun-ness – Ostojenka, Ordynka, Sivtsev Vrazhek – unlike 3rd Sovetskaya or East 23rd Street. I'd missed such streets the most at lunchtime in Midtown Manhattan, where I'd had to search frantically for a quiet bench on which to eat my sandwich during the 20 minutes allowed for lunch outside the office.

I looked up and saw a glass-and-metal concoction of a building, ten stories high, with darkened windows slanted in multiple directions, as was the fashion in mid-'90s Moscow. An ornamental sign above a heavy wooden door read *Tamerlane*, with carvings that could have been inscriptions from the Koran.

"The first Korean restaurant in Moscow," said Sanjay.

We entered a sprawling room with rows of large square tables on the left, alongside floor-to-ceiling windows adorned with silk yellow curtains. Three large barbecue mangals were lined up on the right. Behind each, a chef in national costume – embroidered maroon caftan and a round skullcap – prepared meals.

A hostess in a long, heavy silk gown, also maroon, escorted us to a table by the window, smiling shyly. It felt as if we had entered an ethnic museum. Despite the early hour, most of the tables were occupied: by young men in business attire; couples – heavyset men in suits with gold watches on their wrists and young women half their age in miniskirts across the table; and expats, mostly American, drinking beer and conversing loudly.

As we devoured our food, Sanjay filled me in on Moscow's new noteworthy establishments of 1997, speaking in Russian with a Georgian accent, as most Americans in Moscow did. There were two nightclubs run by Yugoslavs, the best being *Jazz Café*; a few upscale restaurants, *Mao* and *Justo* the trendiest of all; and a dozen or so fashion boutiques on Tverskaya Street and nearby. Sanjay then stopped short, swallowed hard, and pointed to a table across the aisle. "You know who that is?" He switched to English.

"Who?"

"That small woman with short dark hair. It's Alexandra Veil, publisher of *Poise*."

"So?"

"I have a meeting with her tomorrow, but I'm afraid of her."

"Why? And isn't she too young to be a magazine publisher?"

"She's 28. And she eats men for breakfast."

I studied her as she gesticulated to a man across from her. She moved her chopsticks as if they were a baton.

"Are you sure? She looks like an excited child. How did she get to be a publisher so fast?"

"Anything is possible in Moscow, my dear," Sanjay said. "She launched the damn thing."

"Why are you afraid of her?"

"She's the smartest person you'll meet in Moscow. Razor-sharp. Every time I talk to her, I feel like my balls are in her hands."

"That should feel nice, no? She's very cute." I imagined Alexandra's small hand on Sanjay's crotch, my laugh escaping into the wine glass.

"She's a lesbian. A business shark who treats men like shit. And I'm assigned a story on her: *Top Women of Russian Business*." I nodded. Sanjay kept looking at Alexandra across the aisle, a piece of chicken stuck on his immobile fork. "I wish I had a career like hers. She rules her kingdom – total control over the editorial, creative direction, you name it. Has the largest subscription base among young Russians, and their advertising revenue is through the roof." He opened his notebook as if to confirm his facts. "Every new brand that's launched in Russia becomes her advertiser. They run features on drugs and S&M and anything else that can shock and entice the youth. And they just got Coke to advertise with them – the first-ever print ad for Coke in Russia."

I listened with my head down, slowly succumbing to jetlag under the information overload. Why should I care about Alexandra Veil? I had my own business aspirations. Just then, a petite brunette approached our table. I stared at Alexandra Veil's small breasts, which were unfettered by a bra. Under a tight yellow T-shirt, separated by a *Prada* bag belt running diagonally across her chest, the nipples stared back at me insolently. I averted my eyes before looking up at her face. She was short and slender, something boyish about her, with a mischievous smile and a twinkle in her brown eyes, resin-black bangs falling over them. She studied me a moment, straightening her black pants. Before I knew it, she was joining our table.

"Sanjay, good to see you," she said, looking at me. She seated herself next to him, then held out her small hand across the table.

"Alexandra Veil."

"Inga Belova. Nice to meet you," I said and paused, sensing she wanted to know my connection to Sanjay. "I'm not his date," I added, wondering why I felt compelled to do so.

"Good."

She noticed the issue of *Poise* next to Sanjay's plate, and the smile disappeared from her lips. She put her small hand on top of Sanjay's, and he shrunk in his chair, managing a grunt of a hello. I could see his previous night's adventures were costing him dearly.

"Inga is a friend from New York," he said, his eyes begging me to carry on a conversation.

"I haven't been to New York in ages." Alexandra handed me her business card and I felt accepted, even though I wasn't sure into what. "I just need a quick word with Sanjay, if you don't mind. Can I treat you both to a drink for interrupting?" She gulped my water, raised a hand for the waitress, and ordered a bottle of Cuvée. I looked at the card. *Alexandra Veil. Publisher. Poise.* Cell phone and email.

"Sanjay, I know I owe you an interview, but I have to postpone it till next month."

"My deadline is the end of next week, you know," he said mournfully, but I could see his shoulders relax with the postponement.

Did Sanjay plan to write about her for *Newsweek* or was it for one of the local Moscow papers?

"Fine, we'll do it next week, then," she said, "but I was wondering if you might have some insider info for me. I've been trying to salvage fifty grand. Unsuccessfully, so far. That's the price of doing business with friends. This is off the record." She looked at me, inviting me to be her audience. "Friends of mine launched a company, an Internet provider. Perfect timing. They have a ton of money for advertising, including *Poise*." She paused and took down her bag, freeing her breasts from the separating strap. "Today they called the deal off. Despite the signed contract." She took a sip of water. "You know what they said? '*Poise* is too risqué.' Hello? We have their demographic by the balls!"

I looked at Sanjay, who shifted in his seat.

"And I know the guy loves the magazine," continued Alexandra. "It's his father, the investor, who pulled the string. I could have sued them – if we had laws, that is. Or I could send my *krysha* over to make them uphold the contract. But he's a friend, and we actually have the same *krysha* which makes it impossible to threaten them."

The wine arrived, and we watched the waitress pour, as if the solution to Alexandra's problem was hidden in the bottle and would come out any minute now. *My first*

lessons, I thought. *No friends in business. No laws in Russia.*
And you have to have a *krysha*, a roof – people with guns
protecting your business – something I'd neglected to
mention in my proposal to McLadley.

As I listened to her explaining all this, I was thinking
that her lost deal equaled the salary of a mid-level manager
in New York. I admired her guts and self-deprecation for
confessing her "failure" to a journalist who was supposed
to hail her achievements. I realized I wanted to sparkle
like her.

Sanjay sipped his tea, his narrow eyes toggling from
side to side, as if he were watching a tennis match.

"I think I know the company," he said. "InterCity?"

"Yes. Damn them."

"How can I help?"

"Can you maybe talk to these guys and explain that our
magazine is a mix of *Paper* and *Details*? Explain to those
stiffs that provocative is the best guarantee for consistent
readership and advertising revenue. *Everybody* wants to
read about sex and drugs and masturbation and everything
else we never talked about until five years ago. Talk to
InterCity, will you? If *Poise* gets an endorsement from
a foreign journalist, maybe they'll understand that advertising with me is safe. Look at Coke and Snickers and
Dialogue Bank already on my pages."

"On the subject of advertising, Inga is starting with

Obundy Moscow tomorrow," interjected Sanjay. "Maybe she can be useful to you."

I couldn't believe Sanjay was putting me on the spot. Alexandra looked at me as if she knew something I didn't, but should have.

"Really?" she said. "Why in Moscow and not in New York?"

"Things happen faster here," I replied.

"Well, maybe we should have lunch one day and talk advertising," she said curtly, as if dismissing the subject.

"I'll see what I can do," Sanjay said, turning back to Alexandra. "Can I have a favor, in return?" he added without blinking.

"What?"

"I want to mention your personal life in my article. We try to paint the whole picture: work and life balance type of thing."

"Must you? First of all, there is no such thing as work and life balance; it was invented by shrinks who charge you a shitload of money to give you an illusion that you're getting there. Second, I don't talk about my private life in Russia. Those who need to know already do." She looked at me, a complete stranger, considering her answer. She squinted, then smacked her lips as if stumbling upon an idea and said, "Off the record, I have a girlfriend. We've been together for three years. She's my partner in the magazine. Emma Krapivina."

The idiosyncrasy between her previously stated credo of having no friends in business, coupled with the admission that she worked with her lover, turned my impression of her upside down. But I had no time to ponder it. I was starting my new job in Moscow the next morning; my stellar career was waiting for me. Soon enough, I'd be interviewed by a business glossy myself. I was sure of it. I couldn't wait to get back to Sanjay's, to crash on the pullout couch in his yellow living room. I had to sleep off the jetlag before meeting my new boss in the morning.

· 3 ·

A few minutes before nine o'clock, I walked into Obundy's office on Tverskaya Street to find it empty and silent. I approached the reception desk and stood there, waiting. A moment later, a twenty-something woman with a short, spiky haircut appeared from underneath it. She wore red-rimmed rectangular glasses, and a tight red sleeveless shirt, that hugged her small breasts and exposed slim, tan biceps.

"Inga Belova?" she asked me with a professional smile.

"Good morning," I answered.

"I'm Natasha, office manager. We're expecting you," she said in English before switching to Russian. "Laura called. She's running a few minutes late: traffic on Rublevka as usual. Can I offer you some coffee while you wait?"

"Thank you."

She went to a coffee machine, walking on three-inch heels as if they were slippers, softly swaying her hips hugged by an abbreviated black skirt – just long enough so as not to cross the border between the hired employee of a Western advertising agency and one of the hookers that would flood the pavements just below those windows come nightfall. I couldn't help thinking of the many shapeless secretaries of an unidentifiable age, with "New Jersey" haircuts, oversized jackets, and sneakers worn under colorless skirts, that I'd encountered in clients' offices in New York.

I sat in a plush white leather chair observing the spacious office – all white, with red geometrical figures drawn on the walls corresponding to Obundy's logo, and white cubicles. Such offices hadn't existed in pre-*perestroika* Russia; back then, it had been all drab and gloom, from teacher's offices to factory director's suites, the monotonous repetitions of gray-blue walls and neon lights, shabby brown furniture and portraits of the Soviet leaders on the walls. This Natasha, a new breed of young professional, so self-assured and proud of her position, must have gotten the job through her family's connections to people in power, *po blatu*. She was too young to find employment like this on her own. None of my friends could have scored a job like hers. Natasha's father was probably one of Obundy's clients. Or partners. Or maybe I was underestimating the new generation of twenty-somethings.

I sipped my coffee. I myself was of that generation, yet not of Natasha's kind. At her age, after a brief honeymoon with the exchange program, I'd found myself on my own in New York City, with no money or family, spending close to a decade scraping through the granite of New York life: posing as a live model in a window of a fashion store, handing out leaflets on the streets for a newly-opened restaurant, waiting on tables until the restaurant closed at 1 AM, my feet buzzing and eyes burning from the smoke. And once, I was almost lured into sex for money under pretense of a photo shoot; I should have known better than to trust that sleazy, aging man at The Russian Samovar. I felt goose bumps running down my neck. Natasha nodded, her eyebrows slightly raised, as if asking whether everything was fine. I smiled.

"Beautiful office. Nicer than where I worked in New York."

"Everyone says so," she replied. "We just moved here a month ago."

I wondered if I'd get my own office – or, at least, a desk by the window, since I was their new special projects consultant – or whether I'd be locked up in one of the white cubicles.

"Let me show you to your desk." Natasha led me into

the labyrinth of cubicles, filled with employees who all seemed no older than 25, and introduced me as we passed. We stopped by my desk, which had a partial view of the side street. I approached the window. The lines to the world's largest McDonalds, down below, were already forming despite the early hour, the rest of Tverskaya Street still sleepy. I looked over the tops of the buildings, contemplating how I'd finally be making deals worthy of my MBA, advising Fortune 500 clients on their online-advertising strategy in the murky waters of the evolving Russian Internet.

We were on our way back to reception when the glass door opened and a woman in her late twenties walked in wearing a black skirt suit, white formal shirt, and sharp-toed Prada shoes, a bright red briefcase in her hand. She, too, wore rectangular glasses (with a red rim) and a short haircut, which made me wonder if Natasha was styling herself after her boss. The woman gave me a curt smile, nodded, and went into her office. Natasha followed. She returned a minute later and announced, "Laura will see you now."

I felt strange entering the large, loft-like office of Laura Paulson: windows floor-to-ceiling, Moscow's traffic humming below, street banners at eye level. I'd expected her to be a woman in her mid-forties, with a long career in advertising behind her and a welcoming attitude toward new employees. Instead, I saw my American peer, one who eyed me surreptitiously while trying her best to conceal her mistrust. *I could have been that woman,* I thought.

"Sorry I'm late. Please sit down."

I took a seat across from her desk and gave her my most sincere smile.

"We're glad to have you join us this summer. We have a tremendous amount of work in the regions ahead of us."

I sank into my chair. *Regions.* No, that couldn't be. Yet my English couldn't have been so poor. I must have heard her correctly. Even so, I wanted to make sure.

"You mean 'regions' as in 'provinces'? And 'us' would be 'me'?"

She looked at me as if trying to decipher whether I was dumb or just pretending to be.

"We'll bring you up-to-speed with our regional projects, and on Wednesday you should head to Tver'," she said. "It's the first one we're doing for the cola" – she named the brand – "a street festival. A lot of work – you'll need to make some 'ins' with the local government. Natasha will give you the details."

I was speechless for a moment. But then I thought that maybe this was a test. Or a joke. To see how I'd react to an assignment that couldn't possibly have been given to someone with an MBA from NYU. Because one didn't need that to navigate the Russian provinces. That much I knew. And so did Laura. In provinces, one needed connections, which I didn't have, and the ability to consume ungodly amounts of vodka, which I didn't drink.

She must have read the disappointment on my face. I detected a badly-concealed satisfaction. So I decided to play her game. I straightened up in my chair, put my hands on my knees, and let my eyebrows arch as if I were pleasantly surprised.

"I see… Well, I'm excited to help you with this challenging project! And once it's over – you know I'm here to help you with online advertising. The cola must have it in their plans, right?"

"We don't know yet," she said dismissively. "Tver' is the first stop; there are ten other cities after that. You're in charge of the whole campaign." I couldn't believe what I was hearing. "I fired the person who was supposed to run it. So you're his replacement. There'll be two junior account managers assisting you once you're done with Tver'. As for online ads, let me worry about getting additional budgets from our clients."

My throat was itching. I couldn't utter a sound. To run away from New York only to get entangled in someone else's old business in Moscow! What irony! My time was to be spent in obscure provinces, with muddy roads and one pub for the entire town, where I'd be in charge of changing the consuming habits of provincial punks. I inhaled and held my breath. Laura looked at me curiously. *Fine*, I thought. *You want tough? I'll show you tough. Russian provinces are nothing compared to the loneliness of New York.*

"Sounds great." I exhaled. "Can I go now? I'd like to look through the files right away."

"By all means." She looked at me as if she had pulled the wings off a bumblebee and was observing whether it would manage to fly again. Why was she such a bitch? I strode to my desk with my head high, smiling at the sea of faces, which blurred into a white fuzzy mass by the time I reached my desk.

I sat down in my chair, no longer savoring the June morning, feeling the news of how I'd be spending my summer adding to the depression I'd carried from New York. I mechanically flipped through a pile of brochures and folders that Natasha had brought me, becoming more depressed.

One of the files was dedicated to *Poise*. I opened it. Sanjay hadn't lied. The soft drinks, sportswear, and health clubs that had entered Russia in the last few years all had budget allocations for the magazine. I felt that the vision for my career in Russia and the actual career with which I had been presented were pointed in completely different directions. But I decided to fight. After all, I was a New

Yorker, and New Yorkers can deal with anything. Or anybody. Or so they think.

· 4 ·

On Wednesday, I found myself on a train. Obundy hadn't provided me with a car, as all of their cars had been assigned to other accounts. Mine was no ordinary train, but a *platzkart*, similar to the one we'd taken to the Black Sea back in the 1970s, with cramped, stuffy communal cabins occupied by overweight, sweat-and-sour smelling people – middle-aged women with disheveled hair, half-drunk men missing half of their teeth – all eating fried chicken and hardboiled eggs, their screaming kids running the length of the car because there were no doors between *platzcart* compartments. I had four hours of this to go – four hours to reach the heart of Russia.

As I sat on a wooden bench that made my ass feel as stiff as the wood itself, a large woman in her mid-sixties across from me, dressed in a light-blue, washed-out robe, started cursing Yeltsin and his government for letting the country go into a freefall. *"Yebanye raspizdyai, shtoby ix zadralo!"* Sweating profusely, her unwashed gray hair covered with a black net, the woman spit out curses so spicy and tangible that I felt Russia taking me over. I couldn't resist.

Her son, Kirill, was a war veteran and an invalid: both of his legs had been amputated during the war in Afghanistan in the 1980s, when he was 22. Upon his return to Moscow, Kirill had been promised an apartment of his own, but after nine years, he was still living in a communal flat with his mother and three other families – nine people to four rooms. I took out my notepad and jotted down some of her expressions to remember for later. *"Pizdoblyatstvo! Chtoby u nix khuj ne stoyal!"* She kept pointing her finger at me and other listeners, cursing the government. The woman had probably mistaken me for a journalist, and she made sure not to hold back. She told us how she walked to the local government office every week, each time being told that Kirill's case was being worked on. He'd been entitled to food stamps, but they'd become useless in the early '90s. The rest of her story drowned under such a thick flow of expletives that I could no longer decipher the facts. She swore like a person who had lost all hope, whose only consolation was her furor made public. I wanted to hold her hand and to run away from her at the same time. *What are my problems compared to hers?* I thought. A few trips to the Russian provinces paled in comparison. *I should count my blessings.* Could I help her? Perhaps. I'd ask Sanjay to write an article for *Newsweek* about it. A story in an American magazine would solve the issue faster than any official complaint to the Russian authorities. That much I knew.

I wished her luck and fled the moment the train came to a halt. I was so drenched in the tales of Russian reality that I jumped onto the platform as if escaping from prison. Unknowingly, the poor woman had taught me how to swear properly – which would come in handy later on.

To get to my motel, I hailed a so-called "private" taxi, a 1980s green and rusty Lada with a chain-smoking driver affixed to its driver seat. We agreed on fifty rubles, a hefty sum for a province, but I had no strength to negotiate. The old car, covered with dirt, reeked of stale cigarettes and vinegar, and its seats were sticky with soot. It stumbled on the unpaved country road. The windows didn't close, and by the time we reached the motel, my hair looked like a haystack after a tornado. I hadn't imagined that potholes of such size could exist; the car nearly fell through a couple of them. When I arrived, sweaty and sporting a bruise on my shin caused by a particularly unfortunate turn, I discovered that the elevator was broken.

I crawled up three flights of dark, crooked steps, dragging my two suitcases filled with business suits, only to discover a prison cell: a narrow, fenced window; a single naked light bulb on a ceiling so low I could reach it with my arms half-bent; a creaking floor smeared with evidence of a cockroach infestation; and a twin bed covered with a thin, yellowish sheet, practically transparent after millions of washes, with a scabrous, military-style maroon blanket under it. I hadn't seen a room like this even before I had left for the U.S.

I was dying to take a shower and turned on the faucet. It farted a few times and let out a trickle of rusty ice water. I couldn't believe Obundy would put its employees up in such a hole. Had this been devised by Laura specially for me? But why?

The next morning, my talks in the mayor's office overseen by the portraits of Yeltsin and Luzhkov produced zero results in advancing the cola's street festival – the same cola that Alexandra, the publisher of *Poise*, had signed as an advertiser for the magazine. Sitting on a metal stool with faded, dark-green upholstery across from the deputy mayor, Mr. Dobrynin – a five-foot clown, dressed in a soiled suit the color of pea soup, stuck behind a plywood desk – I tried not to shudder at his protruding yellow teeth. In my beige blouse and black skirt, I felt like a schoolgirl in front of a teacher – looked upon with condescension and suspicion (*How does a woman get into position to make deals like that?*). Yet he was the one with dirty nails. I knew the conversation had to be moved to a more informal setting and remembered that the only way to establish an understanding with a Russian official was with the help of alcohol. I'd done my research before leaving Moscow, and I invited him to the best nightclub in town.

"Shall we discuss this over a glass of wine?" I asked him.

"Cognac," he said. "Great idea!"

A few hours later, we sat in a dim lounge, surrounded by dancing teenagers whose bodies multiplied in the mirrors all around us. The deafening noises of 1980s Russian pop songs drowned out our conversation. Mr. Dobrynin kept stroking three solitary hairs sticking out like scallions on his bald, glistening head, pretending to be listening while his eyes darted from one dancing girl to another. I shivered just looking at him. And then the moment came when I had to drink vodka…which I didn't drink. At all. But I had to down four shots or he wouldn't budge.

At last, he allowed street banners for the cola festival to be hung around his town. As we were about to shake hands, or so I thought, he put his hand on my knee. I gasped and almost slapped him in the face, my blood boiling with anger and vodka, but threw my napkin at him instead.

"How dare you! You useless pig!" I screamed. "You should be ashamed of yourself!" A few women turned to look at me. "It's because of you women are afraid to enter into business in Russia!"

A hiccup interrupted my flow of anger. I saw a waiter approach, his face crinkled in alarm. I stood up and turned around. "*Ebanyj karas'*," (*fucking cod*) I hissed, the expression I'd learned from the woman on the train. Two deep breaths. Unsteady walk to the exit. Taxi waiting outside (a blurry thought that they had cabs in Tver', after all). 200 rubles to get back to the motel. I couldn't care less about the Cola or its street festival. I had to get out.

As I mounted the steps to my prison cell, I knew I couldn't deal with this scene ten times over in towns across Russia. *Fuck it*, I thought. *I quit.* Yet I knew I couldn't quit. But I couldn't go on drinking vodka with slimy men pawing me, either.

The last thought before I passed out: *I have to call Alexandra Veil.* She was my only hope.

· 5 ·

A rusty, choking ring woke me up the next morning (the room had a phone!). My head a bag full of boulders, my eyes glued shut, I couldn't turn my head or lift an arm. The phone rang for another full minute before it stopped. A question hammered in my temples: *What do I do now?* I recalled insulting the Deputy Mayor and running out of the club, but the details were blurry. I fell back asleep.

Two hours later – a knock on the door. *KGB*, I thought. *They've come to lock me up for committing a federal offense.* I would have prayed if I knew how. I kept quiet. The knock persisted, then stopped. Then keys shuffling, one entering my door lock. I hid under the blanket.

"Oh, I'm sorry." A soft female voice. "Maid service. I'll come back later."

I gulped the water from the nightstand, throwing back my head to catch the remaining drops of the last bottled water brought from Moscow. *They do need to start selling the damn cola in this town*, I thought.

I shuffled to the bathroom and put my head under the icy water from the faucet. I had to deal with Laura. I dialed Alexandra's cell phone. There was no surprise in her voice when she heard it was me.

"Can we meet tonight, please? I'm coming back from Tver' and need to talk about something," I said.

"Tver'? Seriously? I'd love to, but I'm going to Paris for the weekend. Let's do next week."

She hung up. As she did so, I thought I heard laughter.

At the checkout twenty minutes later, the concierge handed me a piece of paper.

"A message for you."

I opened it.

Dear Inga,

Sorry if my call this morning woke you up. I'm happy to confirm the dates for the Cola Festival, July 25-27, 1997. Please call me to discuss logistics.

Signed,

A.S. Dobrynin,

Deputy Mayor.

I folded the piece of paper four times and put it in my pocket. *Was this how deals were really done in Russia?* I thought. Did they know about it at Stern when lecturing on emerging markets? In any case, Laura would be pleased… which also meant a dozen more trips to provincial Russian towns. I couldn't wait to speak with Alexandra and prayed Laura wouldn't send me anywhere else before that time came.

#

The following Wednesday, Alexandra called me at my office.

"Still want to talk?" she said without a hello.

"Absolutely."

"Come to Starlight Diner in an hour. I'm already here."

The Starlight Diner was modeled on the American ideal: a stainless-steel train car sat in the middle of a park behind Mayakovsky metro. When I got there, the place was full, mostly with expats extending their lunches into early cocktail hours and New Russians imitating their lifestyle. This ordinary place that I wouldn't have visited twice in New York turned out to be the trendiest place to be seen in Moscow, as the concept of diners hadn't existed there before. Ketchup and Tabasco sauce sat on every table, and posters from the '50s adorned the walls – Marlon Brando astride his motorcycle, Marilyn Monroe in *Some Like It Hot*. They made the place nostalgically inviting.

I saw Alexandra surrounded by a group of people and was glad I'd dressed in my nicest jacket and skirt ensemble. They *all* had probably just returned from a weekend of shopping in Paris. These people didn't go to developing regions; they sent their employees to do it for them. I ruffled my hair to make sure it covered two red spots on my face, each the size of a quarter, a rude reminder of my ill-fated business trip to Tver', where bed bugs had invaded my mattress. As I approached the table, I held my purse with both hands to keep them away from the burning itch on my right temple. Alexandra finished her speech and motioned to the group to leave. She rose to greet me.

"I wanted you to meet my girlfriend." She smiled and clinked her glass with a petite blonde who sat next to her. "Please meet Emma."

Hiding my disappointment at Alexandra's postponing our conversation, I smiled at Emma. Her blue eyes penetrated me, pinning me down as if I were a butterfly in a frame, daring me to answer a question she hadn't asked. Emma squinted, cocking her head slightly to the right, then broke into a shy smile, allowing innocence to settle on her face. She ran her left hand through her spiked hair, touched the sunglasses on top of her head (I noticed a Prada logo), adjusted a formal black jacket (again Prada), then stretched her hand across the table.

"*Emmochka,*" she said with a smile that revealed her pearl-white teeth, so uncommon among Russians, and produced a dimple on her right cheek. "Friends call me that."

I stared at her, studying her features – a slight birthmark on the lower lip, the bluest eyes, curves of black eyebrows in sharp contrast to the dyed blonde hair – mesmerized by the fact that she'd introduced herself with an endearing nickname. Did it mean that she wanted me to be part of her inner circle of friends, or was she acting the part of a child used to being indulged and spoiled? I couldn't define what else stopped me in my tracks so firmly. A web of sexuality that hung around her? Her poise? Is that why their magazine had been given that name?

"Inga," I answered. Her warm perfume reached my nostrils, and, inhaling it in, I sat down across from Alexandra, who'd already ordered a glass of white wine for me.

"What's with the face?" Alexandra asked. I had wished she wouldn't start with that, yet I thought that this might at least give me a chance to tell her about my trip and to scratch the bites. However, she continued without waiting for my answer. "There's a dinner tonight," she said. "You should come. I want you to meet some people. Emma might be there if she behaves herself." The two exchanged looks.

It sounded strange but intriguing, and I looked at them trying to understand what Alexandra was implying with her last phrase. Had they had a fight? Was Alexandra the boss and Emma the servant? Did Emma really obey Alexandra's every edict?

"I'd love to come."

"Our driver will pick you up at eight at Sanjay's."

On hearing Sanjay's name, Emma looked inquisitively at Alexandra, who muttered with a grin, "She's not dating him." Emma gave me a quick smile and said, "Alexandra said you worked in advertising in New York. Maybe you could help us bring in some clients?"

"Slow down," Alexandra said. "She just got here."

"All the best companies already advertise in *Poise*," I countered. "And I don't have that kind of power in the New York office. Not that I have any in the Moscow one, as it turns out...." I looked at Alexandra.

"Laura didn't like you?"

"Doesn't look like it." I was glad to be able to mention my problem.

Alexandra and Emma exchanged looks again.

"How do you know?" Emma asked.

"Let's just say I was supposed to run their online ad department – here in Moscow – and she sent me to Tver' instead!" I took a long sip of wine. "Let me tell you about my trip last week. First of all, they didn't provide me with a car, as every car had supposedly been taken for other accounts. So I had to take a God-awful regional train." I told them about my ride and the woman with her Afghan vet son and the motel without hot water.

I knew that my audience only traveled first-class and had a dedicated driver wherever they went, so I wondered if they were listening. Emma had a thin smile on her face, while Alexandra's look was a mix of pity and condescension. I needed more wine, and I almost asked Emma for a cigarette. I worried that, after hearing my story, the women would cancel their dinner invitation. Yet I couldn't stop. I felt like someone had to listen to my diatribe, especially considering they were indirectly related to it. At least I didn't tell them about the brown water farting out of the bathroom sink taps or the bed bugs, since those were just too disgusting.

"Am I boring you?" I finally asked.

"On the contrary," Alexandra said. "Go on. It's very amusing."

"Okay. I went there to arrange a street festival for the cola that you had signed as an advertiser for *Poise*. I had to get drunk with a deputy mayor, a truly revolting creature, to make it happen. And just when we'd almost reached an agreement, he put his hand on my knee! Need I say more? I told him everything I thought about him and ran away, yet the next morning he confirmed that the festival had been given a green light. Insanity. I've dealt with worse shit in New York, but I can't bear the thought of living through this again. Yet Laura thinks I've done a superb job and wants me in Ryazan' next week. I have to break this cycle. Do you know someone they could hire for their regional projects?" I poured myself another glass of wine. "Sorry I'm dumping all this on you."

I looked at Alexandra, hoping for magic. She scribbled something in her small, black, leather-bound notepad, then looked up at me.

"We'll see what we can do," she said, lighting a cigarette. "Have another drink. Relax. It's not the end of the world. Anything can be fixed with the right connections and the right amount of money." She looked at Emma. "Let's talk to that Vanessa friend of yours. She's been looking for work. I'll deal with Laura."

She turned back to me. "Now, tell us why the hell you came here in the first place. Emma here is very curious."

I looked at them and pursed my lips, the wine running through my veins, the relief from their promise to "fix" Laura giving me a glimmer of hope.

"What do you want to know?"

"Everything – love, work. Imagine it's like when I first met you, only now you're the one being interviewed."

I finished my wine and bit my lips, which were suddenly

dry, then inhaled as if preparing to take a deep dive. "I lived in New York for nine years. Got married, got divorced, got a Green Card, got an MBA. Got this job, thinking it would get my career going. Now it looks like I might return to New York sooner than I thought. Unless something wonderful happens here before that." I stopped, wondering if I had already said too much.

"Like what?"

"Like my own company, or a great man, or both."

Emma raised an eyebrow, as if dismissing the notion that men could be great. Alexandra said, "What about a great woman?"

I looked at her, then at Emma.

"I never considered that," I said and leaned under the table, pretending I had dropped a napkin. I looked at the floor tiles, and wished I could stay there for a while.

Emma excused herself and went to the bathroom. Alexandra's phone rang. I saw her small feet in black sneakers move sideways as she got up to take the call.

· 6 ·

When I returned to my apartment, there were nine messages on the answering machine. The women had changed their plan several times, concluding with the announcement that their driver would pick me up two hours later, at 10 PM, without a mention of where the dinner would take place. It was still hard to fathom that these two twenty-eight-year-olds had a personal driver.

Sanjay wasn't home. I walked around in a thong and a bra, deciding on an outfit, passing by the mirror in the hall, back and forth. Formal? Funky? Who'd be there? I stopped to assess myself. Strong body, flowing blond hair, high cheekbones – the look was stubborn and determined. But my eyes! The sadness never went away. I was forever the child of St. Petersburg, Dostoevsky's city, and a scared child at that – afraid that Moscow wouldn't accept me, that there was too much of New York in me, that coming back to Russia was a mistake after all. I contemplated the last thought, recalling the chain of events that had brought me here.

In 1992, my third year in New York, I'd been hired by McLadley. Pure luck: a friend knew someone inside the company; rumor had it they were looking to open an operation in Russia at some point in the future. My nationality was to my advantage, and I was hired to help them with research and "initial assessment." They paid me peanuts, but, for three years, I lived vicariously though Russia's transformation until they had sent me on a trip to Moscow to "test the waters." The two weeks that followed, in the summer of 1995, had either poisoned me or brought me back to life; I still couldn't decide. I was intoxicated. The transformation of the country from a Soviet sleepy beast into a leaping newcomer to capitalism – "The Wild East" – was exhilarating and scary. I fell in love with Anton. I fell in love with the possibilities. All events, small and big, seemed historical and important. Many lives had been changed forever.

I'd made a decision: graduate school in New York, then back to Moscow. Yet nothing was turning out the way I'd hoped.

It was nearly 10 PM, and I was still naked. I decided on a strapless black top, tight red skirt, and high heels, which made me six feet tall. I didn't mind. I'd always loved being tall. Moscow men, like their New York counterparts, enjoyed being around models. I'd let them think I was one. I put a touch of shadow on my eyelids and a light shimmer on my cheeks.

A car honked outside: Alexandra's Audi. I ran downstairs feeling important, as if thinking of her made me stronger, and I almost believed I could finally realize my potential in life, whatever that was supposed to be. The car flew onto the boulevard, the Garden Ring, and then on to Kutuzovsky Prospect, the Upper West Side of Moscow. The lights glittered along the Prospect, weaving a blurry line of yellow. Buildings with tired, dim windows blinked their monotonous TV lights at the evening crowd outside. I felt comfortable in Alexandra's car, as if I were inside a magic circle – the one from Gogol's *Viy*, which guarded you against all evil as long as you remained inside.

The elevator let me out straight into the apartment, the only one on the entire floor. The high-ceilinged building could have stood on a corner of West End Avenue or Broadway in the lower 80s; it had the same royal feel. The mirrored walls of an enormous entry hall reflected a giant bouquet of red and white roses on an antique table in the center. The beige and brown upholstery matched the paint on the doors. Polished parquet floors gleamed with candlelight. I felt – at last – like Cinderella entering the ball.

I had taken only a few steps towards the noise in the next room when a door opened and Alexandra, draped in a long black sleeveless dress, stepped out. Her hair fell in black bangs over her high forehead, covering her eyes.

"*Molodets, moya krasavitsa*" – *Good job, my beauty* – she said, and kissed me on the right cheek. She led me to the dining room, where a group of young men and women whose outfits were right out of the pages of *Vogue* – the women in open-back, tight summer dresses, the men in bright shirts with oversized cuffs – sat around a long wooden table. Small bouquets of red and white roses in square vases sat next to every plate; long, white candles added their glow to the silver and crystal arranged on the white tablecloth. A murmur filled the room. It didn't stop when I entered. I put away my smile. I could have been stepping into a deluxe suite in the Ansonia – only here, the people were better dressed, less polite, and spoke Russian.

Alexandra had Emma moved over and sat me down between them. Emma looked different from how I remembered her at the Starlight Diner. In a black strapless gown, with the diamond drop of a pendant reaching between her breasts, she looked more feminine. I kept staring at her deep blue eyes, glittering skin, and small hands. *Such tiny fingers*, I thought. Emma smiled, soft dimples appearing on her cheeks.

"This is our friend Inga from New York," Alexandra announced, handing me a plate of sashimi. A few men lifted their eyes and said hello. I nodded. Directly across from me, a man in his mid-twenties, in a heavily-starched pink shirt with a bright yellow tie, smiled faintly and went back to his sushi. On his left, a slender young woman with wavy blonde hair, wearing a *décolleté* blue cocktail dress, reached her hand out to me. A fat diamond ring adorned her finger.

"Olga," she introduced herself. "This is my husband, Sergey." Olga couldn't have been over 25, yet her bearing was that of an older woman, with a self-assurance doubtlessly earned through her husband's salary and position in society. I swallowed hard. "What brings you to Moscow?" she asked.

"Advertising." I answered reluctantly. Moscow was turning into New York, where the answer to "What do you do?" was more important than who you were.

"How fabulous." She raised a glass to me. "I write. My first book of poetry came out last week."

"Congratulations! I love poetry. Brodsky and Akhmatova

are my all-time favorites."

"Tsvetayeva is mine," Olga answered. "I'm still heavily influenced by her, which I'm sure shows in my book. I've been working on it for the last six years." She smiled. "It has every poem I've written since age 18."

I smiled back, wondering how one could put *all* the poems one had ever written into a book.

"I'd love to read it," I said.

Emma, sitting on my right, touched my shoulder. I excused myself.

"Don't believe everything you hear," she whispered, pouring me a glass of wine. "Sergey, her husband, is an investment banker. He bought a publishing house to have his wife's scribbles published. She hasn't worked a day in her life."

As I sipped the wine, I turned to Sergey, now in a conversation with a fortysomething woman on his right. Her nest of reddish-blonde hair, heavily spiked, was one of her many distinctive features, along with the triangular glasses sitting on her potato nose. She wore a three-piece men's suit and laughed a little too loudly at Sergey's jokes. She was avoiding eye contact with me.

"That's Svetlana Kollegan, a TV personality," whispered Alexandra, following my gaze. "A crazy bitch, but totally fun. Her show is on Channel 5, Thursdays at midnight. She mocks Russian politicians, and she's great at it."

"She's a brave woman."

"That she is," Alexandra said, turning to the head of the table. "And these are our hosts, fresh from Paris," she said, "René and Katerina."

A small man in his sixties – balding, wrinkled, and twitching with excitement – offered me a glass of Merlot. In French. A young, sturdy woman almost twice his size, the type that could be found in a nineteenth-century Russian novel (heavy bosom, wide hips, large hands), looked on with approval. As she raised her glass to meet the bottle that he held, I observed that her palms were like frying pans compared to his, tiny saucers. He filled her glass and kissed her forehead, which was flanked by blonde curls. His daughter, I guessed.

"Katerina is my high school friend," Alexandra whispered to me. "They met in Paris and married for love, though he is French and 30 years older." I scrutinized the couple. Nothing here turned out to be what it seemed.

Emma propped her head on her hand and leaned in to me. "You look fantastic," she said.

Then she put her hand on my knee, and I felt a rush of warm blood run to my cheeks. Emma served me sushi and moved even closer.

"Why don't you move to Moscow for good?" she asked.

I stopped chewing. "Why?"

"There are lots of great things to be done here. Look at

these people – do you know how much they are worth?" She paused. "Sergey, across from you, made half a million last year. He's managing the gas sector or something at an investment bank. Olga just got back from a long weekend in Paris. The woman next to her started her own chain of upscale health clubs two years ago and is now one of the richest women in Russia."

It was the woman I'd read about in the *New York Times*. I'd learned that she started her sports club empire with an investment from her oligarch husband. Not only was she one of the richest women in Russia; she was running for Parliament. Did women blossom in Russia only when men poured money into them? Or was it the same everywhere? What about Emma and Alexandra?

"Alexandra and I are different," said Emma, as if reading my thoughts. "We have always been self-funded."

"How?" I couldn't help asking, the wine having reached my bloodstream and Emma's hand still on my knee.

"I'll tell you later," she whispered, her lips touching my hair.

Her eyes hard on Emma, Alexandra put a hand around my shoulder and leaned behind me.

"I need to talk to you," she said to Emma through gritted teeth. Together, they left the room.

I was left alone, an empty chair on either side of me, sliding into the warmth of mild inebriation and trying to focus on the flickering candles. Then I noticed two men looking at me attentively. They sat diagonally from me, next to the TV woman, murmuring as they studied me. One wore a black suit with a white shirt and silver cufflinks; another had a fiery orange linen shirt on. I thought they were gay, yet their stares grew more insolent. I felt naked without Emma and Alexandra by my side. I turned my gaze to my plate, which now held an arrangement of grilled fish, albino asparagus, and a bowl of mashed potatoes that I'd somehow failed to notice before. Finally, Emma and Alexandra returned.

"Thank God," I whispered to Alexandra. "Who are these men staring at me?"

"Nobody," said Alexandra. "They publish *The Bulletin* magazine. Our competition. The one in the suit is gay; the orange shirt is an asshole. Ignore them."

We ate silently, sipping our wine, the clunking of forks and knives the only sounds for a few minutes, as if the three of us had to think something over and come up with a decision before dessert was served. I found out later that the decision had indeed already been made, without my participation.

"It's time to dance," Alexandra announced before floating off to another room. Most of the guests followed. I observed the setting, as if in a dream, and didn't move. Then I emptied a glass of water into my parched throat and joined the rest of the guests.

Three couples moved around the room in a slow dance to the sounds of the first Hotel Costes album. Emma went over to Alexandra and kissed her slowly. I was mesmerized, having never seen women kiss before, except in movies, most memorably in *Henry and June*. Only a decade ago, such a scene wouldn't have possibly been allowed in Russia, as homosexuality had been banned, along with drugs and prostitution. These kissing women, swaying to the music, were truly a scene from a new world.

They danced as if no one was watching them. In fact, no one was – except for me. Suddenly, I realized what bothered me: I was jealous of Emma. I wanted Alexandra's undivided attention. I was her guest. Every time she talked to me, I had a stamp of approval, and when she didn't, I felt left out. And I was curious, for the first time, about what it was like to be kissed by a woman. What if she kissed me? What if Emma did? I licked my lips. The orange shirt that'd been staring at me earlier approached.

"New York, huh?" he said condescendingly. "Are you with Emma?"

I looked at him silently, my eyebrows raised to my hairline.

"Never mind," he said with a smirk and went off to the

dining room.

A moment later, without looking at me, Alexandra and Emma whiffed through the room and disappeared into the bathroom. I took my wine and sat down on the couch, saddened by the feeling of not belonging. Were they having sex there? After fifteen minutes, I got up to go home.

Just then, they appeared, flushed and smiling, their eyes wet and glowing. Emma wrinkled her nose, rubbed one nostril with the back of her index finger. As I looked at them, I felt like a guest at one of Gatsby's parties, where nobody would remember my name or care who I was the moment I closed the door behind me. And that included Emma and Alexandra.

"I'm fading," I said. "I'll call you tomorrow."

I didn't want to be caught in the web of Moscow secrets. I still believed I could be just an observer, with New York serving as my shield against local intrigues.

"You can't leave yet." Alexandra took my hand and pulled me into the room. Emma took my other hand and I found myself dancing with them, my hips touching theirs, their hands gliding over my skirt, their open smiles erasing my sadness from a minute before.

The door opened, and Laura Paulson walked into the room. She seemed stunned at the sight of me, unable to close her mouth, but I couldn't tell whether it was because of my dancing with Emma and Alexandra, her clients, or because I'd just witnessed her arrival on the hand of an imposing black man. We stared at one another.

Alexandra went to greet them, high-fiving the man, whose tall body towered over hers at over six and a half feet and whose shyness was concealed by an enormous smile, his white teeth contrasting with the night of his skin. Laura gave me a puzzled look as Alexandra led them into the dining room, and I turned to Emma.

"Laura's dating him? Where did she find a black man in Moscow?"

"She didn't. She found him in Nepal, on a trekking trip. He's why you won't be going to the provinces again any time soon."

I wondered how Laura Paulson's boyfriend could be the reason for altering my career path, but didn't finish the thought as Emma took me by my shoulders and led me out of the room.

"We're going clubbing."

· 7 ·

Two weeks later, on a Saturday, I woke up and couldn't open my eyes. When I did, the clock showed 2:06 PM. The night before had been spent dancing and drinking with Emma and Alexandra at Justo, the latest *It* place, its metal black door opening only for *svoi*, those who belonged – either because of their net worth or connections or social status. It was the same place they'd taken me clubbing after the penthouse dinner. We'd become regulars there.

My days passed in a whirl of meetings, business lunches, dinners, and after-hours lounging. As Alexandra had promised, I didn't go to the regions, yet still had to manage those regional ad campaigns – only now, from Moscow. I felt like I was drowning in the tediousness of production and media buying, impatient to leave the office come 5 PM – very un-American of me.

Every night, Emma, Alexandra, and I closed another club or restaurant, and I'd met nearly a hundred new people – businessmen and artists, fashionistas and posers, some self-made millionaires, and many wannabes, mostly Russian, with a few expats. I'd become accepted into the inner circle of Moscow's high society, as a protégé of Emma and Alexandra, to whom I'd grown attached like a little sister. My social calendar left no room for pondering what my life would be once the Obundy job was over. And I couldn't think serious thoughts on Saturday afternoon anyway.

The air in the room hung heavy and silent. The door was closed, although, being a claustrophobe, I remembered having left it open. I put on my shorts and peeked into the corridor – a pair of women's shoes next to mine, size six or so.

In the kitchen, I put the kettle on. As it hummed, I leaned out the window to air my throbbing head. Saturday. In the backyard, kids played in the sandbox; mothers pushed strollers; babushkas fed pigeons. My stomach twisted with hunger; my mouth tasted like dead leaves; my legs felt like cardboard cutouts. I moved a *taburetka*, a Russian version of a bar stool, short and square, closer to the refrigerator, sat down and opened it: stale crackers, old cheese, water, and wine. It could have been my fridge in New York. I needed to go shopping.

When I turned, a girl stood in the doorway. I recognized her. Sanjay had courted her the previous night, kissing her hands and shoulders, whispering things into her ear that made her smile and kiss him. His devotion so impressed me that I felt certain true feelings were easier found in Russia than in the U.S. I even commented on that to Emma and Alexandra, who only snorted in response. Even so, I was jealous that Anton, my former lover from the band Airplanes, hadn't been around to court me – despite the fact that I'd told him I was in Moscow.

"Hi, Inga. I'm Tanya," the girl said. "Sorry we didn't get to talk last night."

In a tight bodysuit, short and slim, her hair carefully combed, full make-up still untouched, she looked as if she'd never left the nightclub.

"Anything to eat?" she asked.

"Just crackers and cheese."

"Want to go shopping?"

"Sure."

"Let me find Sanjay's wallet." Tanya disappeared into his room.

I tried to remember how the previous night had ended, and vaguely recalled that I'd managed to fall asleep on the stage at Justo while some band was still playing. Emma and Alexandra put me in a cab around 3 AM.

"Sanjay told me about you. And New York," Tanya said when she returned.

I went into the hallway to get my shoes. "What did he say?"

She followed me. "That you've survived in New York on your own, which is admirable." Tanya stood in front of the mirror, evaluating herself, straightened the wrinkles around her straw-thin waist, glided her palms over her buttocks, then turned to me. "Maybe I'll marry a New Yorker and go live there," she added, turning back to the mirror.

"Sanjay?" I suppressed a yawn.

"*Da ladno!*" – *No way.* "We just sleep together. He's not the marrying type."

I looked at her with interest.

"I'm only 18," she explained. "Why would I want to marry now? I just finished my first year of journalism at *MGU.* That's how I met Sanjay. He's helping me with my English."

"I can certainly hear that."

"I want to marry a rich American, and Sanjay is just a journalist. Plus, he's not white. My parents wouldn't approve of it."

"Why American?"

"They are the easiest to fool."

While I had never thought of it that way, it was common knowledge in Russia that American males in their twenties largely lived like kids in a sandbox, unburdened by family or other obligations. And I had my own reasons to think that marrying an American man wasn't such a hot idea for a Russian woman.

"What about love?" I asked.

"I have plenty of time to be with someone I love. After that, I'll marry someone reliable and financially secure. Marriage and love are two separate things."

You could have fooled me last night, I thought. I remembered being Tanya's age, walking on the banks of the Neva, holding hands with a guy, looking at the dark water glistening under the elusive light of a white night, dreaming of marrying someone I loved. I still dreamed of it.

"I might marry a Russian after all," said Tanya. "A New Russian, that is. I just want to practice my English first. Plus, Sanjay pays for my drinks and introduces me to cool people. As a journalist, I need connections."

"Does Sanjay know about this?"

"I don't care. He's using me, too. I'm sure it's nice to have sex with an 18-year old when you are 30. He probably can't get that in the States."

Maybe that was the reason why Sanjay had come to Russia in the first place. I wondered what my friend

Kristina in New York, with her unwavering opinion that marriage had to be based *solely* on love, would have to say to Tanya.

I put on my jean jacket and walked out to call the elevator. Tanya followed.

On the street, the morning breeze erased the last traces of my hangover. We walked to the corner store. Rows of white shelves decorated with blue paper bulged with Russian and foreign foods, from *muesli* and Swiss cheeses to pickled herring and dry soups – a scene unimaginable several years earlier, when people would have swarmed empty-shelved stores waving their useless vouchers for a kilo of sugar or a brick of butter, rows of canned fish and rotting cabbage staring at them through the closed doors, and an overweight salesperson waving at them to leave. There was no promise of real food unless you had connections or knew when a truckload of perishables would arrive, which nobody did.

I'd been lucky to be invited for a semester in New York just then, and I went. The borders had opened up, and nothing could hold me in Russia except for my parents, left behind in St. Petersburg, and the magic of my home city. I took my chances with America and had been diligently sending parcels of macaroni and cookies back to St. Petersburg ever since. When my mother and grandmother died, my parcels became smaller, as father said he didn't need that much food for himself. When he remarried, his new wife refused to accept my packages. She said my "handouts" were degrading, never mind the empty shelves in grocery stores.

I bought a round of black bread, still warm from the bakery, a can of instant coffee, and a can of *sgushyonka*, condensed sweet milk, so hard to find in Manhattan stores. Tanya chose smoked salmon, salami, eggs, and cold cuts from the refrigerator. She looked at my selection and frowned, then added butter, cheese, two bars of Swiss chocolate – white and dark – and some homemade salads to her cart. I couldn't tell if it was all meant for Sanjay and her, or if that was how she supported her family. I didn't ask.

We paid separately and took three plastic bags – the same kind I would collect in New York and send back home, where disposable plastic bags hadn't yet been available until recently. I might have been the first person recycling plastic across the Atlantic.

When we came back, the smell of fried eggs filled the apartment. I almost hugged Sanjay. I made coffee for myself, and tea for him and Tanya, who flipped through *Time Out Moscow*.

"Want to go out later?" she asked Sanjay.

"No, I have to work tonight."

"Fine, I'll go with someone else."

"I'm sure."

As he served the omelets, I quietly watched this scene, which could have been lifted straight from a typical Sunday morning in New York. We ate in silence, Tanya bent over the magazine, Sanjay reading the *Moscow Times*. I looked at the tree branches outside the window, wondering if the Airplanes concert had been written about in either paper. I hadn't invited anyone to join me later that night, not even Emma and Alexandra. I would be meeting Anton backstage an hour before the show.

"What's *Time Out* offering for tonight?" I broke the silence.

"There is Bartenev at the Manezh, but it will be hard to get in without tickets. The Airplanes at the Chinese Pilot Dzhao Da. And *Three of Hearts* is playing at the Pushkin," read Tanya.

"That's a great movie," I said. "About a threesome in New York."

"Sanjay, maybe we should go?" Tanya said.

"I'm working – I told you," he replied without looking at her.

Tanya finished her food, fished two chocolate bars out of the bag, and left, her plate and cup still on the table.

"Why were you so rude to her?" I asked once the door

closed behind Tanya.

"Was I rude?"

"She wanted to be with you, and you pushed her away. Quite a change from last night."

Sanjay looked at me like he knew something I didn't, raised his eyebrows as if considering an explanation, and said, "She wanted to be with my wallet, not with me. And she got plenty of both last night."

When had everyone managed to become so cynical? I still believed in everlasting love, but it must have been hard to come by in a Moscow dripping with money. I was certain such a scene between me and Anton was not possible. He'd never send me away. I couldn't wait for the day to end, to look into his eyes and feel his hands on me.

· 8 ·

An hour before the band was scheduled to perform, I went to the Chinese Pilot Dzhao Da Club at Kuznetsky Most. As I entered the dim, low-ceilinged room that reeked of stale smoke and alcohol fumes, I clutched my purse closer to my body, wondering how Anton could continue playing in such run-down clubs.

I remembered the first time I met him, in 1995.

I noticed him at a small underground nightclub as he played bass guitar, stage right, in my friends' band. First, I saw his brown Robert Downey Jr. eyes, which drew me like magnets. He looked directly at me, smiling and nodding, tapping his foot on the floor, his whole body saying, "I know you'll like me." I loved the song and sang the words back to him. Hot waves traveled up and down my back. First, I resisted the urge to throw myself into his arms. Afterwards, there was a nightlong train from Moscow to St. Petersburg, with me traveling *sans billet* in the band's compartment.

That night, I couldn't sleep, watching the moonlit landscape roll by through the dirtied train window. Before the first rays of sun broke the darkness, he took me by the hand and led me out of the compartment, walked me to the vestibule, and made me come perched against the wall, as the wind from the window blew through my hair. He then led me back inside and spread me on the bottom berth. His friends pretended not to notice, playing guitar and looking at the starry darkness out the window. Anton made me laugh, whispering in Russian as he loved me right there, on the train. My exhausted soul had finally found its way home. He'd written me a song; I would hear it later on the radio. We used to make love everywhere: backstage in clubs, in friends' apartments, once in a park; never in my own bed, as my father wouldn't have approved of it. I was in love.

A year later, they played at Joe's Pub in New York. We were reunited for a week, then separated for another year. Yet I still wanted to be with him: I'd never known such chemistry before; he was the reason I'd left my husband; and no man had touched me for six months. *Nobody* had touched me for half a year!

I made my way backstage at Dzhao Da, my heart ticking like a timer, thinking he could fuck me on the side of a highway or in a cowshed for all I cared – as long as he wanted to. Just then, I tripped over the cords hanging like snakes from the stage, and torpedoed through a narrow door in the back wall, almost landing on a coffee table littered with empty bottles. Anton, dressed in black, lunged forward just in time to catch me. Five other musicians sat on a worn-out velour maroon couch, each holding a beer. They lifted their bottles in unison, greeting me, but I hardly said hello.

"Inga, *devochka moya*," muttered Anton. He held me – and was as handsome and stylish as I remembered, a twinkle in his brown eyes, his lips pursed in a half-smile. "You're here after all!"

He kissed me slowly on the lips, tracing their outline, his hands on my shoulders. I leaned into him. I felt my life's mishaps and anxieties settle like a sheet on a bed: the man who had inspired me to leave my husband still loved me. We kissed and kissed until he remembered that he had an unfinished beer, a *Baltika*, in his hand. He offered me one, and I took it, even though I didn't usually drink beer. But its smell was the same as Anton's breath, and I found it a turn-on. The other musicians left. I sat down next to him on the couch, trying not to notice the stains; our hands intertwined, the warmth enveloping my body.

I wished I could stay like that, that we could make love right there: his eyes and hands on me, his lips whispering into my ear, him pulling me down to the floor and loving me so hard that there'd be no room left for loneliness, not in my body, not in my heart.

"I missed you so much," I whispered to him.

He brought me closer and took a sip of beer while studying me. Then he placed a hand on my thigh. "I've been waiting for you to come back."

"Is there another room?" I asked.

"After the concert."

He pushed me onto the couch, covering my face with kisses, his hands on my breasts. *Take me right here,* I thought. *The guys don't care; they've seen us make love before.*

And they've probably seen you make out with a bunch of other women, I thought, but chose not to dwell on it.

A short, fat man in a black T-shirt, with *Poise* written across it in lemony yellow, walked in to announce it was five minutes before show time. *The magazine really is everywhere.* Anton lifted himself onto his elbows, kissed my eyes, gave me a last quick rub between the thighs for good measure, and followed his fellow musicians out of the room. I sat up on the couch and straightened up. I wished the concert would already be over. I wished we could be left alone to study each other's bodies, inch by inch, every birthmark, every curve. Nothing else mattered.

I sat on the couch for a few minutes, staring at the floor stained with old beer spills, trying to catch my breath. I didn't need to be strong or proper with Anton. I could just be me.

I stood in the middle of a roaring crowd in front of the stage. The Airplanes started with their first hit and my mind returned to the time of our affair. I watched Anton embrace his bass guitar as if it were his lover, looking above the crowds, tapping his foot to the rhythm, serious, focused. Then he locked eyes with me and, for a moment, his face melted into a quick smile that I was convinced was meant for me alone. That special moment, the fleeting connection that pierced through the crowd and held us together at his concerts, had always filled me with happiness, our special communication amidst the concert's frenzy.

The next moment, he existed only for his music, and his guitar was his only woman. As I watched him play it, humming along with the soloist, I knew he'd had other women. But as long as I didn't see them, it was fine with me. In that department, I subscribed to the notion of *Ignorance is bliss.* Yet one of the girls dancing next to me could be a lover he hadn't bothered to mention, and that was no longer fine. I watched him closely. He smiled at someone else. I followed his eyes. A slim brunette in a white T-shirt sparkled under Anton's grin, singing to the tune of the song. She blew him a kiss, and I watched him purse his lips in a kiss and close his eyes, the exact replica of what was mine a minute earlier, now an affirmation of *their* intimacy. I stared and stared at the girl, tears pushing at the corners of my eyes – hot, salty, burning tears that I tried to hold back by lifting my face to the ceiling.

Anton was no longer mine. He never had been. The raving, sweating crowd pushed in on me, and I hit a speaker with my hip. Pain shot through my body. I almost fell over but straightened up, looked back one more time, and maneuvered through the crowd towards the exit, tears flowing freely, at last. Once on the street, I dialed Alexandra's number.

"Where can I meet you tonight?"

She gave me the address of a nightclub, and I hailed a cab. The driver stared at me through the rear window, at the tears that wouldn't stop streaming down my cheeks. I lifted my face and breathed deeply. I still loved Anton, if only for his having made me feel alive for the past two years. He'd given me that, and it was mine to keep. But I shouldn't have been trying to step twice into the same river.

"Easier on the turns," I told the driver as I pulled out a mirror to fix my running mascara.

The Jazz Café on Ordynka was surrounded by dozens of

Mercedes, BMWs and Audis. I felt as if I'd arrived at the Oscars. Had Emma not met me outside, I'd have had no chance of getting in. I tried to hide my face from her as we walked towards the metal gate, my eyes still burning. Yellow lights in the garden depicted moving silhouettes of well-built men attempting to convince two giant security men of their VIP status. Gorgeous, slender girls – some in low-cut, sheer, spaghetti-strap gowns, others in jeans so tight you expected them to burst at the seams, with silky hair and perfect makeup – sized up our group as we pushed towards the entrance. Everyone looked detached and uninterested, as if being stuck outside wasn't an obstacle but a purposeful delay. The combination of ennui and condescension on their faces, so common for Moscow's golden youth, contrasted greatly with my red, puffy eyes. Alexandra said multiple hellos, nodded to the guy at the door, and told him to get the owner.

She turned to me. "What happened?"

"Nothing. Leftover boy troubles."

She looked at Emma, who stared at me, as if pondering whether they should have invited me to join them. They must have had plans for me even then, but the thought hadn't crossed my mind. A moment later, a tall bald man in his thirties, with a skeptical expression on his oval face, let us in.

"Meet Inga, fresh from New York," said Alexandra,

pushing me forward. The owner, a Yugoslav, as I found out later, took my hand and led me down the spiral staircase, where Emma had already disappeared. Alexandra remained in the garden, sharing laughs and high-fives with two models we had passed on the way. "What a pretty bird you are," I overheard her tell one of the blondes before I went downstairs.

Inside, the club was a replica of a SoHo loft – open brick walls, dim lights, low-set glass tables, and fuzzy chairs. Men in three-piece suits with manicures elbowed each other, struggling for the attention of the barman to serve their *femmes de nuit*. One of them had a tiny dog on her lap, another accepted compliments for her purple and orange hat, which covered her face completely. They all briefly turned to me and gave me a once-over as I followed the owner through the crowd. I wished I were in New York.

"Dance floor slash chill-out," said the baldie, parting the curtain. Half-naked girls pirouetted around the room as their boyfriends shouted encouragement, and suddenly I was alone in the middle of the dancing frenzy – sweaty faces and white shirts shivering to the latest techno selection from London. I moved towards the back and, at the second bar, spotted Emma talking to a young woman. I wondered whether Alexandra would be jealous if she saw her girlfriend flirting with another woman or whether it was their accepted ritual in public. I wanted my New York Kristina by my side.

Emma waved me over.

"My sister, Maria."

I shook the limp hand of a woman who bore no resemblance to Emma – short, with bad skin and twitching lips. Thankfully, I didn't need to speak: the bald owner appeared from the back room announcing a stripper performance. The crowd separated us and carried me to the front room.

A woman scarcely old enough to vote, who looked as if she had swallowed a series of French curves, climbed on top of a round coffee table in the middle of the floor and lifted herself up by a chain hooked to the ceiling. She slowly moved her hips to the music, the chain between her knees. As the rhythm quickened, so did her performance. She slithered from her silver dress – a mermaid shedding her tail, her breasts bouncing up to the ceiling. Trembling with excitement, the gentlemen – having totally forgotten about their dates – stared at the diva in the center of the room. One of those noble men, I realized with a mixture of horror and amusement, was Sanjay, who stood gawking in the very first row as the girl flicked the dress off the painted toe of her right foot and into the crowd – the sort of gesture, I thought, that

Toulouse-Lautrec had captured so well at the Moulin Rouge.

One of the expats caught the dress and buried his face in it. A moment later, on top of the table, he approached the girl from behind and put his hands on her bare breasts. She covered his hands with hers. Whistles from the crowd urged him to undress. I moved closer. In a blink, the man's trousers dropped to his ankles and his naked *chlen* bounced up to touch the girl's buttocks.

I was looking around to see if Alexandra was in the crowd of observers when a smashing noise ripped through the place. I turned back in time to witness a piece of the ceiling above the girl give out under the weight of two people. A square of dry plaster smashed on top of her and her admirer, as if in slow motion. The table tilted over, and the couple toppled to the floor, pushing the crowd towards the walls. The man tried to cover himself, folds of fat rolling over his stomach, his *chlen* no longer attentive, while she looked around in panic as if she'd forgotten her clothes. She winced in pain while trying to free herself from the torn chain that coiled around her breasts like an iron snake. The observers, so involved only a moment before, rushed towards the door, pushing each other, screaming. Frightened, I headed towards the exit. A stocky man in a bright yellow shirt stepped on my foot as he made for the door, and I pushed him away. "Bitch, what are you doing?" he hissed.

"Shut up!"

I threw the dress to the girl, and ran upstairs. Alexandra caught me at the gate.

"Where are you going?"

"As far from here as possible."

"Wait," she said. "Don't go yet."

I didn't have the strength to argue. It was 1 AM. I ran towards the gate and stopped on the sidewalk. A car drove through a puddle, and I felt the chill of cold water on my feet and shins. It stopped a few feet away, and I saw Anton get out of it, the T-shirted brunette on his arm. I turned away so he wouldn't notice me. The air left my lungs as I shuffled several steps in my wet shoes to lean against a wall, my knees giving in. I felt like a kid lost on an unfamiliar playground, forgotten by her parents, with nobody around to ask for help because she'd been taught not to talk to strangers. I watched Alexandra say hello to them as the two entered the club. I bit my lower lip and held it between my teeth until the pain became dominant. My mouth felt salty.

Alexandra returned.

"Are you okay?" she asked.

"Fine."

"Your mouth is bleeding."

"I tripped and bit my lip."

She studied my face and took my hand, leading me to her car. Emma followed us. I chose to sit in the front, next to the driver, so I wouldn't have to talk.

· 9 ·

The long ride soothed me. I even fixed my make-up, looking at the mirror above me, stealing glances at Emma in the backseat. The car stopped on the outskirts of the city. Four-story pre-fab buildings identical in their gray monotony crowded around an empty soccer field with yellowing grass and an enormous puddle in its center. Beyond the tunnels of square archways, fields of worn-out grass stretched as far as my eyes could see, the wind howling its empty lullaby to no one. It was 2 AM.

We walked on the unfinished pavement, puddled with mud, to one of the gray façades and entered a vast, unadorned lobby, where I squeezed into a tiny elevator. Emma's sister's apartment wasn't as glorious as the one I'd visited for a penthouse dinner, but it had all the fixtures typical of a recently designed space, with new window frames, parquet floors, and stainless steel kitchen appliances.

Maria greeted us at the door. "Come in," she said, gesturing us towards the living room and fixing her unruly copper hair with both hands. We followed her into the dining room, and I froze at the entrance. Four couples, all women, lounged on the couches and on the carpet, drinking, touching, and kissing. They scanned us with their eyes before returning to their conversations. A stocky creature, dressed in overalls, bent over a giant bong on the floor, inhaling the thick smoke. A short blonde girl in her mid-twenties, her eyes glazed, rose from the carpet, climbed on another woman's lap, and hugged her with her knees. The woman, with dry skin and a crew cut, put her hands on the blonde's round butt, and they blew smoke into each other's open mouths until there was none left. They sealed the exchange with a long kiss.

Alexandra turned to me. "Close your mouth and stop staring," she said. "I want you to meet Jane – Maria's girlfriend. She is an anchor on a daytime TV show on Channel One."

I shook hands with the beautiful dark-haired girl. I noticed her height; she was almost as tall as I. Her slender figure and her marble-white hands made her look like a piece of art. Her face lit up with a smile as she embraced

Maria at the waist.

Alexandra took my hand. "Let's get a drink. I'll tell you her story." She pulled me into the kitchen.

"Jane has a five-year old son," Alexandra said as she poured wine. "She's separated from her husband. It's been a year. The man is devastated; the love of his life left him for a woman! After they had their son and he bought her an apartment and all that jazz. Not bad, huh? He was a good catch – a diplomat, with real connections. He got her the TV job, too. And there you are – along comes Emma's sister Maria, with her sensitive nature, female intuition, and no patronizing, and woos our perfectly heterosexual Jane away. Strange how things work, right?" She winked at me. I stood with my mouth partially open, unable to swallow a sip of wine.

"I didn't even know things like this happened in real life," I muttered and turned to look at Maria at the other end of the apartment. The woman wouldn't have caught my eye in a crowd – a plain-looking, skinny girl, with curly hair and a shy smile. How she'd managed to seduce beautiful Jane was a mystery to me, but then I had little experience when it came to lesbian sexual undercurrents.

I walked back into the room and settled on a soft beige couch to study this scene, so far removed from my New York reality. On our girls' nights out in New York, Kristina and I would flirt mercilessly with young men

– never women, our wedding bands shielding us against unwanted advances. We thought we had it all, until we no longer did.

The girl in overalls approached and offered me a toke. I inhaled from the bong. The smoke's sweet warmth filled my body. Moments later, my hands and feet didn't weigh an ounce, and I felt myself floating around the room, Emma's smile following me all the while – a feather tickling my ego. I leaned my head against the back of the couch and looked up at the ceiling, smiling for the first time since I'd left the club. I no longer had a husband, or a lover. The possibilities were endless.

I like her, I thought to myself. I watched Emma in the corner blow marijuana smoke out of the eight-floor window, her body silhouetted against the white curtain. *What about Alexandra?* Yes, very much so... *I shouldn't have inhaled that smoke.* I liked both of them – Alexandra for her quick wit, Emma for her... I quivered and felt my cheeks burn. *I like them both! Is that what I mean? Is this liking, or something else, something more, something more like lust? Or is it both? Oh, God.* It felt awful and delicious, splendid and stupid. If I spent more time with them, maybe I could even become like them – independent, carefree, and confident.

As more wine flowed and more smoke was inhaled, my head started to feel like a giant haystack. I no longer felt awkward staring at the kissing girls at my feet, nor did I find it strange. As I succumbed to the haziness in my brain, I saw two couples get up and leave, then two more. Maria and Jane went into the bedroom. Alexandra announced it was getting late and they would crash right there for the night. I looked around the room.

"What about me?" I asked.

Alexandra pointed to a recliner chair next to the beige couch. "You should fit, Miss America."

By the time I went to the bathroom and back, the curtains in the room had been drawn and two beds made – not far from each other. Soft, gray light filtered through the windows – a reminder of St. Petersburg's White Nights. I saw the silhouettes of two bodies, Alexandra and Emma, entangled in a tight embrace under white sheets. It looked like a Rodin sculpture.

Exhausted, I undressed and got under the covers. Yet sleep eluded me, and I just lay there, staring at the ceiling, glancing at the Rodin sculpture breathing evenly three feet away from me.

I needed to talk to someone, about tonight, about my first weeks in Moscow. Emma and Alexandra weren't available. I had to get to my laptop at home and write to Kristina. She was my sounding board for all things complex in life, and I hadn't written to her in two weeks! As I put my skirt on, I noticed a movement under the sheets on the bed next to me and looked closer. The women were kissing as they undressed each other. In the early morning light, the shapes became white waves lingering on the surface of the ocean. The noises grew louder, wet and breathless. Then a hand appeared from under the sheet, reaching out to me.

I dropped my skirt to the floor and approached their bed. I stood next to it, immobile. What was I supposed to do? Was anything expected of me? Had this been planned? My brain was foggy, incapable of answers. I counted till five. The two people I felt closest to in Moscow lay naked underneath that sheet. This was an invitation, but was it from both of them? I held the hand, Emma's. Our palms touched. She stroked my fingers, and I answered. I didn't know if Alexandra was aware of what was happening. The hand tugged at my fingers, and I followed the signal, moving to the bed – between them. Not a word was uttered. They turned to me; their breath hot under the sheet. I melted under the slow caresses from both sides, surrendering to the girls' touch. Emma kissed me on the mouth, my first kiss with a woman. The gentleness of that kiss, warm and tender, made me want to hold on to Emma for a long time, without letting go, ever. My eyes closed, I kissed her back. Alexandra's lips traveled slowly over my breasts, towards my navel. I still couldn't let go of Emma's lips.

Alexandra surfaced, and all three of us kissed. I tasted myself on Alexandra's lips – sweet and sour, moldy warmth. Emma got up on her elbows, her eyes wild. She looked at me and lowered her head on my chest. Was she listening to my heartbeat? Her lips traced my belly down to my navel, and lower. I obeyed her. Clutching the sheets, I had to turn away from Alexandra, to inhale, my body arching under Emma's lips and hands. My moans reverberated off the coffered ceiling. Her hands were golden, her tongue magic. My fingers twisted her spiky hair as I convulsed in surrender.

"Bozhe moi," – *My God* – I whispered to the ceiling. *"Bozhe moi, kak mne horosho."*

I closed my eyes, brought Emma to my chest, and held her. Her cheek was hot on my breasts, her heartbeat furious against my navel. She initiated me into a ritual that I'd never thought would have been for me. Yet this was beautiful and intoxicating, and I wanted more. I understood why women might not need men. Alexandra smiled at us, leaned over Emma, and kissed her back.

Emma and I switched places. I let my lips and hands improvise on the smooth landscape of her white skin, tight belly, and cleanly-shaved halves of her beautiful vulva. My tongue entered her. She tasted salty and sweet, and I didn't find it strange that I liked being there. I wanted her, this woman who had seduced me at the first "Hello." My hand entered her, and Emma rolled her head on the pillow, hot whispers on her lips. "Yes – like that!" she screamed. Reassured, I continued to move my hand the way I normally did when pleasuring myself. It made me hot to think that I was the reason for Emma's impending orgasm. "*Da, da, da!*" Emma tensed up, an electrical wire charged by me, and then her body went limp. I put my chin on her bellybutton, admiring the view: her flushed cheeks, sparkling eyes, messy hair. Emma traced my eyebrows. "Thank you," she said. Her smile said much more.

"Sweet Emma," I whispered. She was mine.

"Are you sure it's your first time with a woman?" Alexandra asked, giving me an approving nod.

"I'm sure."

"Good girl," Alexandra said, and moved closer to the wall, freeing the room between them, for me.

As the three of us lay on that foldout couch in complete silence, I felt the room spinning around me, smelling of sweat and lust. Shafts of pre-dawn light poked through the frilly white curtains. I couldn't stop smiling. Emma's hand found mine under the sheet. I gave it a squeeze and fell asleep.

· 10 ·

When I woke up, the room seemed bigger than it had the night before, washed in the yellow afternoon light diffused by the white curtains. My skin was on fire; Emma's and Alexandra's bodies were pressing against me on each side; and my mouth felt like the Sahara. I'd never felt embarrassed being naked in front of a man, yet at that moment caught myself thinking that I couldn't just get up and start looking for my underwear in my Eve's suit. I lay there, waiting for something. Alexandra opened her eyes first and turned to me, propping herself up on an elbow.

"You're still beautiful in the morning," she said.

"Isn't that what middle-aged men say to their 20-year-olds?" I answered.

"Maybe I *am* a middle-aged man." She took my hand and kissed it. "And you are a 20-year old."

"No talk of men, please." Emma sat up in bed and reached for her jacket. She lit a cigarette and fell back on the bed. "*Emmochka* is very happy this morning," she said. "And hungry."

"She's always happy when she's hungry. Especially for more sex. Aren't you, *Emmochka*?" Alexandra asked.

Saying nothing to this, Emma got up, put on her white bra and knickers, and started hopping around the room on one leg and singing a little "*Twee-twee-twee*" song, her stomach showing traces of a six-pack on every jump. She pirouetted in a circle, switched legs, and hopped back to bed, bringing me my underwear.

Alexandra reached out to her over me, and they kissed. "My baby *is* happy today," Alexandra said.

I heard voices behind the wall.

"What will you tell your sister?" I asked Emma.

"Should I tell her anything?"

"She surely heard me last night."

"Good for her. Free aphrodisiac," said Alexandra, kissing me on the lips.

We gathered our clothes, laughing and pushing each other. Then we made up the beds and snuck out.

It started raining – a good omen. The staccato raindrops

pinged against the car as we sped towards the center of the city. The windshield wipers waved their slim, crooked arms in the fight to clear the view ahead. *Could a threesome be the answer?* I thought, dozing off against Emma's shoulder. *Can one be in love with two people at once? Maybe I should see* Three of Hearts.

I fell asleep to the sound of raindrops against the windows, Alexandra watching me in the rearview mirror. I didn't know where we were going, and that was fine. For once, I didn't want to be in control.

I woke up from the flood of lights beaming at the car. For a moment, I thought we were in Times Square or had been stopped by the police. I looked out. We'd pulled up to *Kodak Kinomir*, a recently built American Cineplex in the Moscow center – flashy posters of American block-busters, popcorn stands, and DVD rentals.

"Movies? But I'm famished!"

"We're getting DVDs for our perfect rainy afternoon," said Alexandra as she got out of the car.

"We'll also get some yummies, and I'll make us brunch in bed," Emma whispered once we were alone. "Wouldn't you like that, Sweetness?"

"I would love that."

She leaned over and kissed me.

"Wait." I exhaled. "We shouldn't without Alexandra."

"You're probably right." She caressed my knee, moved her hand up under my skirt and gave me a long kiss on the lips. "Sweet Inga," she said, her eyes sparkling.

I edged my hips into Emma's hand. The rain hid us from the street crowd. I breathed into her neck, inhaling the scent that had enveloped me the first time we met, surrendering to her knowing hands.

"Please go," I whispered minutes later, finally pulling away from her, my legs like cotton, my body pleased.

She left, slamming the door, and ran for cover, becoming a blurry silhouette in the strings of rain. I moved to the front seat and checked myself in the mirror. My cheeks flushed, hair tangled, and yesterday's makeup still lingering under my eyes: I looked undeniably happy. I closed my eyes and fell asleep, a smile teasing my lips.

They returned together – Alexandra with a stack of DVDs, Emma with shopping bags from the supermarket.

"Your place?" Alexandra turned to me.

"If you don't mind Sanjay for the audience."

"Right. Our place, then." And we sped down Tverskaya Street.

* * *

As we parked near Alexandra's building, she pointed at the newly-installed white windows on the top floor. She owned a penthouse. I felt my desire stirring somewhere below my belly button: every step with Alexandra was a turn-on. She opened the door, and we entered Asia: a green and yellow loft with human-sized vases in the corners, each vase lacquered with black and red ornaments; a worn-out, brown leather couch in the center; and a coffee table covered with issues of *Vogue* and *Poise*. Bookcases, nested inside the columns in the middle, held volumes by contemporary Russian writers, while white lilies in transparent, square vases graced windowsills still gleaming with fresh white paint. Despite its size, the apartment felt cozy, with sheets of rain striking and sliding down the windowpanes and thick clouds crowding together outside.

A large bed filled a pink bedroom. Dozens of teddy bears sat and lay on the covers. Some were tiny, some huge; they were of all colors and textiles. They lived their own lives in the toy kingdom.

"*Emmochka* loves *mishkas*," explained Alexandra, dropping her bag on the floor.

And I thought how I loved summer rain, with the air filled with longing, every tree sharing its best aroma, warm fog rising from the ground, and soft drops caressing your skin. I opened the windows in the living room.

"Are you mad, *Amerikanka*?" Alexandra turned around. "We'll get flooded."

"Let her be," said Emma – the first time that I had heard her contradict Alexandra. "I love the smell of rain, too."

Alexandra shrugged and went up to the TV in the bedroom. "What are we in the mood for?" she asked, spilling the DVDs on the floor.

"*High Art*, the story of a straight girl falling in love with a lesbian artist." She winked at me. "Or *Henry and June*, highly praised by *Amerikanka*. There is also *Fear and Loathing in Las Vegas* and *M. Butterfly*. Preferences?"

"*High Art*," said Emma.

"I really wanted you to see *Henry and June*," I said. "But we can do it later."

"A whole weekend devoted to nothing but food and love. Perfect," said Alexandra. "Let's whip something up real quick first." She went to the kitchen to help Emma with the shopping bags.

I sat on the antique brown leather couch in the living room and watched them. I knew they'd been together for over three years. According to Emma, they were the envy of Moscow – successful in business, with a loving relationship. "They just don't understand how we keep our relationship so fresh and vibrant, as if we'd just met a month ago," she once said. *By bringing in a third*, I thought at the time. Had there been others before me? Either way, I wouldn't ruin the balance of their world. I didn't think they could ruin the balance of my life, either, since I didn't have much balance to start with.

Emma brought in a tray of hot appetizers. Smells of roasted potatoes, garlic, dill, and parsley filled the room. Alexandra followed her, holding a bottle of white wine and glasses. The three of us climbed on the bed: the rain, the food, the movie, and the girls on both sides of me. We fed each other and kissed in between, our faces and hands smothered with food. Emma poured wine into my mouth and unhooked my top. A drop of wine landed on my right breast. Alexandra unzipped my skirt. The movie played in the background, as I surrendered to their knowing hands. I felt like I had boarded a ship of hope and it had carried me to *Tikhaya Bukhta*, the Quiet Bay – this time not in the Crimea, on the Black Sea, but in my own heart.

We had until Monday – an eternity.

· 11 ·

We made love for two days and two nights. On Sunday afternoon, my insides aching, and with no shower since we'd parked on their enormous pink bed, we lounged in the bedroom, *Henry and June* playing on mute. I'd never written that letter to Kristina in New York. I didn't want to think of anything. I was in that rare state of bliss that lovers achieve after crossing the divide between guarded interest and unbridled vulnerability, allowing yourself to believe that another had not only enjoyed the erotic encounter but had accepted all of you, with flaws, insecurities and quirks, giving you a way out of loneliness, a promise of belonging.

I kept watching the film, mesmerized by the bed scene – in which June asks Anaïs to be with her – when, stroking my hand, Alexandra said:

"We should start a business together."

I looked at her, then turned to Emma, who nodded and smiled softly.

"You said not to mix friends and business," I reminded her.

"I never said you shouldn't do it with lovers."

Oh, they still want to be with me, I thought with relief. But that meant staying in Moscow indefinitely... And I hadn't planned on becoming a Moscovite. I'd hoped for a quick success on my own and a subsequent return to New York a year later. Yet I couldn't find a better business partner than Alexandra. But what about Emma? And what about my McLadley plans? I could break the Obundy contract, but it would have to be for something worthwhile. I felt a headache approaching and got up for a glass of water.

When I returned, Alexandra continued, "During the three years that Emma and I have been together, the magazine we created has become the most widely-read on the market – not in spite of our being lovers, but because of it. It's a family business. We had the biggest revenue of all the glossies last year. I'll tell you how: we're not afraid. I know Emma is always behind me, and she knows I'll never lead her in the wrong direction. We might argue. But we know what we are doing, and we're

good at it. Plus, there is always make-up sex after a fight."
Alexandra winked at me and slapped her knee. "Think
it over. You know business as Americans do. We're the
trendsetters. You'll help us get all those American firms
that have flooded Moscow in the hope of getting their
products to the Russian market yet don't have a clue
about the Russian mentality. We'll be their consultants
of choice."

Emma blew smoke at the ceiling.

"We can run this town. How is that?" Alexandra lit a
cigarette and crawled over to Emma.

On the one hand, I loved this idea, but on the other,
I wanted to think about it alone, away from the teddy
bears and soft hands exploring my body. "This is too fast
for me," I said.

"Since when are you a slow one, *Amerikanka?*" Alexandra
got up. "Don't drag it out. You know you're too good to be
a lowly account manager at an ad agency. And *Emmochka*
and I love the idea of a new business. We are tired of
the same-old with *Poise.*" She kissed Emma, and, leaving
me alone with my thoughts, they went out to buy more
cigarettes.

Once they left, I kept thinking that Alexandra's proposition
was exactly what I, Inga Belova, wanted to do in Russia. It
should have been my idea, this forging of a new company,

a new enterprise with me near the top. And it had been, in a way – except McLadley hadn't responded to it, and I had done nothing about it since. Alexandra, on the other hand, didn't need anyone's permission or backing to do what she envisioned. She plowed ahead on her own.

I tried to think, staring at the TV screen. If I accepted the offer, would I become a local businesswoman? Or would I be an expat joining a Russian business? The muddle of identities became unbearable. I knew that the gates to life in Russia – that is, Russia as I'd known it – had closed. I could only enter the new life with the help of someone like Alexandra. But that wouldn't be *my* business. On the other hand, that could be the best reason for staying in Russia – a business with lovers who had already oiled the wheels.

When they returned, I asked for a week to make a decision.

"What will change in a week?" asked Alexandra.

"I still have the Obundy job, and I need to sort out how to leave before my contract is up. More importantly, I'd like you to come to St. Petersburg with me next weekend. I want you to meet my father."

Emma looked at Alexandra, who said, "Really? That's big. You're a strange animal, *Amerikanka*. But so is everyone from St. Pete. You all need to nurse your melancholy and indecisiveness, and take it slow, and have others tell you what they think. I thought New York changed people."

"It does. But some things never change."

"Like what?"

Like wanting to be in love or needing your parents to be on your side no matter what, I thought. But instead, I kept silent.

· 12 ·

The *Red Arrow* – the same train where Anton had once loved me – would be the one to carry me again to St. Petersburg, this time with Emma and Alexandra. We entered the last car as the train pulled away from the station and walked the entire length before finding our compartment on the other end.

As we passed through several cars, with people smoking out the windows in the vestibules between them, I saw Anton at the far end of the corridor. Indeed, I had known that the band would be returning from Moscow that weekend. All the same, after we locked eyes for a moment, I passed him without a word.

In the next compartment, I discovered another band from St. Petersburg that was returning home. Alexandra high-fived these men – some handsome, some worn-out, all wearing a mysterious look of slight disillusionment with life, yet ready to celebrate it at any opportunity. Most were famous in certain underground circles, their songs played more and more often on the radio.

"Let's hit the bar. Moscow's treating." Alexandra beckoned them to follow us to the restaurant car to the sound of loud cheers. I squeezed her hand.

She ordered half a dozen bottles of red wine, and almost everyone lit a cigarette. Clouds of cheap smoke enveloped me with their acrid smell. After the second bottle of wine was emptied, I no longer cared that one could hang an axe in the air. It felt as if we were in someone's kitchen or on the set of *Henry and June*. Not that I bore any resemblance to Anaïs Nin, married to a banker and having an affair with a writer – or living in Paris, for that matter – but I was involved with two semi-celebrities, surrounded by excellent musicians. Our conversations about art and sex and money seemed to me the stuff of the French bistros of the 1920s. It was all very bohemian. And, crazy as it was, as fast as it may have happened, I was in love. With two women.

Emma and Alexandra took my hands in theirs and held them under the table. They took turns bringing a glass of wine to my lips, every sip a turn-on. Meanwhile, one of the musicians started impersonating himself, as if onstage. He jumped high in the air, twisting his whole body, his bald head almost touching the ceiling, lip-synching to the famous oldie by Alla Pugacheva, Russia's Cher, on the radio. The laughter grew more contagious, and all eyes were on the musician, allowing me to be with my girls. I felt as if I were standing on a mountaintop on a crisp summer day – ready to take off and start flying; a colored paraglider against the brilliant blue sky, a fireworks ready to light up the whole world.

At 4 AM, three hours before our arrival, we made to leave the dining car. As I turned back, I saw Anton's face in a cloud of smoke, his eyes on me. Then the door closed.

We didn't sleep. The berths happened to be an excellent prop for making out with two people at once. With my feet on the lower couchette, my hands on the upper, and my crotch somewhere in between, Emma's and Alexandra's lips and hands delivered me to ecstasy just as the train delivered us to the city of my youth.

* * *

The calm of St. Petersburg: sooty clouds low in the still air; the heavy sky familiar and comforting. I'd always thought that the tentative character of St. Petersburg's weather left an imprint on its residents, making them quiet, somber, and slightly melancholy. Time took slower steps here, as if it paused to observe the royal waters of the Neva or sift through the woven railings of the Summer Garden. Here, everything was pure and magical, yet real, like the White Nights.

The orderly skyline of the Nevsky Prospect was festooned with advertising banners and billboards, their awkward size and bad taste ruining the harmony of the Northern capital. Yet it was still my beloved St. Petersburg, and I wanted Emma and Alexandra to fall in love with it, too, for they'd only been there once before.

The cab sped through the sleepy city, weaving through a spider's web of bridges and canals, with pastel facades of Baroque buildings in regimented rows along the Neva embankment, their windows sparkling in the morning sun. We arrived in the quiet backyard of a large, yellow Stalin-era building. The intercom was broken, the lobby door lock torn out. The cramped entrance smelled of urine and cats, and the inner panels of the small elevator were filigreed with graffiti – everything familiar and unchanged for decades.

Emma and Alexandra grew quiet, as if the city had already made an imprint on them. But the truth may have been simpler: they weren't sure how to behave in front of my father. Neither one had come out to their own parents, yet they were to share a bed in my father's apartment. We held hands one last time before ringing the doorbell.

I hadn't seen my father in two years. He was approaching 60, but his eyes sparkled with youth and intellect. As he opened the door, I could tell he was happy to see me, yet apprehensive about the guests: he was nervous about meeting new people. The slight awkwardness of his appearance was always present on first encounters with strangers: a shy smile, hunched shoulders, hands trying to calm each other, and kind eyes hiding behind spectacles. In these moments, I watched the professor turn into a shy student in need of reassurance from his teacher, and I wanted to run to his rescue, embarrassed for him at the same time.

"*Papochka, privet!* So happy to see you!"

I wrapped my hands around his neck. "Meet my good friends from Moscow, Emma and Alexandra, publishers of a magazine," I said, putting the latest issue of *Poise* on the side table.

Alexandra stepped forward and shook his hand with both of hers, something she had probably seen President Clinton do on TV when greeting supporters.

"Welcome, welcome," my father said with a wide smile, holding Alexandra's hands a second too long.

Emma stood behind her, nodding.

"So good to see you," he said, hugging me again. "Come on in. I made breakfast."

He led us to the kitchen and pointed to a table with

steaming *bliny*, coffee and jars of homemade preserves. I kissed him, frazzled after the sleepless night on the train, but trying hard to hide it.

"Let me show the girls their room first," I said. "We'll be right out."

We walked into my old room instead. Instantly, I was transported back to my childhood: the wallpaper with miniscule maroon flowers, slightly faded but still more or less the same as when I was six; the map of the world above the couch, with "My dream" written next to New York; my childhood photographs on glassed-in book-shelves. The room had shrunk since I'd last seen it. I walked to my desk, postcards of roses and puppies still above it, Sophia Loren in black and white, smiling luxuriously, and a photo of little me – a burst of blond hair and piercing blue eyes. I paused for a moment, wishing I were alone, so that I could turn around and become a six-year-old again, running out to the kitchen, where Dad had prepared his usual Sunday omelet feast. Mom was there, too, looking on with approval. It was almost as if I could smell the eggs cooking if I tried hard enough.

Emma tugged at my shoulder, then kissed me on the neck, and I had joined the threesome again.

"What a girly girl you are!" Alexandra said, observing the room. "Who knew you'd keep all this fluff!"

"They haven't touched anything for eight years," I said with a sigh. "They still hope I'll come back."

I showed them to my grandmother's room, untouched since her death, with a royal bed in the corner, flowery curtains, an armchair under a reading light, and walls covered with black-and-white photos of her ancestors, the Russian nobility that had lost everything after the 1917 revolution. Back in my room, alone, I put my head on a pillow and fell asleep.

I woke up from a touch on my neck – a soft touch that I recognized as my father's. I looked at the flowers on the wallpaper, this time thinking, suddenly and surprisingly, that something had been lost forever. With my head facing the wall, I whispered, "I missed you, Papa."

"I miss you, too, *malysh*," he said touching my shoulder.

I turned around and managed a smile.

"Shall we have breakfast?" he said.

"In a minute."

I lay on my side and counted till ten, pushing back the tears, then went to wash my face. I peeked into the adjacent room. Emma and Alexandra were fast asleep, embracing on grandmother's enormous bed, adorned with half a dozen pillows. I didn't wake them.

The kitchen, unchanged since I'd left home, was still dominated by the familiar worn-out beige cushions on the corner bench. I reclaimed my seat by the window. The sight of the white-and-black brick of a radio, an anachronism from Soviet times that only broadcasted three stations, warmed my heart.

"How is it going in Moscow?" Father asked, searching my face, sipping steaming tea from his enormous mug.

"Great. I'm thinking of starting my own business. With partners, of course," I admitted for the first time.

"In Moscow? With whom?"

"With Emma and Alexandra."

He frowned and quickly sipped the tea – too quickly, burning his tongue – but didn't object, practicing his old rule of letting me make my own life decisions.

"How long have you known them?" he asked.

"About a month."

"And you trust them enough to go into business?"

Why not? I thought. *Sometimes one day is enough to get to know a person.* But I couldn't tell him that we were lovers.

"They were highly recommended by people I trust," I said, looking at the tea flakes floating in my cup. "And they helped me with my current situation at Obundy. If it weren't for them, I'd be sitting somewhere in Ryazan' right now."

"Make sure you weigh all your options," he said after another pause. "You're a big girl. To run your own business is interesting, but risky. But I'm sure you know that."

I wished he'd ask me more questions, be more curious. Why did he have to keep his distance, like a diplomat? I wanted him to endorse my choice, so that the burden of making a decision didn't rest solely on me.

"I always wanted to run my own business. It's much easier to do in Russia than in New York."

Why did I feel compelled to convince my father? Why had he let me doubt myself? I was already full of doubt as it was. He made me feel the same as he had in 1989, before I had left for New York: I was free to do whatever I wished, no matter what he thought of it. It didn't feel like support at all. Indifference, maybe.

Alexandra's head appeared from behind the kitchen door. "Good morning!"

"Please join us," said my father. He went to the kitchen counter, making himself invisible, as Russian parents do in the company of younger people.

"Stay with us," I pleaded.

But he only smiled, refreshed the platter with more hot pancakes, and excused himself.

I poured more tea into my large yellow mug and returned to the corner seat, my own for as long as I could remember. Alexandra devoured the pancakes while Emma looked out the window, not touching the food, slowly sipping her coffee.

"Something happen?" I asked.

"We had sex. Emma says she's really into you," Alexandra said, looking at me.

"And you said?"

"Me, too."

If they like me so much, why do they have sex without me?

"A little insane to have sex while my father is at home, don't you think?" I asked.

"We can be quiet when we want to," Alexandra replied and gave me a steely look.

"I'm sure," I said, and went to get the teakettle. I poured tea for both of them. My hands shook, but I wasn't about to make a scene. Not in my family apartment. Emma took my other hand.

"I told my father about the business."

"And?" Alexandra asked.

"He loves the idea." I freed my hand from Emma's and returned to my seat.

"Great! Do you still need to go to New York? Because we can start right away. Why wait?"

"I have to deal with Obundy. Terminating a contract with one of the best advertising firms, no matter how crappy the actual job turned out to be, won't look good on my résumé. I also have to tie up some lose ends. And I hope you'll visit. We can go to South Beach together before returning to Moscow," I said, looking at Emma.

She turned from the window, bit her lower lip and

stared at me. Then she exploded.

"You can break your contract right here, in Moscow. We'll take care of Laura. We've done this once already. What's in New York? An apartment you can hardly afford, and a bunch of ex-boyfriends who don't give a shit about you? Who needs you there? Nobody! That's why you are here. Choosing between nothing and a sure path to success shouldn't be that hard. You can do much better here, and you know it." There was no trace of affection in her voice. I stared at her numbly. Alexandra got up, went around the table, and set on the bench next to me.

"Okay, okay. Don't get upset," she said. "Of course you need to go to New York, and we'll go to Miami with you – right, *Emmochka*?" Alexandra took my hand. "We'll help you with your apartment sublet, and come back to Moscow in the fall, together."

I felt a tear escape from my right eye. I wiped it and said, "I'm going for a walk. Join me if you'd like." I wished they wouldn't. I cursed myself for bringing them to St. Petersburg, for agreeing to their business idea, for meeting them at all.

· 13 ·

By the time the cab dropped us off on the corner of Nevsky Prospect and Griboedov Canal a few hours later, *Kazan* and *The Savior of the Spilled Blood* cathedrals in full view, my anger had subsided. I was taking Emma and Alexandra on a boat cruise along the canals. I wanted them to see the city as I did: an airy presence of longing and melancholy.

As had been the case for three centuries, all roads in St. Petersburg led to the grand Nevsky Prospect, with people strolling its entire length in their best weekend outfits. It still was the Champs Elysées of St. Petersburg, where French had once been heard as often as Russian. Nevsky displayed the usual array of personalities and types, from teenage girls in tight skirts looking to pick up men, to young couples with toddlers in tow, to aged couples returning from the matinee at the Philharmonic. An occasional Mercedes or BMW flew by, though most of the cars were still old dirty Ladas and Moskviches.

As we stood in line for the tickets, I wanted to recite poetry, but I couldn't think of anything aside from Blok's famous "Night. Street. Light. Apotheca." The heavy steel waters licked the granite walls below our feet. If I could move to Moscow, why couldn't they move to St. Petersburg?

So I asked Alexandra. "Would you move to St. Pete with me?"

She turned to me with a squint, her eyebrows raised. Emma kissed me with slight embarrassment.

"*Amerikanka*, you're full of surprises," said Alexandra before running down the pass to the boat. "What the hell would we do here? There is no money, no businesses, and everyone is half-asleep. You're the only person I know from St. Pete who has the energy of a Moscovite."

"A New Yorker."

"Just don't try to pull the nostalgia bit on us. All right, dear?"

"What if there were businesses here? Hypothetically speaking, would you move with me?"

"We don't live hypothetically, do we?" Alexandra said.

Without speaking, I followed her onto a small cruise

boat, the awkwardness hanging above us like an umbrella.

We settled in the back, the only tourists on our boat. Emma and Alexandra lit cigarettes. As the boat moved slowly under low bridges, almost touching the granite banks of Griboedov Canal, then Neva, then Fontanka, I watched the water sparkle under the late afternoon sun and thought of my high school friends, Igor and Elena, with whom I had once walked on these granite embankments, talking of future plans and aspirations. I wanted to tell someone about my two lovers, but who would understand? Maybe Kristina in New York.

"I brought wine," said Emma, pulling out a bottle of Cuvée, plastic cups, and some grapes.

As if speaking might ruin the beauty surrounding us, we grew quiet. The boat plied the glistening waters of the Neva, and I remembered the first time I had seen the Hudson, in 1989, from the air, onboard a Czech Airlines flight – my first encounter with New York. Almost nine years earlier. I couldn't tell if, since then, things had changed too much or not enough.

Sam, the exchange student I'd met in St. Petersburg (then Leningrad), had greeted me at JFK in an old maroon Cadillac – rented, the height of luxury. The ride to the city had been a revelation, the wide road smooth as silk, unlike the half-ruined pavements of Leningrad. My behind drowned in the plush leather seat, more comfortable than any couch. And I'd never seen so many lights and billboards. As I admired them, my first-ever brush with *zagranitsa*, the abroad, Sam paid the Triboro Bridge toll and warned me, "Only the air is free here."

We arrived at his apartment, on the corner of Central Park West and 110th Street, where, the next morning, I woke up to see a half-naked young woman sitting on top of another one, lying on a bed, in the living room. "This is my roommate and her girlfriend," explained Sam. I was stunned by the matter-of-factness of that indecency. I could never imagine seeing such a scene unfolding in Leningrad. But I kept it to myself. Maybe it was normal in New York, I thought. I'd watched American students clip their nails and pick at their toes in front of each other. This could have been another one of those customary things. What did I know at the time? I had just arrived the night before.

Alexandra waved at me, and I realized I'd become the one on whom other women sat, half-naked.

"Inga, if we go to Miami with you, we'll have to miss our annual trip to Sardinia," she said. "Your South Beach'd better be good!"

"I promise," I said.

I took photos of them. They looked serene – a brunette

and a blonde, so contrasting yet so alike, their faces almost touching, as if two birds perched atop a tree and washed over by the August sun reflected in the heavy waters of the Neva. As I looked at the women, I was filled with a happy feeling: that magic moment when you don't need to seek any answers or wonder what you're doing with your life. The sureness of knowing that everything has fallen into place, as it would on a good day in childhood, when you got a perfect score on a school exam and your parents let you go to the movies and the boy you liked chose you among all the other girls in class to smile at.

I kissed Emma, then Alexandra, on the lips, St. Petersburg the only witness to this show. Or so I had assumed. When I looked up, I saw that Dmitry Vernik and his wife, of all people, were staring down at us from the wide *Potseluyev* (the Kissing) Bridge. Dmitry seemed to recognize the women. *Great*, I thought. *Now the rumors will start.* Embarrassment. Regret for a moment ruined. Dmitry Vernik, true to himself, always appearing at the most inopportune time, always witnessing the juiciest scenes. How many times had he walked into the girls' locker room during phys ed – as if by mistake – only to catch me changing, topless?

"Fuck," I said through gritted teeth, waving at him.

Emma and Alexandra lifted their wine glasses in greeting.

"Who are they?" Alexandra asked.

"Dmitry, my high school friend, and his wife."

"Looks like you'll have to tell people what you're doing with us and why." She pierced me with her brown eyes. "Are you ready?"

"Are you?" I fired back.

"I don't have to explain anything to anybody," Alexandra said, then went on to do just that: "I live my life, and I have nothing to hide. I'm not sorry about the things I do. It's a gut thing. And I don't hesitate once I've made up my mind."

Having to answer questions just when all the ripples had begun to settle. Why? This was mine and nobody else's. And I wasn't ready to share this with the rest of the world. Everything was too new and precious, and I didn't want to scare this romance off. I was scared myself.

"He won't ask any questions," I finally said. "And if he does, I don't have to answer. Falling in love with two women isn't something I can explain. Especially to a man."

Alexandra got up and gave me a long kiss. I closed my eyes, my body weightless, only registering the sounds of the water lapping against the boat, my lips answering hers. When I sat back down, I saw that Dmitry was still staring at me from the bridge.

And then I felt a chill, either because of the wind that had picked up as the day was winding down or because I knew that the bubble of my privacy had burst. If I felt embarrassed about my connection with the women in front of Dmitry, one of my oldest friends, what was I thinking starting a business with them? I was committing everything to these two: both my career and my love life would be in their hands. Yet it would all end, sooner or later, and when it did, everything else would end at once, too. I'd be like the old lady from the fairy tale who had too many wishes for the goldfish her husband had once caught, only to end up with her old beat-up bucket, forever straining and failing to fetch the goldfish again.

I looked at Emma and Alexandra, who were sitting on a bench kissing as if I didn't exist. Just then, Emma got up and pulled me in. And I let the wind erase my worries, as my girlfriends kissed the palms of my hands.

Half an hour later, tipsy and famished, we stepped on the pier and walked along the embankment, *The Savior on the Blood* Cathedral greeting us solemnly. Opening the door to the first place in sight with a promise of food, we entered a Japanese restaurant, with white linen and yellow chandeliers.

"Three, please," Alexandra said, speeding by the hostess, a tall brunette with pearly teeth. After a few steps, Alexandra stopped and turned around, winking at Emma and pointing to the woman. Both smiled with approval.

Dining at Japanese restaurants, still a novelty in

post-*perestroika* Russia, was the ultimate sign of success among the locals, yet Alexandra took it further. She lunched in Japanese restaurants almost daily, entertaining clients and friends alike, doling out crisp hundreds at the end of every meal without flinching. I was not to pay in restaurants – the rule firmly established by Alexandra. She treated everybody. Always. Fine with me: men always paid in Russia, and in this relationship Alexandra filled that role.

We sat at the corner table, in a booth nested in an alcove with a waterfall streaming down one wall and tea candles flickering on the other. Exposed brick, soft cushions on low couches, delicate Japanese porcelain on wooden tables, a half-empty restaurant – a refuge in a city when the day hadn't quite ended and the evening had yet to begin.

Then I saw it: at the other end of the restaurant sat Nick, Kristina's husband. He was speaking with a woman whose face I couldn't see, but who was certainly not his wife.

"Looks like you'll meet some of my New York friends before you even get there." I turned to Alexandra, pointing toward Nick. I tapped my fingers on the table. "My best friend's husband."

"Kristina is here?" Emma asked.

"No, just Nick."

"Who's the woman with him?" Alexandra asked.

Long, dark hair, very white skin, large eyes. I couldn't see more, but could tell she was a beauty. No older than 22. They were holding hands.

"I don't know," I said, watching the waiter place our sushi order in front of us. Then I saw Nick heading towards us. I had the sinking feeling that something was very wrong and that I didn't want to know the details.

A moment later, Nick hovered over the table.

"Inga, is that you?"

I wondered why he even had to ask.

"Nick? What are you doing here?" I tried to act natural, scanning his face for signs of how to behave. His companion remained seated, fiddling with a napkin.

"I'm working on some new deals with local musicians." He gestured towards his table. I nodded, feeling that I couldn't display any proper reaction, as I had no clue what people did in such situations.

Alexandra stared at him, trying to hide a smile. She glanced at Emma, who lowered her gaze.

"May I steal you for a moment?" Nick asked.

I followed him outside, mouthing "just a second" to the girls. We passed by the woman at his table; she didn't lift her eyes. Outside, Nick waved me closer to the railing of the canal, away from the crowds.

"You didn't see me here today, okay?"

I reminded him that Kristina was my best friend.

"All the more reason not to mention anything to her." He wasn't nervous. He seemed unmoved, a man who'd probably been in this situation before and knew his way out. "The girl is a loyal friend. She's no threat to Kristina or my family. So I'd appreciate it if you didn't tell anyone. Just between us, right?" He winked.

"I have to go," I said.

I turned around, a nagging feeling inside my stomach. Why had we come to this restaurant?

"A girl in every port, heh?" said Alexandra.

I folded my napkin into the smallest possible square, then unfolded it. I repeated this several times, staring at their half-eaten sushi. "Can we talk about something else, please?"

"Sure. Tell us more about your other friends in New York."

"Stop it," Emma interrupted. "Don't worry about it," she said, turning to me. "It's none of our business, and we won't mention anything to your friends when we're in New York." She looked directly at Alexandra. "And we won't talk about this now, either." She finished her glass of wine and returned it to the table with a loud knock.

"I do want you to meet my friends. Kristina, especially." I was close to tears, yet tried to remain civilized. I gulped my wine.

"Sure, Sweetness." Emma took my hand and kissed

my palm.

"*Emmochka's* never been to New York," Alexandra said. "I was there ages ago. Can't wait to say hi again to the Big Fucking Apple."

I poked at my sushi.

Emma pulled at my sleeve. "I want you," she whispered and put her hand on my crotch. She unzipped my pants and pulled me closer, spreading my legs. I didn't resist. I felt as if she could read my thoughts and had decided to cure me the best way she knew how – by loving me. Alexandra enclosed me from my left and put her hands on mine. They each fixed their eyes on me as I gave in, half-sliding under the table, my forehead on Emma's shoulder to muffle the moans. "Emma…" I whispered. "I'm going to scream…" I buried my face in the curve of her neck.

"Good girl," she said, kissing me.

When I looked up, Alexandra was sitting across the table twisting a dead cigarette, her eyes sad. I hadn't seen her move away from us. The waiter, several feet from our table, dropped the dessert menu on the floor.

· 14 ·

The new lock my father had installed was complicated; the door wasn't opening. When I finally conquered it, the apartment greeted us quietly, specks of dust hanging in the air, lit up by the setting sun. The floor-to-ceiling hall mirror, a constant witness to our lives, reflected the familiar plaid wallpaper, faded over the years to a dull beige and tired yellow, rows of dusty book shelves, and a collection of gardening tools near the door.

I approached the mirror and saw the note left by my father, saying that he would be back at eight, after a trip to a hardware store, the never-ending tale of fixing cabinets and windowsills and installing new fixtures, his lifelong hobby. I looked at myself, hair tangled from the wind, eyes wild with anticipation. I knew that I'd left a part of myself in that mirror before, that it would preserve this moment – before the sunset, before the words were spoken – and the next time I'd look into it, a different Inga would emerge.

"Belova!" Alexandra said. "We're wasting time!"

We dropped the bags to the floor, kicked off our shoes, and ran to my grandmother's room, our blood thick with alcohol. Alexandra spread me on the royal bed by the window, taking over the top of my body, planting airy kisses on the edges of my lips, while Emma worked me from the waist down: she unzipped my jeans, threw them on the floor, and took me in her hands, her tongue drawing a line from my navel to the edge of my polka-dotted underwear. She pulled the waistband down with her teeth, and her tongue traveled over my skin with a precision and mastery I had come to admire.

Her lips arrived, her tongue moving ever so softly, extracting the first "Ah" from me. Alexandra whispered, "Give it to her, baby."

I did. I gave Emma all of me. My heart pounding, I repeated, "I love you, I love you…What are we doing? How can it be? I'm so happy…" Words entangled and meshed, tears…

They smiled at me, their hands gliding over my breasts from each side. I pulled Emma close to my face, tasted me on her lips. As she put her head on my chest, I noticed an old photo of my grandmother observing us from the dresser. I reached out and turned it face-down. A loyal communist throughout her life, this grandma would have probably denounced my behavior along with the actual existence of my girlfriends, these women who could engage in such unbecoming conduct, which I was enjoying so thoroughly.

Emma moved over to Alexandra and pinned her to the flowery pillow. In bed, Emma played the dominant role, with Alexandra taking a back seat, a page-turner for a concert pianist. Theirs was a different kind of love-making, that of lovers who'd mastered their favorite primal dance, bold and powerful. Emma straddled Alexandra, who rolled back her head, shiny black hair spread over the pillow, bangs covering closed eyes. She bit her lips with a remnant of a smile, moaning softly. I withdrew to the corner of the bed, covered my feet with a sheet, and watched. There was no jealousy. I watched them as they had been before me, two lovers without the third. Alexandra hit the bed with her small hands as she gave herself to Emma, who stared at her with a look of a hunter in her blue eyes. "*Da, da, da!*" Emma shouted to Alexandra's climax and fell beside her, panting. A drop of sweat slid over her left temple. Alexandra brought Emma's face to hers, whispering, "My girl... My sweet girl."

We lost track of time, succumbing to sleep. At midnight, I left grandmother's room and tiptoed into mine. My father must have gotten home while we napped. I hoped he hadn't peeked into either room, one empty, the other with three sleeping women embraced on a bed. I unfolded the sofa bed, making an indent in the pillow where my head would have been, and sat quietly. After a while I mustered enough courage to join my father in the dining room, across the hall. He was having tea with his wife, watching a late-night movie.

"I'll have some tea with you, okay?" I whispered and ran into the kitchen to get a cup. On the way, I peeked into the other room, at the women fast asleep. Father and I watched the movie in silence, sipping tea. It was good to be home, at last. I was wondering if he had an idea about me, and them. Even if he did, he wouldn't ask. We didn't need to talk. Just sitting next to him as he watched TV in his faded yellow shirt and worn-out dark blue sweatpants made me feel anchored. I had my father by my side, and he approved of me.

Or did he? A worm of doubt in my heart.

And the women… Why did they need me? To be a Band-Aid for their flailing relationship? I recalled how they had argued the night of our departure for St. Petersburg, Alexandra accusing Emma of being irresponsible (how?) and Emma shouting at the top of her lungs, "Leave me alone! I've had enough of you!" To which Alexandra had hissed, "I'll show you 'enough'!"

I walked back to my room, palms sweaty, heart accelerating.

Back in my bed, alone, I couldn't sleep, my internal motor idling. In New York, Kristina might be online. I opened my laptop. I needed to speak to somebody from my "other reality," to bounce my life off of a friend who knew me well, before Moscow and the threesome, who wouldn't ask too many questions. And I had to find out if Kristina knew about Nick.

"*Privet*," I wrote. "I'm coming back next week, but only for a few weeks. Someone offered me the chance to start a business in Moscow. Well, not just 'someone.' Two women – very cool, successful, and smart. I agreed. I've been spending most of my time with them. Actually, they're coming to New York with me soon. I'm curious what you'll think of them. There is more to this, but I'll write later. It's after 2 AM here. Kisses."

I hit the "Send" button and sat there, waiting for something, not sure what. I couldn't muster the courage to tell my best friend about my love affair or her husband's. Ours was so beautiful, so magical – as long as we remained unburdened by the outside world, with its curious glances and the need for gossip. Once I attempted to describe or explain the threesome to someone (in my mind), it seemed unnatural, almost freaky. I didn't know what I should tell my friends. Or perhaps I didn't need to say anything; I'd simply introduce the women in New York and let everyone figure it out.

My screen displayed a new email coming in.

"I thought you'd fallen off the face of the Earth. We all miss you here," Kristina wrote. "I can't tell you how much has happened this summer. Lisa's boyfriend finally came over from Germany – still hoping to score an exhibit here. I'm not sure how things are between them, though. You missed lots of great parties, too, but I'm sure you had plenty of that in Moscow. Did you go to St. Petersburg? Nick is there right now signing new bands – do you want his number? Maybe he can take a look at Anton's band and bring them over to New York."

Why hadn't I thought of it myself? But I was no longer interested in Anton's band or in his future; in fact, I almost hoped for his sake that the eternal high-school world he'd built for himself would come crumbling down. Or maybe that was just my bitter sense of injustice spinning its wheels. In any case, it was too late now.

"I would love to meet your new friends," Kristina's letter continued. "Are you sure you want to go into business with women, though? I remember you don't trust them, except for me. But things change, right? Can't wait to see you! Gotta run. Kisses. K."

I let out a sigh. Kristina... I knew I couldn't tell her about being in love with two women. She wouldn't understand. Even I didn't understand. But I didn't have to, I just lived it and it made sense. And what about Nick and the girl in the restaurant? I stared at the screen. She was my best friend. I had to protect her. I couldn't decide what to do, so I turned off the laptop and went back to bed.

Images of the Airplanes onstage and of Nick in the restaurant floated over me, then of Emma on top of Alexandra. Finally, sleep enveloped me, and I dozed off to the sounds of hushed whispers behind the wall.

· 15 ·

I saw a silhouette in the doorway. It paused, then entered the room. Another appeared. They approached my bed. I couldn't tell if these were men or women. Curious to know the dream's end, I made no effort to wake up. The first figure pulled the sheet down and slid off my underwear. My legs tingled, and I felt warm spirals traveling through me. I wanted to stay in that place forever, swimming in the vanilla mousse of being touched in the right places, when I heard my own moaning. I woke up. Emma's face was at my crotch.

"I think I'll die now," I whispered.

"Please don't," said Alexandra. "I have no interest in necrophilia."

She got into bed with me. The three of us lay there,

holding hands and whispering about whether my father had heard anything. My plans didn't include his knowing of my affair, and I knew that neither Emma nor Alexandra's parents were aware of their daughters' interest in women.

"Why do you hide it from your parents?" I asked.

"My mother lives in her own little world, with church bells and home-cooked meals," Alexandra said. "My father divorced her when I was nine – went for a younger woman, so she's had enough reality checks as far as I am concerned. Do you think I'll make her happy by announcing that I sleep with women? She knows something is out of the ordinary, but it's easier to leave things as they are."

She added, "Emma's mother became a nun when she suspected something was going on with both of her daughters. She used to be a gorgeous woman, stylish and sharp. Then, about ten years ago," Alexandra propped herself up on one elbow to better see Emma, "she donned long skirts, grew her hair into a braid, stopped using makeup, and went for the church. Her poor husband still doesn't know what to make of it. Can you imagine? Marries a knockout who turns into a nun? And two lesbian daughters to top it off. I mean, he must see the reality. Emma – what do you say?"

"We don't talk about it," she replied. "I just wish my

mother would go back to her normal life."

"She probably thinks the same about you and Maria," suggested Alexandra.

"I doubt my father would become a monk if he thought I was a lesbian," I said.

"You're not a lesbian," Alexandra answered. "You slept with men most of your life. And probably will again, even though *Emmochka* and I can't stand to think about it."

"Shut up," hissed Emma. "Both of you."

"What? You don't think she still likes men? Even *Emmochka* was once married. When she was 21. I guess the man wasn't that great in bed, so she became one instead." Alexandra laughed into her knuckles.

"Really? You were married?" I felt my eyebrows arch into extreme curves.

"It was in my previous life. And I left him not because he wasn't good in bed, but because I found male energy offensive," said Emma, turning to Alexandra. "Better share your story."

"My story? There is no story. I once had sex with a guy and didn't like it. I've been a lesbian ever since."

I thought there was much to learn about my girls, and I hoped there was more to our togetherness than sex.

"Okay, enough. Let's go to sleep," I said. "I have an errand to run early in the morning."

We kissed, and the girls tiptoed out, stocky Emma in

dark-blue silk pajamas, and slender Alexandra in a white T-shirt and green boxers. They'd make love again before falling asleep.

· 16 ·

I left early, without breakfast. Visiting the cemetery was traditionally an early-morning affair and, with no food in my stomach, I felt cleansed from the previous night's adventures, purer for meeting with Mom. I went to buy flowers first: white chrysanthemums, her favorites.

I took the metro. It calmed me. Unlike the filth of the New York subway, with muddy puddles, litter scattered on the tracks, and rats crossing the rails, St. Petersburg metro stations were museum halls, sparkling clean despite the utter absence of trash bins. With trains running every sixty seconds and men still giving up their seats to women, it brought order back into my life, helped me find much-needed grounding before visiting my mother's grave. The regular people around me, most of them reading, brought me back to the life I'd had when she was still around, before New York and the threesome.

A long escalator carried me up to a busy market square, peppered with stalls of food and flowers for sale. A couple of lines had formed near the stands with freshly baked bread, nobody interested in flowers, their prices exorbitant. I picked six long chrysanthemums without bargaining over the price. The number of flowers had to be odd for all occasions except in matters of death – an old tradition, strictly observed by every Russian. The six, then, was almost a lucky seven.

A twenty-minute walk brought me to the cemetery, laid out among the pine trees – the oldest and largest in St. Petersburg. At the entrance, a large monument to the victims of the 900-day Siege of Leningrad guarded the graves.

I stepped into a small church in the opening of the pine forest, my head covered with a maroon shawl, and crossed myself. Babushkas, their wrinkled faces framed by bright scarves, mumbled prayers in front of large, glittering icons on the walls, lit up by dozens of candles on the altars below them. I smelled hot wax and incense, looked around, hoping I didn't provoke disapproving glances from the babushkas, always ready to reprimand people for not knowing the Church rituals. I bought a thick yellow candle and lit it at the square altar, crossing myself again and wishing for Mom to rest in peace. I stood there for a while, inhaling the stale damp air of the church, staring at the candlelight. The choir started singing. I thought of my grandmother, who, unlike my paternal grandma – the communist (in whose bed my lovers now slept) – had been a believer all her life and had brought me to church once, when I was five or so. It had taken twenty years and leaving Russia for me to come back to her church.

The sounds reached the wooden ceiling and reverberated, enveloping me in peace and sadness. I stood with my head bowed, crossing myself to the priest's words (which I couldn't decipher) each time the others around me did, checking the babushkas' faces after every crossing to see if they registered disapproval. I waited for the psalm to end before leaving the church.

I walked along the wide road, which was crowded with monuments on both sides: some recent, with large headstones and golden engravings, drowning in fresh flowers; others old and sickly – simple crosses over dry bumps of soil, forgotten and listless, visited only by wind and rain.

Dry leaves covered the small hill where both my mother and grandmother, the believer, were buried. A large spider web had spread over the photos, and wild grass ran rampant under my feet. The iron gate was stuck in the mud and covered by dead leaves. I had to push with my whole body to open it.

The maple tree shrub that my father had planted had grown into a beautiful tree, its orange leaves casting a soft shadow. I stood there, listening to my heartbeat and to the wind rustling through the leaves.

"*Zdravstvuj, Mamochka.*"

I put on the gloves, took the broom, and set to work. First, the leaves had to be swept and the grass torn out. Then, the mums in the beds pruned and watered. I cleaned the photographs, removed the wilted roses from the plastic vase in the corner, and put white chrysanthemums in their place. Twenty minutes later, I was sitting down on a crooked bench, rubbing my hands, and I began as I always did.

"I miss you so much." I spoke softly but out loud, looking at her already-faded photograph in its small porcelain frame. "I know you can see me from there. I see you, too. I got an MBA in New York and now work in Moscow. I returned to Russia – something you'd always hoped I'd do. And here I am – a little too late." I paused and looked around, wondering if those buried nearby could hear my monologue.

"Dad is doing well. I see he hasn't visited in a while, but you know how busy he is. I think of you often. Wanted to ask you – how were things between you and Dad? I never saw you quarrel, yet we never talked about how it was being married to him. Like a woman to a woman. Did he love you enough? Did I? Or were we too busy with our own lives? Oh, how I could use your advice, especially now."

I paused again, looking over to the treetops. I had never really discussed any matters of the heart with my mother – neither hers nor my own: her first boyfriend or how she had lost her virginity or plans for a family of my own. As in every Soviet family, a mother never brought the subject up, and a daughter never asked. And it had remained like this until my mother had died. The daughter had finally grown up enough to seek advice, but there was no longer anyone to provide it. I felt the tears approaching, yet I wouldn't cry at the cemetery. Never. I'd cry for Mom when least expected, and then it was real – and the only honest way to miss her.

I thought of mentioning Emma and Alexandra, but decided against it. She probably already knew about us.

"I'm sorry I didn't come sooner."

These last words formed a lump in my throat. I lost my balance and nearly fell on my face, but at the last moment regained my footing. I imagined my mother smiling at me, as mothers will at their clumsy children. I returned her imagined smile.

"I'll be back soon. *Do svidaniya, Mamochka.* I miss you."

I lingered a moment longer before closing the gate behind me. I didn't know when we would talk like this again. I didn't know when I'd have another moment to reflect on my family and what my leaving had meant to them. I had a nagging feeling that my mother died because I'd left and there was nobody to love her. She could have stopped me from going, but she hadn't. Because she loved me.

I was now on the main alley toward the exit, passing babushkas trotting in single file, with their flowers and cleaning tools, walking past middle-aged couples with sour facial expressions. Babushkas were probably visiting their friends. And the couples? Most likely, their older relatives. I wondered who'd visit my grave when I died. I didn't imagine when it might be. And where. But I wished that Mom could be with me.

The tears came as the revolving doors let me into the metro.

· 17 ·

I didn't get back to the apartment until noon. I expected to find it empty, with the girls out for breakfast in the city, my father on errands. But when I opened the door, everyone, including my father's wife, was gathered at the kitchen table.

"We're just finishing breakfast," Father said, getting up from the kitchen table to greet me. "Where did you go? Are you hungry?"

"I visited Mom. I'm starving," I said, looking down, since I knew that the subject made him uncomfortable if discussed in front of his wife.

We went into the kitchen. Half-eaten omelets, half-empty coffee cups, a crumbled newspaper on the table – breakfast unfinished, as if there'd been a discussion that hadn't left enough time for food.

"We should go walk around," I said to the girls to change the subject.

"Alexandra and Emma mentioned The Hermitage in your plans for today." For some reason unknown to me, my father sounded very satisfied. "I was suggesting Petrodvorets, though. Imagine – they've never been!"

"Good idea. Ladies, are you ready for a trip to the Russian Versailles?" I asked.

"Absolutely," Alexandra said, getting up.

"Did I miss something?" I asked.

"Your father thinks highly of our magazine," Alexandra replied. "He even said he wished that there had been a publication like that when he was coming of age."

I looked at my father. He had never discussed his coming-of-age with me, let alone the magazines he'd read as a youth. I had no idea he knew *Poise* even existed.

He turned to me with a soft smile. Perhaps he wanted to "fit in" with my friends. But why now? He had never discussed things like that with me: what moved him, what it was like living with Stalin in power and his mother a devoted Communist (who had hardly cared about me, her only granddaughter). The only thing I knew was that he had never joined the Communist Party, and I respected him for that.

Alexandra sat back down and went on talking with my

father. I poured myself a cup of coffee and sat next to Emma, who, as usual, kept to herself in the company of strangers. Elena, Dad's wife, also kept quiet. I marveled at Alexandra's ability to charm my father in so little time. The same powers that had seduced me worked for him – wit, a sparkling personality, open-mindedness. Maybe that was the power of true artists – to inspire people. I knew Alexandra had been an artist in her "previous life" and had only turned to magazine publishing after graduate school. I'd never seen her paint, though, had never seen any of her artworks – though I had heard them praised – and couldn't imagine Alexandra at an easel. As for Emma's past, it was a complete mystery to me, nor did I quite understand her role at the magazine, save for being Alexandra's lover. Perhaps Emma's enormous energy, so well-displayed during sex, was the driving force behind many of their business deals.

I stared at the tablecloth, yellow and red flowers on white, letting the conversation float above and around me without entering my ears or touching any part of my brain. I wasn't ready yet to return to the world of the living; I wanted to linger a while longer at my mother's grave. So I got up and left the table. In my room, a new issue of *Poise* sat on the desk. I came closer. It was spread open to an article, its title looming large over the pages: "Three in Love." I stared in disbelief. Maybe my father had guessed something about me after all. He had been the one receiving my mail while I was away. Maybe he had connected the dots when I'd arrived with two women at his front door. Maybe it hadn't been that hard to figure out. I'd never brought out-of-towners to spend the night before. I felt the blood rushing to my cheeks and forehead. I went to the bathroom, turned the spigot, and splashed cold water on my face.

I looked in the square mirror. What if the threesome had been set up by Emma and Alexandra, after all? What was the true reason behind it? To get me as a business partner or to spice up their relationship? I dismissed the thoughts. I wanted them myself, both of them: Alexandra as a business partner, Emma as a lover.

Emma. I shivered thinking of her.

"I think Emma is ready to go solo with me, too," I mouthed into the mirror—the same mirror into which, at age seven, I had spelled out words in English and Russian, wondering, for example, how it was possible that the number of letters for the word "dog" didn't match in different languages. *DOG.* Three letters. *SOBAKA.* Six. How could two such different words possibly stand for the same thing? Or (on the other hand) could two similar words refer to completely unrelated things? Dish and fish. Mountain and fountain. Lust and trust.

I suspected that if I went solo with Emma it would be

a disaster. I couldn't do it. A threesome was the only way, and I did revel in it – being the little sister, the protégé, with few responsibilities and plenty of attention. "We'll see what happens," I told the mirror, and went back to the kitchen.

The table was cleared, but my cup of coffee was still sitting in the middle of it. Elena was washing the dishes and my girls, surely happy that no help had been asked of them, had gone to prepare for the trip to Petrodvorets. I looked for Dad and found him in the living room.

"Mom's grave hasn't been visited for a while," I said, looking off to the side, my hands trying to find their way into my jeans' pockets. "I know it's none of my business, but maybe you could visit her sometime?" I looked at his pale and serious face. "I mean, you spent a quarter of a century together. And yet there's not a single picture of her in this apartment. You don't visit her grave."

"Sure I do."

"When? When was the last time?"

"I don't know. A month ago, maybe two."

"Longer."

"Why does it matter?"

"Didn't you love her?"

I wished I hadn't started. But even though I was happy he had a new woman to love him in the twilight of his years, I believed one shouldn't erase important people from memory.

"Inga, I've been sick for the last two months," he said quietly. "It's been hard to move around. I haven't told you because I didn't want to upset you."

"Why didn't you say anything before?" It sounded cold, but I didn't believe him yet. "And anyway, it's been much longer since you last went to her grave. I could tell. It's been at least six months. Or maybe even a year."

He said nothing. His silence made something inside me collapse. I was lecturing my father and not even asking about his illness. Did he have cancer? For all I knew, he was dying. Entrenched in my own feelings, obsessed with my two lovers, feeling sad for my mother, I had turned against the most important person in my life.

"I'm sorry, Papa," I said, touching his hand. "I'm really sorry. I don't know what came over me. What was wrong with you? Are you okay now?"

"It's really nothing, dear. Don't worry about it." He put his arms around me. "My heart was acting up, so they told me to take it easy for a while."

"What do you mean 'acting up'? Did you have a heart attack?"

"No, nothing that serious. Arrhythmia. It wasn't a big deal. Just some tests, so I was in and out of a hospital. It's all behind us now. I'm fine. I'm sorry. I should have told you about it when it happened. I didn't want to upset you.

I thought you had enough on your plate."

"I guess I've become a complete egotist, living by myself."
I said, ready to cry. "Not the daughter you raised."

"Nonsense. I know how difficult it is for you. She is your
mother. So don't be sorry, just don't rush to conclusions.
And please take care of yourself. Yes?"

I wasn't sure what he meant by my having "enough" on
my plate, and why he wanted me to take care of myself,
as if I hadn't been. I didn't elaborate. I kissed him, turned
around and quietly closed the door behind me. We never
talked about these things in my family. Illness, hospitals,
tests. For that matter, we never talked about love, either.
Maybe that was the reason I needed two lovers – to catch
up for the past 28 years by talking about everything, and
exploring everything, no holds barred.

· 18 ·

I leaned over the railing and lifted my feet off the ground, as I always had on the Palace Embankment of the Neva. The Hermitage stood behind me, noble and silent in its majesty, surveying the spectacular vista across the river through its thousand windows. Peter and Paul Fortress, the Spit of the Vassilievsky Island, the Rostra columns, all reflected in the shimmering waters of the Neva, the quintessence of St. Petersburg's elegance and beauty. The view always made my heart beat a little faster. In that moment, I didn't know how I could have ever left all of it.

In the minutes before the final boarding to Peterhoff, as the locals still called Petrodvorets, I watched boats, small and large, nestled at the pier, with swarms of tourists getting on and off. With my body balancing on the railing over the water, the crowds outside of my field of vision, I could be one with St. Petersburg. Emma and Alexandra stood nearby, the wind dancing in their hair. The final boarding was announced, and we got on the passenger boat, settling by the window in a half-empty salon.

The boat roared past the palaces on the Neva embankments and entered the Gulf of Finland. It was easy to forget that St. Petersburg was a city by the sea, but so nice to be reminded of it. Half an hour later, we disembarked, paid the fifty-ruble admission fee at the gate, and entered the sprawling parks. A flock of foreign tourists behind us was stopped by the ever-observant babushka checking the entrance tickets. Her small, withered body stood up well against the wind as she held back the crowd of tourists.

"*Inostrancy, bilet – dvadcat' dollarov!*" she commanded. They struggled to understand why they had to pay twenty dollars to get in. An obese man in his late fifties who seemed to understand some Russian tried to reason with her. "But we just saw those women pay two dollars! That's not fair!"

The babushka, holding onto the gate, looked him up and down, as if in awe of how a man could let his body grow to such proportions, and didn't utter another word. Not only because the gibberish of the English was not for her but because *inostrancy* should have known the rules before visiting: foreigners paid ten-fold to enter all museums because their banks wouldn't be broken by the amount. She stared at him. The man and the rest of his group doled out 800 rubles each. I pretended that I spoke no English: I had nothing in common with that American.

I walked toward the main alley to the Upper Palace. The Grand Cascade of fountains in front of me, with the famous "Samson" in the middle, made me feel proud every time, as I was certain it did all Russians. It was the monument to Russia's victory over Sweden. I stopped to admire the view.

"Versailles doesn't stand a chance," Alexandra said standing next to me, smoking. "Peter the Great knew his desires and had them served. The results speak for themselves."

"Sounds like what we want," added Emma.

I found the comparison strange, if not inappropriate.

"To build something that will last beyond us and make us rich," Alexandra explained.

"Haven't you already?"

"We have, but not on the scale we want." Alexandra's tone had become impatient. "Have you been away for too long? Russia is practically begging for things to be introduced! What's common in the States is mostly unheard-of in our country. And you can't just bring a new brand and expect Russians to go for it. We don't trust advertising, remember?" She puffed on her cigarette. "That's exactly the niche for our future agency – to 'translate' Western products for Russians, to make them cool and desirable. Think of banks, restaurant chains, travel agencies, even detergents, for crying out loud."

"I'm all for it," I said. Alexandra was right. Russia and the West could use some closer connections. I had even dedicated part of my thesis at Stern to the subject.

I looked around. Peter the Great had probably had similar thoughts when introducing Western culture to Russia three centuries ago. His legacy, started in the 1700s and interrupted in 1917, was again becoming a reality eighty years later. I relished the thought of working toward the same profound ideal as Russia's most "Western" tsar – opening the world to Russia while re-introducing her to the world. Suddenly, all of the answers I'd been searching for seemed to fall into place. I'd build a bridge between my two homes. I walked faster. Soon, I had outpaced the crowd, Alexandra, Emma, everyone.

I was six again, visiting Peterhoff with Mom and Dad. I stood between the two mini-fountains, through which kids were running, trying not to get wet, searching for that special cobblestone that triggered the water flow. Only when I was a teenager had I found out there was no magic stone, only a retired old man pushing the buttons in a shack behind the tree hedges, away from kids' eyes. I stepped into one of the fountains. Its icy droplets played a staccato rhythm on my face, hair, and shoulders. I stood there, with my face turned upward, letting the cold stream wash away sadness and doubts. "Mom, I'm back," I whispered as the cool water drops rolled over my cheeks.

Emma pulled me out. As we kissed, I felt the warmth of her breasts pressed against mine and knew that I'd do anything to stay with her. And with Alexandra. They were my fortress against all the Northern winds of life. Nothing bad could happen as long as we stayed together. I might have been naïve, yet I was most certainly happy. Which was a major improvement over New York.

II. NEW YORK

· 19 ·

New York was sweltering: I was inside an oven. As I left the air-conditioned JFK terminal, hot air crawled inside my lungs and sweat flowed down my back. The nine-hour flight across the Atlantic had left me exhausted, yet I quickly composed myself: no sentiment was allowed in this city, a rule I'd learned to follow strictly. I was once again on my own, and nobody cared what or how I felt.

"*Privet*, Home Number Two," I said out loud, dragging my bags to the bus stop. A cab would have been too expensive, and the thought of a personal driver picking me up was as unreal as the fact that I had two female lovers in Moscow.

It always happened: the moment a plane touched the ground, the other reality was no longer tangible. During the past two months in Moscow, I'd grown accustomed to the changed Russia, overflowing with money for some and in shambles for others. Yet, alone in New York, all the money- and sex-filled Moscow escapades seemed grotesque and unnatural. The Inga of New York bore no resemblance to the Inga of Moscow; the two didn't connect. Here I needed to pay rent, student loans, and utility bills, and I needed to try to ignore the slight condescension in people's eyes once they detected my accent.

On the bus, I settled by the window. Despite the stress that New York always filled me with, I was glad to be back. Kristina was here, as was Lisa, and Central Park and sunsets over the Hudson. And a trip to South Beach with the girls in a week. Emma and Alexandra would bring their carefree lifestyle with them, dressed in Prada and Kawakubo – with loads of cash packed into every purse – and dote on me, their Inga.

The familiar skyline appeared through the hazy air, and I thought of the city's inhabitants. Kristina. Should I tell her about Nick? Lisa. Was her boyfriend still in New York, or had he left for Germany? I thought of my own ex-boyfriends, roaming the streets of the city, no longer caring for me.

I took a cab from Grand Central to my apartment. The subtenant had just moved out, leaving the small studio clean, still smelling of Windex, the backyard swept. But it didn't feel like my place, so devoid of coziness and deprived of its photos and little souvenirs from across the world, all stashed away while I'd been overseas. I dropped the bags on the floor and hit the play button on the phone machine. "You have four messages," announced the female electronic voice.

"Privet, *Amerikanka!*" Alexandra's voice greeted me. "We just dropped you off at the airport, and we already miss you. Be a good girl there, and we'll see you soon!"

I smiled as the voice from Moscow bubbled into my New York existence.

"Welcome back! I know you'll be tired, but maybe you can meet us downtown tonight," Kristina said. "We're having a going-away dinner for Lisa's boyfriend, 8 PM. You should totally meet him before he leaves."

Lisa's voice joined the ensemble. "Inga, dear. I know you're back tonight, and I'd like you to meet Vlad. He's going to Moscow soon, and I hear you met some important people there, so we need to talk about it."

Lisa. Always straight to the point. No matter that I was exhausted, drowning in the storm of two colliding realities. She wanted me to facilitate the artistic career of her boyfriend. And not even a "How are you?" before she got to her point. Not a single email while I'd been away (or perhaps Lisa still couldn't afford a computer). I sighed and sat down on the bed.

"This is an automated recording. Your Con Edison bill is past due. If you do not submit your payment by September 1st, your service will be disconnected." In two weeks.

I called Kristina.

"*Privet*, I'm back. What's all this about Lisa's boyfriend? And why should I meet him?"

"You're back! I missed you so much!" She, indeed, sounded happy to hear from me. "It turns out Vlad is having an exhibit in Moscow, and since you know the women who publish *Poise*, maybe you could help him with publicity."

"How do you know they publish the magazine? I never mentioned it."

"Lisa talked to one of her friends in Moscow the other night and was informed you'd been seen in their company everywhere for the past two months," Kristina explained. "I guess they're the ones you mentioned in the last email. Sounds like they have some serious connections in Moscow – should be great for your business."

I kept quiet. The world was much smaller than I'd realized, and I had no desire to talk about Vlad's business.

"Listen, you don't have to talk about it," Kristina said. "Just come over for a bite to eat, and we'll raise a glass to your return."

I hadn't been to a Mexican restaurant in two months and found myself smiling with satisfaction that New York, unlike Moscow, really did have it all. I stopped behind the curtains at the entrance to observe the table in the middle, a quick pang of self-consciousness running through me. Lisa, a conceptual artist, and Kristina, a sociology researcher, were grand dames of fashion, even though neither could afford it. *Daffy's*, the notorious outlet for European brands, served them well: their outfits could have appeared on the cover of *Vogue* any day. I couldn't match their elaborate creations. I had neither the time nor patience for sifting through the clutter of shitty outfits in the hopes of finding a gem that would evoke "wows" from onlookers. And I had no money for *Barney's*, either, unless Alexandra would want to take me shopping there.

They sat around a small table, laughing and gesticulating, two margarita pitchers almost empty, their plates filled with burritos, quesadillas, and other mashed, crumbled, and refried Mexican dishes. Observing Lisa was like watching a favorite movie, only with new scenes added each time. I always felt drawn to her mix of warmth and cynical honesty. Her 1920s style bob haircut matched her sarcastic energy. Tough on the surface, a lost puppy inside – very much like me.

Next to Lisa sat a handsome, even beautiful, man in

his early thirties. There was something feminine in his appearance, in his large green eyes and soft, curly hair. His crumpled, dark gray jacket hung loosely over his shoulders, the white, crisp shirt exposing both collarbones, giving him the aura of a decadent *artiste*, the type with whom women easily fell in love. He drew smooth circular lines in the air as he spoke, a fork in his right hand, as if directing his thoughts to a logical conclusion. I couldn't hear what he was saying, but Kristina was listening to him attentively. Lisa beamed with pride, perhaps because she was finally the one with a man by her side. I lingered a moment before approaching the table.

Kristina got up to greet me with open arms and covered my face with kisses. "Finally! Welcome home!" A warm feeling, like smooth cocoa, spread inside me.

"*Privet!*" I went around the table to kiss Lisa and to shake Vlad's hand.

He smiled back and rose to greet me. He has manners, too, I thought, looking him in the eyes a bit longer than necessary while the busboy searched for an extra chair.

"So, how was fucking Moscow?" Lisa emptied her water glass and poured me a margarita. "The service is too slow here," she explained. "Have a drink."

I took a sip of a strong, heavenly strawberry cocktail.

"Moscow was… interesting," I said, looking for words to best describe my two months in the Russian capital. I wondered if I should mention my worry-free life under the wing of Emma and Alexandra, or the obscene amounts of money the New Russians had made, or the beauty of the pastel, cake-like buildings in downtown Moscow and the intrusion of the ever-present advertising billboards in the city center – or how stunning the women of Moscow and St. Petersburg were, and my own infatuation with two of them.

"What's all this talk about starting a business there?" Lisa fired again. "Have you lost your mind? Aren't you sick of that place yet?"

I didn't have a chance to answer. Lisa poured out her disapproval via another margarita from the pitcher. "Anyway, welcome back. Vlad here, my long-lost and newly-found lover of six years, is also going to Moscow. Unlike you, Miss St. Petersburg, he was born and raised there, but hasn't been back in over five years." She looked at Vlad with satisfaction in her eyes, that of an owner who had found a long-missing possession. "But he isn't staying or anything like that." She paused. "Right?" she asked him with a touch of hysteria in her voice, squeezing his elbow.

"Right," he said, freeing his hand.

"You'll be a foreigner there," I said to him. "It's a different world from when you left it. Why are you going?"

"I was offered a personal exhibit at *The Manezh*. They

must have heard about my shows in Germany and wanted one of their prodigal sons to come back home," he said without a trace of pretension, lighting a cigarette.

"You don't sound too happy about it."

"I'd rather be offered an exhibit – of any kind – here. I tried for a while, but, of course, they don't care for you if you don't already have a name. And my shows in Germany failed to impress any of the galleries here."

"Welcome to New York, the city that doesn't give a shit. And in Moscow?"

"A solo exhibit. They priced my work nicely and are taking care of the publicity. Several New York curators will be there. With a show like that under my belt, I'll have a better chance here," he said, taking a bite of his burrito.

I looked at him again before opening the menu. Vlad didn't need my help with publicity. But this man seemed to be going through the same doubts and hopes as I was. I, too, hoped my Moscow business would have the same effect: once I'd built my Russian empire and sold it to McCann or some other big agency, I could return to New York for good, on a winner's white horse.

"So, how was Moscow?" Kristina asked. "We almost never heard from you."

"Fantastic." I asked the waiter for a regular glass for my next margarita. "Let's just say it's happening – the business, the nightlife. It feels like everyone is on a fast track to somewhere, and you're forced to join them in this frenzy. So far, I love it." I took a sip of the margarita that the waiter had brought me, trying to better phrase my main news. "And I guess I want more." I smiled at Kristina, who, of all the people at the table, knew exactly what I meant. "My future business partners are visiting soon. I'll be showing them the city, then we're off for a week in South Beach, and then –'*Goodbye, America, oh!*' – it's back to Moscow." Just then the waiter leaned back over me, saving me from elaborating on any of my statements, and I ordered a chicken burrito.

"Nick is still in Russia." Kristina said suddenly.

"I saw him there by accident."

Kristina sat up. "Really? Where? He didn't mention anything."

"Oh, at some restaurant. He was having lunch with one of his protégées, I think, so I didn't really get to talk to him."

"He told me he needed to stay longer this time because of all the bands he's signing for the fall tour," Kristina said. "I've never met any of his musicians. Can you believe it? I went to concerts and all, but he never invited me backstage."

I couldn't stand to be the only one who was in on Nick's secret. Or did Lisa know? I needed to unload my doubts on someone – preferably right away.

"I definitely want to meet them this time." Kristina looked through me again, sipping her margarita.

"You don't want to meet any of those musicians," Lisa said. "The half-civilized *muzhiks* who think their shitty, post-Soviet rock is music and that they're the carriers of the underground freedom torch."

"What's up with you tonight?" I asked.

"Her last project fell though," Kristina confided, leaning close. "She's broke and hating everyone."

"But Vlad is here. Shouldn't that make everything look better, at least for tonight?"

Kristina didn't respond, so I attended to the burrito that the waiter had swiftly brought me. Jet lag was starting to kick in. I dreaded going home – to my lonely apartment, a computer, and the girls thousands of miles away. I missed them, their warmth and cynicism, their easy way of falling into laughter, and their conviction that nothing was impossible. I noticed Vlad's stare from across the table.

"Can we hang out tomorrow?" I whispered to Lisa. "Just the two of us?"

"Sure, come over for brunch. Vlad has some meetings, so we can have our girls' afternoon out."

Fighting the jet lag, rubbing my eyes and trying to stay awake at any cost, I followed the group to our next desti-

nation, a small, dimly-lit lounge several blocks down the
street. I felt light-headed, as if orbiting around my real
self, observing from above. I asked Vlad to tell me more
about his art and walked close to him, our hands slightly
touching. I also made sure my jacket was open to reveal
the outline of my breasts under a tight red shirt. Then
it hit me: I was flirting with him and enjoying it. Did I
miss the attention of men, whom I'd willed to disappear
from my life for the past two months? Was I drawn to
Vlad because he could understand the torment of living
between two countries better than anyone in the group?
Or was I just testing the level of his interest in me – a
sport that women practice at every opportunity? If so, I
wasn't being much of a friend to Lisa. But I was too tired
to think about it.

The bar was small, with candles flickering on the walls
and on the low-set tables. I found the bar experience in
New York to be a hundred light years more pleasant than
in Moscow. Here, nobody gave you once-overs when you
walked in. Nobody lowered her gaze to check on your
shoes. Nobody turned a head at your appearance – none
of the haughty attitude, so well adopted by Moscow's
New Russians. Here, you could be anything or nothing.
New York didn't care.

We settled on high chairs at the bar, and I ordered a
glass of red wine. I tried to muster the courage to talk to

Kristina, the image of Nick and his lover in the Japanese restaurant still hovering in my mind. I leaned towards her.

"Can you keep a secret?"

"I hope so."

"Promise not to act weird?" My palms sweaty, my heart racing.

"I'll do my best." Kristina looked at me attentively.

"Remember the two women I mentioned, the ones I met in Moscow?"

"Emma and Alexandra?"

"Right. Well, they're not just my business partners," I paused and gulped some wine. I stared at the candle for a moment and then dropped the bomb: "We're lovers."

Kristina choked on her wine but composed herself. She gripped the glass, as if trying to maintain her balance, and stared at me. "What do you mean?"

"Do you know what it is to be a lover?"

"Who's lovers – all three of you?"

"Yep. A threesome. And I think I'm in love. And it's crazy and wrong somehow, but this is the best thing that's been going on in my life in a long time. The sex is out of this world. We laugh all the time. I'm stronger around them."

I asked the bartender for a refill and looked for more words to describe my experience.

"I'm in love. With... two... women."

For a while, we were quiet. Kristina stared at the barman, a thin-as-a-rail musician type, as if he could explain to her what I'd just said, while I tore my napkin to pieces.

"Say something," I pleaded.

Kristina looked sad, her eyes hollow in the light of the candles.

"What do you want me to say? I've never heard of such a thing, but if this works for you – I'm very happy for all involved. I'm sure it's a thousand times better to have two lovers who want you than one husband who doesn't."

Can't we talk about me for a moment? I snapped inside. Immediately, guilt spread through me. Was anyone happy in their marriages?

"You and Nick are having problems?" I asked as if I knew nothing of his extramarital affairs.

"Why do you think he's away so long?" Kristina replied. "We decided to take a break from each other, so he agreed to an extended business trip for work."

"When is he back?"

"In a month."

I covered her hand with mine. "Do you want to stay over at my place tonight?"

"No, I'm fine. Let's talk about you." Kristina moved closer. "Are you happy?"

"Ecstatic. And scared. I don't know how to tell my

friends. I know less than I did before I went to Moscow: only that I'm involved with two amazing people, and even thinking about it gives me butterflies," I said, smiling.

"Listen, you're a big girl. And I'm happy to see you happy. We were getting a little worried about you, to tell you the truth."

"So, what do you think?"

"What does it matter what I think? It's your life. I admit it's a bit strange, but then again, we only live once. The one potential issue I see is working with lovers. I tried it once with one of my ex-boyfriends, and it failed miserably."

"What are you two whispering about over there?" Lisa leaned forward from the other end of the bar, visibly drunk. Kristina waved at her not to bother and ordered another glass of wine.

"I thought about this," I said. "This will be our own company, so hopefully we can manage. I just believe it will work."

"Then you're all set. Congrats! Just don't tell Lisa yet – she'll make a mockery of it."

I realized Vlad's knee was touching mine. I didn't have the strength to sort out if it was on purpose or by accident and withdrew my knee while looking at Vlad's face from the side. He turned to face me. *What a handsome devil,* I couldn't help thinking before turning back to Kristina.

"Do you want to talk about Nick?" I asked, praying for

a "No."

"Not tonight. You already have enough on your plate."
She laid her hand over mine. She sounded like my father.

"I have to go," I announced. "It's almost 7 AM for me.
Let's do this again soon."

I looked at Vlad as I got off my barstool. Maybe he'd be
here or maybe not, next time, when Emma and Alexandra
were in New York. I left a twenty-dollar bill on the bar,
gave everyone a kiss, and went to catch a cab.

Tired. Horny. Excited. Guilty. Lonely. City lights sped
by; the buildings looked exhausted from the heat of the
day, welcoming the coolness of night. I registered Astor
Place, then Union Square and the high-rises of Park
Avenue. The rest was a blur.

"Miss… Miss? Madam?" The driver's voice reached
me through the thick of my sleep. "You said 73rd Street,
right?"

"Yes."

"We're there."

"Oh. Thank you."

I paid and got out of the cab, thinking how nice it
would be to land between Emma and Alexandra.

I struggled with the door lock in the lobby and
stumbled downstairs to my ground floor studio. I didn't
pay attention to the blinking of the answering machine.

Face-down, I fell asleep in my clothes. It was midnight in New York, 8 AM in Moscow.

· 20 ·

The next morning, alone and celibate in my sunless apartment, not eager to get up, I reached out to check the messages on the answering machine. Emma's voice broke the silence.

"Sweetie, we really miss you. Please call. Even in the middle of the night. I want to hear your voice." She paused, puffing on a cigarette. "I can't wait to go to Miami with you...." Her voice tapered off, and after some muffled sounds, Alexandra's followed.

"How come you didn't call last night? Are you behaving? Come on now, *Amerikanka*, don't disappear! Kissing you in all the wrong places! Ciao!"

"No more messages," announced the electronic voice.

I looked at the calendar: five more days without them.

An eternity, an inferno. I dialed Alexandra's cell phone.

"Privet, *eto ya*. I miss you, too," I said. "Guess what?"

"What?"

"I told Kristina about us." I paused, trying to assess my feelings about being "out."

"Glad to know we are official now!" Alexandra cracked up. "So, was it shock and awe?"

"Not exactly. But she was happy for me. Her own love life is nothing to speak of, so she was even a bit jealous."

"She should be! Where else can you find such cute, smart, and undemanding lovers?" Alexandra said giggling.

"It's so empty without you. Five more days, right?"

"Hang in there, sweets! We're already packing!"

I hung up and pressed the receiver against my stomach. Why couldn't they live here, in New York?

I decided to go for a run. I put on my worn gray and yellow Nikes, NYU T-shirt, and short black tights. As I pulled my hair into a ponytail on the top of my head – "looking like a palm tree" according to Alexandra – I thought of getting a haircut before the girls' arrival.

With Mozart's *Requiem* streaming from my headphones, I reached the reservoir in seven minutes instead of my usual ten. I stopped on the pavement and contemplated the view through the checkers of the fence, my heart beating in my throat. The Upper West Side basked in the early morning sun, the buildings peaking over the lush green, the windows winking at me with sun bunnies, as such reflections were called in Russia. As I stretched my legs, I remembered why it was that I never ran in Moscow. I had gone running once and collected so many "Look at the crazy" glances that I decided against continuing. Joining a "Western" health club in Moscow was beyond my means, their New York times three prices assuring that simpler folks didn't stand a chance, thus turning the American gym into an oasis of exclusivity and luxury for New Russians and expats.

The running path circled the reservoir in a tight embrace, and I hugged my own shoulders contentedly. The park cured sadness every time, even if I always listened to Mozart's *Requiem*. I completed a circle, passing people of all shapes and ages, a scene unimaginable in Russia, and stopped to greet the gray-haired Reservoir "Godfather." He always smiled at every runner as if they were his close friends, no matter if he was seeing them for the first or last time. I liked that someone greeted me as a friend. I needed that. It gave me strength for what lay ahead.

When I returned, I canceled brunch with Lisa and went to meet Kristina: I had to tell her about Nick's protégée.

"Are you okay?" I asked her an hour later, after we had settled in at the *Silver Spurs* diner on Houston and Lafayette, our usual meeting place for Sunday brunches.

The diner, in blue enamel and stainless steel, had borne witness to many stories, from my being dumped by yet another guy to the ups and downs of Kristina's childless marriage.

"I don't know," Kristina said, her face crinkling as if she'd just gotten up. "I'm so drained by this quiet power struggle with Nick. On the surface it's all fine, but in reality, it's such a mess. I don't know what's wrong with us." She waved at the waiter to bring menus.

"Maybe it's good you're taking a little break from each other. You know – absence makes the heart grow fonder."

"I don't want to talk about it."

We stared at our menus. I couldn't tell if Kristina was avoiding the subject or if this was a cry for help, for a bit of tacit advice. But I wasn't exactly in the position to dispense advice. A divorced woman-turned-lesbian. If only someone could advise me on how to propel my own love life.

The letters of the menu blurred into a blue-gray backdrop for my thoughts. Somehow my life always mirrored the life of the city. Or vice versa. It happened with covers of *The New Yorker* magazines, with movies being released. Whatever the theme of the week, it would be happening with me as well. Traveling to Europe. Threesomes. Subletting apartments to strangers. Graduations. Either I was a general representative of urban life or I was the one living on the edge, about whom those articles were written. I didn't know which.

The letters on the menu morphed back into words, and I found all the things I'd been craving in Moscow – a Western omelet, yogurt and granola. I ordered eggs Benedict. So did Kristina.

"I have to tell you something else," I started hesitantly.

"Someone is in a foursome now?" Kristina asked.

"No. I don't even know if I should say it."

"If you started – finish."

I took a sip of water and wiped my mouth dry. "It's not my secret, but I don't know if I should keep it. Please don't hate me for telling you."

"Come on, already. What is it?" Kristina almost screamed, her face turning red.

"Remember I told you I saw Nick in St. Pete?"

"Yes."

"I don't think he was with his protégée. She looked more like… you know…"

"A hooker?"

I almost knocked over a water glass. Was Nick doing that, too?

"No, no. A young, nice-looking woman."

"I'm not surprised," said Kristina. Indeed, she didn't look it.

"You're not?"

"I always suspected there was someone else," she said, her body caving in as if deflated. "Why else wouldn't he touch me for weeks at a time?" She looked at me with the half-empty stare of a person not present in the moment.

"I'm actually glad it's over there, not in New York," she added.

"Aren't you going to confront him?"

"What for? So he'll leave me? No... I'd rather let him act it out with someone else. Maybe he'll return to me after all." There was no conviction in her voice. She started crying. "Let's eat, please. I can't talk right now," she said through her tears.

We turned to our eggs Benedict. Instead of worrying about Nick and Kristina, I preferred to anticipate Alexandra and Emma's arrival.

We ate slowly. I hardly tasted the food.

"So ironic, it's not funny," she finally said.

"What?"

"I cheated on him, too. On purpose. I knew something was going on, so last week I did it. For the first time in five years, I cheated on my dear husband: went home with an artist I met at a party."

I couldn't help asking, "Was it good?"

"I felt dirty afterwards. I think it's easier for men."

"Isn't everything?"

"Who knew my life would turn into a bad movie?"

Kristina said quietly. "So banal, so trivial."

"So, what are we going to do?" I asked.

She could only shake her head. I felt a slight buzzing in my ears, and the fork slipped from my sweaty hand. I was scared: my main bastion of security in New York was crumbling.

"Don't tell anyone about all this," Kristina whispered.

"Of course."

Guilt. I felt guilty: for being in love with two people while my best friend was loveless, for not writing to her from Moscow earlier, for seeing Nick that weekend in St. Petersburg, and for wanting to be out of this conversation altogether.

"Do you want me to talk to Nick?" I asked, knowing full well I couldn't.

"Are you crazy? Of course not! What would you tell him – 'Please come back to New York before Kristina leaves you?'" She stared at me, a sardonic smile on her lips. "I could never leave him. Where would I go?"

"What do you mean, 'Where would you go'? You don't need to go anywhere! Stay right here in New York, find a nice guy, have a kid!"

"Right, as if finding a nice guy in New York is such an easy proposition. Look at you! You had to go to Moscow and meet two women to find your match," she said, finishing her wine. "Plus, I love him. Did you ever think of that? How terrible it is to love someone and have to cheat on him so that the self-imposed hurt takes over the hurt he caused you?"

I had never considered whether Kristina or Nick truly loved each other. Their union had always seemed strange to me, with him away six months a year, yet both content with their lives. But I did know a thing or two about cheating. Anton had put an end to my marriage. I'd known that I could no longer stay with my husband once I'd been with another man. The cheating had been the resolution of our long-brewing problems, not a reason in itself. Kristina seemed to think differently.

"Do you think he still loves you?"

"He hasn't left me yet, so yes, I think he does."

I didn't agree, but I couldn't tell her that. The more I thought about it, the clearer it was. Yet why Nick hadn't left Kristina, I couldn't tell; I didn't know him that well. But maybe it was just a matter of time.

· 21 ·

My heart paused and then resumed its beating as I went to open the door. Emma and Alexandra stood quietly in the hall, shy smiles on their faces. I felt happy and scared all at once. In the dim, narrow entryway to my New York apartment, their faces looked ashen, almost otherworldly, and their petite bodies appeared even smaller, silhouetted against the open mouth of a brightly-lit elevator. I put my arms around them and pressed their heads, one blonde and one brunette, to my chest. Yet the awkwardness of being apart for a week had crept in. Not a word was uttered.

Emma freed herself from my embrace and kissed me on the lips. Alexandra followed. Peace was restored.

"So happy to see you! This has been the longest week of

my life," I said, leading the girls by their hands through my embarrassingly tiny studio and out to the backyard. The heat had subsided, and a perfect evening had descended on the city – calm, quiet, and slightly sad, as half of Manhattan had already left for the shore.

I had taken time to prepare for their arrival. Orange candles flickered on the glass table. Fire torches lit the back of the yard. Chilled *Chablis* waited to be poured into newly purchased glasses. Several kinds of cheeses, with mozzarella, Emma's favorite, in the middle, were surrounded by green and black olives, prosciutto, grilled vegetables, and artichoke pasta.

"This is lovely, darling," Alexandra said. "Can I take a shower first? Please? I feel violated after sitting for nine hours next to some ex-Soviet *apparatchik* who clearly hadn't washed before boarding the plane."

"Of course. I put out fresh towels for you." I paused. "Are you taking the shower together?"

I was jealous — of their being together in Moscow, falling asleep next to each other, and making love without me for the last week.

"No, not now – too tired," Alexandra said.

"Of course not – unless you join us," added Emma.

I showed Alexandra to the bathroom. When I returned to the backyard, Emma sat at the table with a full glass of wine, smoking, a small smile on her lips. I rushed to her and put my head into her lap.

"My God, how much I missed you," I whispered, burying my face in Emma's knees. She stroked my hair and drew closer.

"I know," she said. "Me too. Don't talk." She leaned forward and put her lips on mine. Hundreds of little drums started in unison inside my heart, and my whole body gave in.

When, after a long while, we had stopped kissing, Alexandra stood at the entryway to the backyard. She leaned forward, smiling, and shook her head, wet dark hair flying in all directions.

"Oh, so much better," she said, approaching the table in my white bathrobe. "I see you two did some catching up already."

I moved to my own chair.

"Let's have a drink to us," said Emma, pulling Alexandra onto her lap, and again a pang of jealousy shot through me. The two bodies, Emma's stocky and Alexandra's petite, were parts of one whole, like two pieces of a puzzle that fell into their proper places. There seemed to be no room for mine. My fantasy of copying their Moscow lifestyle and pasting it into New York was no more than a dream. As if reading my thoughts (for the hundredth time) Alexandra said, "Belova, if I had your command of English, we'd rule this city. No need to go back to Moscow – we could do it all here. The business empire, the future, the money. I still don't understand why you haven't done it all yourself by now." She took a long sip of wine.

"I don't have your guts," I admitted. "I don't want to start again in small steps. Do you think we could do it together here in New York?"

Alexandra looked at me, as if sizing up the idea.

"We could. But let's be realistic – even if we had the language thing down, all our power connections are back in Moscow. It would take us years to establish the same network here, unless, of course, you could speed up the process by getting us into the right circles. Can you?"

I didn't answer. My connections in the city were no match for theirs in Moscow. And I'd witnessed countless times how New York City could strip people of whatever power they might have had in their homelands, turning them into small, unimportant entities. The New York idea didn't hold, even for the three of us.

"I think Moscow is more realistic," I said. "I'd be more useful there." I didn't believe it, yet I didn't want my doubts to ruin our evening together. I wanted to feel carefree, as I had in Moscow.

"Fantastic, all sorted," said Alexandra, turning to Emma. "I'm going to pass out. What time is it in Russia

– 4 AM? I need to crash. Sorry, Sweetness."

"Me too," said Emma, now visibly tired, the dark circles under her eyes more pronounced in the candlelight.

I made the bed and turned down the lights. Alexandra was asleep in minutes, her face to the wall. Emma fell asleep next to her, hugging Alexandra's shoulder. I undressed and got under the sheets, next to Emma, on the edge of the bed. I lay there, smiling at the ceiling, feeling the warmth of Emma's body. I didn't want to think about business in New York, Moscow, or anywhere else. It would all sort itself out. Alexandra wouldn't let us fail. They were with me, and that was all that mattered. Love was more important, and I was certain I'd found mine. Emma turned and spooned me. I kissed her palm and fell asleep holding her hand.

We woke up early, the girls' inner clocks still set to Moscow, and spent hours in bed, losing track of time. They didn't mind my being half-asleep, exploring my body from both sides, finally bringing me to full alert. We had brunch in the backyard and went back to bed.

We made love again and again. They lavished me with their attention, not expecting anything in return, as if releasing their stored desire for me. I'd never been with a man who loved me so generously. I tried to think whether this was the difference in the sexes, in the passion, or in the number of simultaneous lovers, but surrendered to the women instead.

When I finally looked at the clock, it was almost three. I suggested sightseeing, Emma never having been to New York, yet they seemed perfectly content in my bed. I dragged them out onto the street, and we slowly headed towards the Met, my legs Jell-O, the streets quiet and warm – a perfect Manhattan afternoon, with Upper East-siders out in the country or back in their apartments after Sunday brunches.

We went to the Impressionist halls, as Impressionism was Emma's and my favorite. I could stare forever at Monet's water lilies and haystacks. They always brought me back to St. Petersburg, to the halls of The Hermitage, with *London Tower Bridge* and different versions of the pink and green haystacks. Coming to the Impressionist halls always meant visiting my childhood, and that was even more important than the art itself. Doing so with Emma and Alexandra signified true sharing for me.

Not certain where Alexandra had gotten lost, I joined Emma, pausing in front of the *Sunflowers*. "I've only seen this one in albums before. It's my Mom's favorite," she said. We joined hands as Alexandra entered the hall.

"Oh, come on! Let's go see Pollock. This is so overrated," she said.

We breezed through the giant halls of American

Modern art, past Pollock, Lichtenstein, and Warhol. "I'd love Warhol's Marilyn for my bedroom," said Emma as we walked out to the roof sculpture garden, Central Park spreading below us as far as the eye could see.

"We're not there yet, my dear," said Alexandra.

Emma nodded in agreement.

"You mean the original?" I asked in disbelief.

"Why would I want anything else?" Emma asked, smiling at me as if I were a kid incapable of grasping the gist of an adult conversation. She turned to look at the park sprawling before our eyes, treetops in different shades of lush green, hints of yellow here and there.

"Great view. Almost as good as the one from my new apartment in Moscow." Emma winked at me.

"You have another place in Moscow?" I hadn't realized they had each bought an apartment.

"Sure, a great investment: a one-bedroom on the top floor in a Stalin-era building overlooking the horseracing tracks. The sunsets are to die for. It'll be worth a fortune in ten years," Emma explained.

I'd never known she had a flair for real estate, or that their envy-evoking union had room for anything separate, including investments.

"Good for you. I wish I'd done it five years ago, while I still had some money, before prices went through the roof."

"Don't worry. When our business gets going, you'll buy an apartment in no time," Alexandra said. Emma looked at me as if to say her apartment could be ours, that there was no need for another. I turned to look at the tree crowns without responding.

Back in the apartment, we made love until it was dinnertime.

When we arrived at the Italian restaurant downtown – the one where I'd first shared my plans for Russia – Kristina, Lisa, and Vlad greeted us at the entrance. I murmured, "The first ball of Natasha Rostova," as if indeed we were Tolstoy's characters coming out to the public for the first time.

"Please meet Emma and Alexandra," I said, sparkling.

Kristina nodded and introduced herself. Lisa swallowed her name as she looked straight at Emma, who, in turn, couldn't take her eyes off Vlad and Alexandra, both speechless and staring at each other.

"You've got to be kidding me," Alexandra said.

"What?" Emma's voice had a touch of ice in it.

"Vlad?" asked Alexandra, disregarding Emma.

"Yes. How are you?"

"You *know* each other?" I asked.

"We went to art school together. In Moscow. Ages ago," Alexandra said. Vlad kept quiet. I sensed a hesitation in

Alexandra that I'd never seen before. I suggested we at least enter the restaurant and ask for our table. We still stood at the entrance, stopped in our tracks by this development. We shuffled in, and I noticed Emma darting demanding looks at Alexandra, who turned away, shaking her head and frowning.

Once inside, Lisa could no longer hold in her curiosity. "Wait a minute! You seriously have known each other for what – ten years?" She took Vlad's elbow. "And you didn't know that Alexandra was the one running the magazine in Moscow?"

"I've been in Germany for the last five years, remember? I've almost forgotten how to speak Russian."

"To be precise, we met ten years ago and haven't spoken for almost the same amount of time," Alexandra added.

Life was turning into a magic show, with tricks and surprises appearing from the magician's sleeve almost daily. I looked at Vlad, still finding him handsome despite the presence of my girlfriends in New York.

We sat down and scanned our menus. Kristina was attempting small talk to get the dinner going, when Alexandra leaned towards me.

"Remember the story I told you in Moscow?" she whispered.

"What story?"

"About the guy I slept with once?"

"Yes – so?" I looked at her, puzzled.

"Well, now you know," Alexandra said.

"Know what?"

"The guy," she drew out and looked at me. "Just don't tell Emma. She'd kill him. Or both of us."

I closed my menu. I felt like a teakettle filled to the brim with boiling water, about to spew it out. I didn't believe that Vlad could have been so awful in bed that Alexandra had turned into a lesbian after their encounter. I couldn't believe he had been Alexandra's lover to begin with.

"Let's just eat. I can't think about this now," I said, opening the menu again. The meaning of the pastas listed on the pages eluded me as I tried to think. Vlad, Lisa's boyfriend, had been Alexandra's first man, and ten years later we'd all met, and now it was my turn to find him attractive.

Lisa shouldn't know about any of this. We would all see each other in Moscow, at Vlad's exhibit at the Manezh, and at other events, impossible to miss in the small circle of Moscow's high society, while Lisa remained in New York.

Vlad kept his cool, smiling politely at Emma and Alexandra as if he were, indeed, only a distant acquaintance from the past. Emma was tense. I thought of two reasons – Vlad and the fact that the menu was of no use to her until Alexandra or I explained to her what was on it. She didn't speak English. At all. I touched her hand under the table.

"What do you feel like, sweetie? Pastas are great here," I said.

"I want something with mozzarella and truffles," Emma answered glumly.

"No truffles, but the mozzarella pasta is divine here. I'll order for you." I squeezed her hand.

"And a big glass of Chardonnay," Emma added.

I wanted to kiss her, but didn't.

Alexandra and Kristina were deep in conversation while Lisa and Emma eyed each other. I looked at Vlad, saying with my eyes that I knew the whole story. We all assumed he'd been with other women while living in Germany. He smiled. I smiled back, wondering how it was possible for people to forgive so much and forget so completely. I didn't know if it was a Russian thing or an age thing or a singles thing. The waiter took our order, and I turned to join Kristina's conversation with Alexandra about Russian art. Lisa, Emma, and Vlad had plenty to discuss if they chose to, without me.

· 22 ·

Lisa led me by the hand out of the restaurant and across Washington Square Park, in the direction of West Village. Kristina and Alexandra followed, deep in conversation, with Vlad and Emma in tow, in complete silence.

Lisa told me we were on our way to the lesbian part of town. I didn't know if it was for the benefit of Emma and Alexandra. I'd had no idea a separate lesbian part of the city existed.

Henrietta Five, read the red sign above the dark windows in a two-story building. When I opened the door, I was swallowed by the mass of moving bodies, all of them women, many looking like men. Some ogled me; some looked right through me, at Emma. I turned to gauge the girls' reaction. Alexandra approved, with a wide smile, while Emma observed the scene with the look of a hunter on her face. I made my way towards the side bar for breathing room, ordered a round of drinks, and chugged my wine as soon as it appeared. Not the best wine I'd had in my life, yet I ordered another glass: I couldn't take that scene sober. It wasn't my world.

Once the alcohol had found its way into my bloodstream, I took a mental step aside: why was I disappointed at the scene? Because women could pick up women the same way men did? Or because there were so many women looking like men, ruining Emma's theory of being a lesbian to avoid male energy in intimate relations? The most upsetting thing was thinking about it at all.

I noticed Vlad observing me from the end of the bar. Lisa and Emma were next to him, deep in conversation and both visibly drunk, laughing and shouting in each other's ears as they tried to overcome the noise. As if reading my thoughts, Vlad slowly approached and offered me another drink in that gentlemanly way of his. He didn't belong in this place, either, and it made us closer. I wanted to ask about how Alexandra was ten years ago but decided against it. I watched her, the dark-haired girlfriend on the high chair, again in conversation with Kristina, standing next to her. I was glad she was part of my life, yet if someone had asked how long I planned on being with her, I wouldn't have been able to answer. Not that one could plan such things. Being involved with a woman was still strange to me. As long as we were in our cocoon, nothing mattered. Once others knew or guessed about us, I couldn't help feeling awkward, regardless of my friends' sexuality.

Vlad opened his wallet and took out a black-and-white picture of him and Lisa. "Our first trip to Spain, five years ago," he said. "I miss those times." The photo showed a much younger Lisa in a tight embrace with youthful Vlad, both smiling. He moved a candle closer to illuminate the picture, and I felt time shift. Stillness filled the air, blocking the music, the dancing bodies, and the loud conversations, enveloping us, two people looking at the photo as if praying at an altar. *He must still love Lisa,* I thought. *Despite his life in Germany. Despite hers in New York.*

"She misses it, too," I said. "Always talks about it and ends up first laughing and then crying."

If things had worked out the way he'd wished, Vlad would probably have never gone abroad, and Lisa would have stayed in Moscow. But Russia in the early nineties had thrown people around the world in search of a better life and forced them to live away from home, grasping for what had once been the driving force of their lives. Like others, they had traveled through different countries, cultures and times, as if trying to return to the missing warm spot in the tunnel of memory, where they could forgive each other for things that had happened, and had not, while they had been apart. I knew I was such a traveler myself, looking for my permanent home. I thought my Emma and Alexandra provided that, whether temporary or not, and was grateful.

I followed Vlad's eyes and saw Lisa lean towards Emma, craning her neck as if in slow motion. A smile spread over Emma's face. I wondered if Lisa was falling-over drunk, my naiveté a surprise even to myself. A moment later, they kissed. Instead of being surprised, I tried to tell myself that Lisa was being her usual self, hitting on everyone when drunk, and that I shouldn't feel jealous. Yet I was. When I saw Emma answer Lisa's kiss, I became sober.

Vlad leaned over to me and whispered, his breath almost touching my lips, "Interesting friends we have, yes?" I turned to him, looking into his eyes several seconds longer than needed. As I swam in the candlelight reflected in his eyes, caressed with yellow flickers, our lips met.

I kissed him ravenously, as if I had to make up for two months of being with women, and for a year before of being alone. I liked that he was taller and that I could bury my head in his chest, instead of towering over my female lovers. I kissed him because I liked him, and because he'd been Alexandra's first and only man, and because Lisa was kissing Emma, and because he had kissed me first. As if I wanted to kiss my way out of all the confusions of my life, I kissed him and didn't want to let go. I moaned as Lisa and Emma approached us from both sides.

"Hi there!" Lisa barked. "What's going on here?"

"You tell me," I said. Lisa stood silently, looking at Vlad and then at Emma.

Alexandra approached. "I think it's time to go home," she said. I didn't know where she had been this whole time. Talking to Kristina? Alexandra took me and Emma by the hands, and we both succumbed, the adventurous spirit drawn from us. I looked at Kristina, tried to say something, but instead waved goodbye, too tired to find or provide explanations, and followed Alexandra towards the exit.

In the cab on the way home, I dozed off on Emma's shoulder to the urban lullaby of honking cars, the muffled voices of Emma and Alexandra, and the cacophony of the driver's Arabic on a cell phone. I woke up when the cab screeched to a stop in front of the building.

I tried to determine what had happened between the women on the way home, whether Alexandra was upset or Emma defensive, but saw no traces of any serious emotions on their faces. I had often wondered how easily these two could get into a major fight over business, with screaming and name-calling, yet never get angry at each other in matters of love. They managed perfectly the divide between the two, the first never spilling into the other. Or so it seemed to me. And I hoped it could work that way with our future enterprise. Yet I was jealous of Emma's kissing Lisa. As to my kissing Vlad – that would have to wait for its own explanation.

"Did you kiss Lisa, or did she kiss you?" I asked Emma as we entered the apartment.

She looked at me, turned to Alexandra, and answered in a small voice, "*Emmochka* was a little drunk and didn't think about what she was doing. My girls left Emma to be with other guests, and that's what happens when I feel lonely."

While I recalled the hunter's look on Emma's face in the bar, the presentation of a different Emma, small and innocent, worked. She had often become that little girl while giving Alexandra the power to be in charge. Impossible to argue with in such moments, I thought. Emma touched my hand. "Inga knows that Emma loves her, yes?"

I sat down on the couch. The declaration of love, most unexpected and voiced for the first time, was the second of two in my entire life. Nobody had said "I love you" to me except my husband, whom I eventually divorced. Warmth and security spread inside me, as if a cast had been molded and filled with bronze, taking its final shape, solid and strong. I felt guilty for kissing Vlad and for doubting my decision to start a company with the women. Still holding Emma's hand, I said, "I know."

Alexandra took my other hand and sat down next to me. "I love you, too," she said, burying her face in the nook of my neck, turning into the little kid Emma had become a moment ago. A flood of tenderness rushed through me, and I kissed them, first Emma, then Alexandra, repeating, "I'm sorry about tonight. I'm so sorry." Alexandra put her small palm over my mouth and pushed me on the bed. Emma climbed in and put her face next to mine. I saw Emma's black pupils, with streams of yellow spreading into the vast blueness of her eyes, and knew I didn't want to be with anybody else. I let Alexandra undo my pants and gave my lips to Emma.

Our lovemaking was slow and thorough, as if we had discovered each other for the first time that night, with ambiguities erased and questions answered. I couldn't let go of Emma's lips, hoping to erase Vlad's and Lisa's kisses.

· 23 ·

South Beach boasted the usual array of attractions: curvaceous teenage girls rollerblading in bikinis, revealing newly-done breasts; swarms of tourists looking for the best lunch spot on Ocean Drive amidst the cream and yellow facades of Art Deco hotels; and the blue ocean, framed by spiky palm trees against the white sand. Emma was ecstatic. On seeing the ocean, she ran towards the water, her body disappearing in the hazy heat. Alexandra and I followed, smiling at Emma, who was jumping on one leg and then another, trying to save her feet from the oven-hot white sand.

The ocean always calmed me. As I watched Emma jumping in the waves, I caught myself thinking how glad I was to be far away from Moscow. We had five days to play in the sun, swim in the ocean, make love, and eat – all the things new lovers do on vacation, with the realities of their daily lives left at home and the time for fighting not yet arrived.

In our small hotel – a lovely, two-story bed and breakfast painted yellow, well hidden from the street, with a hammock in the back – a green parrot said, "Hello, hello," from a palm tree, as we walked to our rooms. The suite occupied the entire second floor, with two rooms and a kitchenette. Alexandra offered to get wine while I took a shower and Emma unpacked, so that we could have a cocktail party in bed later on. She giggled as she left the room.

I lay down on the bed, tired from the heat, yet excited. I was ready to stifle my desire with a nap after the shower when I felt Emma's body next to mine. Neither of us said a word as Emma took off my robe. Maybe it was the sun that had melted us, or the air filled with jasmine, but we both acted as if we were in heat. I turned around, got up on my knees, face down in the pillow, and arched my back for Emma's tongue and hands to please me. If I could have, I'd have turned myself inside out. I screamed into the pillow. Emma owned me. The surrender was overpowering and complete.

I lay breathless on my stomach, with the pillow stifling

me, yet I couldn't move. I needed a moment, and then I wanted to love Emma the same way... But what about Alexandra? I hadn't finished my thought as I looked up, sweat dripping down my forehead, and saw that Alexandra had been watching us for a while. Not sure whether my one-on-one with Emma was approved of or not, I smiled, as if asking for *post factum* permission to do what had already happened. Alexandra looked at Emma and came to bed, also smiling. They went for it while I watched, as it had been two weeks before in St. Petersburg.

We fell asleep. When we awoke, the sky had turned pale orange. I urged them to dress quickly, to go down to the beach before darkness fell.

Alexandra looked at me with a smile on her fine lips and asked, "Do you really have a schedule of things to do? The sunsets will be there tomorrow and so will the museums of New York. We're happy right where we are." She turned to Emma. "Right, *Emmochka?*"

Emma nodded without opening her eyes and stretched a hand towards Alexandra. Without a pause, Alexandra got up and lit a cigarette for Emma, who inhaled deeply, opening her eyes to let out the puffs of smoke.

"We're in no rush. Totally happy right here," she said.

I couldn't tell if they were simply uncurious or jaded. I decided the answer was neither: theirs was a different approach to life, where putting a checkmark next to things seen and done was not a goal. I thought that maybe being content was the art of shutting out the outside world if your inner world desired as much. If that was true, my girlfriends had mastered it.

An hour later, we strolled down Collins Avenue, Alexandra winking in delight at the number of gay couples heading in both directions.

"Wait till we get to Lincoln Road," I told her. "But first things first."

The Delano Hotel stood tall in its royal whiteness. Emma froze for a moment under the enormous chandelier in the central lobby, and Alexandra nodded appreciatively at the white curtains disappearing in the ceiling twenty feet above us. We walked through the sprawling lobby with its giant couches, handsome people in white reclining here and there, past the elegant crowd at the inner bars, and headed outside, to the open pool framed by white gazebos. Candles flickered on low glass tables. A few couples lounged on the king-sized white beds surrounding the pool as white curtains trembled in the cool wind of the descending evening, guarding the secrets unraveling behind the white walls. Taking off our shoes and rolling up our pants, we landed at the cast-iron table in the middle of the pool, a light that pierced through the glittering blue water exposing our freshly done pedicures. Alexandra waved to the waiter and high-fived me: they didn't have this in Moscow. Yet.

"Not bad, Belova," she said, lighting a cigarette.

A tall, dark waiter approached with a smile.

"Three champagnes, please," said Alexandra.

"What a flamer," she added, turning to us.

I'd never understood the relationship between gay men and gay women, so I turned to look around, taking in the elegance and calm surrounding us.

"I often wish I could bring my Mom to see things like this," I said, unexpectedly for myself. "She died before they opened the borders. Can you imagine? Her whole life inside the Soviet Union."

"My mother hasn't traveled abroad either, and has no desire to," Alexandra said. "Her church is her whole world."

"Same with mine," said Emma.

At least yours are alive, I couldn't help thinking. I stared at the aquamarine water of the pool, lit up from below, and drifted into sadness, in the most inappropriate of moments, as always. Why couldn't our parents have seen the world? Why couldn't we while growing up? Why did we have to learn the real news from jammed foreign radio stations? The champagne arrived in time to stop my stream of self-pity.

"It was my Mom's birthday yesterday," said Emma.

"Happy birthday," I said. "Did you call?"

"I forgot." She paused. "It was my first day in Miami, and I forgot."

"Call her now!" Alexandra said, pulling out her cell phone.

"It's 3 AM there."

"Never mind. She'll love it," we said in unison.

Emma dialed the number, and I couldn't help thinking that the call would cost five dollars a minute. But they never thought about such things.

Emma turned sideways, the water reflecting off her cheek, illuminating it with a soft glow. We heard her murmuring into the receiver. When she turned back, her eyes were glistening.

"She cried. My sister forgot to call, too."

We sat in the middle of the pool, transported into the lives of our parents. Was the real Inga Belova sipping champagne in the middle of an open pool in South Beach, or had she been left behind at the kitchen table with her father in St. Petersburg? Was the real Alexandra the hardened deal-maker or the loving daughter of her divorced, churchgoing mother?

"You should call your mother more often," suggested Alexandra to Emma, ending the subject.

We watched the crowd at the bar grow and couples

settle into the white chaise-lounges around the pool. The candles flickered on every table and around the pool's perimeter as the moon came out from behind pink clouds in the purple after-sunset sky.

"I wonder if I'll ever be a mother," Alexandra said after several minutes of quiet. "I could never imagine the right donor. Blond or dark? Old or young? Extravert or introvert? Seriously, if I don't have to have a relationship with a guy to father a child, I can pretty much program whatever I want."

"Scary," I said.

"*You* can?" Emma asked Alexandra.

"We, we – of course." She got up and kissed Emma. "Let's go eat."

It took me a minute to comprehend what they were talking about. Alexandra put a fifty under her glass and we left, Emma holding my hand, looking away from Alexandra. Were they really planning on having a child together? What were they doing with me, then? Practicing?

Lucky Cheng's on Lincoln Road was a revelation even for my seasoned gay girlfriends. When we entered the sprawling restaurant, decorated in Chinese red and gold, with transvestite waiters dressed in full drag swooshing by, Alexandra couldn't help it; "*Ni khuya sebe*," escaped from her lips.

I felt proud again, as if this were my invention: the only other Lucky Cheng's was in New York, and it would be another century – if ever – before a place like that opened in Moscow or St. Petersburg.

An enormous black waitress, dressed in a red tutu and a push-up bra, approached us on high heels, a smile on her full lips.

"Hello, fabulous," she boomed, towering above us. "What can I get you to drink, honeys?"

"Nice shoes," I said wondering how this man could feel so at home on four-inch heels. I was taken by the gold and the sparkles adorning them; they belonged in a museum.

"Oh, thank you, doll," she said touching my hand, her snow-white teeth sparkling under the lights. "What are you drinking?"

"Get us a bottle of Chablis, please," said Alexandra.

After he had handed us the menus and gone for the wine, Alexandra said, "We should do this for one of our future clients."

"Do what?" I asked.

"Men in drag promoting luxury products. Think about it – these outrageous creatures, promoting Café Vogue or the opening of another Bosco Di Ciliegi boutique. It would be a revolution. And I know Bosco will love the idea. Let's pitch it to them when we get back to Moscow. That's as below-the-line as it gets."

Emma nodded appreciatively while I wondered if such a stunt would really appeal to New Russians. But I trusted Alexandra's intuition and expertise. She had her finger on the pulse of Moscow's desires, and many local socialites turned to her to see what was "in" in the rest of the world. And she was a master of the outrageous. Yet I hadn't envisioned my business in Russia becoming famous for helping to sell luxury goods with the aid of transvestites.

Dolly the waiter poured our wine, her large hand holding the bottle as if it were weightless, her movements precise and delicate. A drop lingered on the bottle's neck, and Dolly caught it with a serviette. I ordered for Emma, our usual ritual in restaurants. The food arrived quickly, but we soon forgot about it: the show had started. I thought we'd been brought onto the set of *Priscilla, Queen of the Desert*. All of the waiters turned into performers, one after another. They sang and danced, a kaleidoscope of twists and poses, some in tight yellow body suits, some in black leather, and one in an enormous white wedding gown with a crystal chandelier for a headpiece. White and gold glitter vibrated in the opaque air of the room, the smoke drifting to the ceiling in the red lights. No Moscow club could have ever topped it.

We kissed at the table in full view of everyone, and I

found it liberating – not having to hide who you were, the way we had in Moscow.

Back at the hotel, I couldn't sleep. The white circle of the wall clock, illuminated by a single yellow light in the yard, showed 2 AM. I touched Emma's leg. I knew it was wrong, but I couldn't help it: my body demanded contact with hers. I stroked her thighs, watched her open her eyes, and pulled her closer. We tried not to wake Alexandra, sleeping on the other side.

I lifted myself on one elbow and covered Emma's neck with kisses while taking off her underwear. We again rushed to satisfy each other, as if in a fever. Emma's eyes sparkled as she fell back on the pillow, panting. I turned to look at Alexandra: she was watching us, without a word, tears in her eyes. Then she slid away, closer to the wall, as if trying to disappear behind it, and let out a small cry, her body shaking. I'd never seen her cry before. In my world, Alexandra could never be defeated or weak. I couldn't bear the depth of my betrayal, multiplied by the pleasure I'd just experienced. I put my hand on her shoulder, tried to say something, but couldn't. She shook off my hand, sobbing, her body trembling under the white sheets.

I looked at Emma and saw no remorse in her eyes. I turned to Alexandra again, who got up from the bed and headed to the bathroom, still crying silently. Emma lit a cigarette. I wished I smoked, too, so I could occupy my restless hands and mind with something specific. I hated myself.

Several minutes later, Alexandra walked out of the bathroom, her face cold and dried of tears, and looked at Emma.

"How could you?" she said.

Then she turned to me. "How could *you*? You! Emma doesn't control her impulses; she is a kid. But how could you betray me like this? Didn't you tell me you loved me? Didn't you say you wanted to be with both of us?" She cringed, tears flowing down her round cheeks again. "I can't believe it," she kept repeating. "I just can't believe it."

"I'm sorry." I said and started crying, too. Who had I become? A sex addict?

"It's all my fault. We were half-asleep. Please don't cry," I whispered, trying to kiss Alexandra's hands and cheeks. She pushed me away.

"It wasn't meant to be without you," I insisted, not knowing what else to say or do, desperately wishing to believe my own half-lie.

Emma stepped closer and took Alexandra's hand. "I couldn't help it," she said, her face contorted. "You should have been with us. I'm sorry I didn't wake you. Hit me if you want."

I watched in amazement as Alexandra wiped her tears,

stepped back, made a fist and hit Emma's left cheek, sharply, with all her strength. Her knuckles landed under Emma's eye, leaving a massive red spot of pain. Emma omphed, but didn't move. There was no blood, but the bruise formed instantly. Alexandra stepped aside, rubbing her hand.

"What are you doing?" I whispered, covering my face with both hands.

"I'm showing Emma how I feel," Alexandra snapped. Then her shoulders dropped and she shuffled back to the bathroom, sobbing, becoming smaller with every step.

I took Emma's face in my hands and looked into her eyes. Tears. I pressed her head to my chest, and we stood there, both crying. Then I ran after Alexandra. This couldn't be happening. I tripped over a towel caught in the door to the bathroom, pushed inside, and found Alexandra on the toilet, sobbing. I'd done this to her. I knelt before her, my hands on her knees.

"*Prosti menya*," I said again, my fingers trying to find their ways into Alexandra's palms. "Forgive me. I thought you'd wake up, but you didn't." I believed my half-lie now.

Alexandra lifted her head and looked at me, her face wet from tears. She stared and stared, as if trying to get to the bottom of it.

"Do you believe this yourself? Emma's in love with you and will do anything to keep you, so watch out how far you go," Alexandra fired off in a rushed whisper, pinning me to the spot with her burning brown eyes.

I brought Alexandra's palms to my lips, kissing them feverishly, and caught a passing thought: If Alexandra was in love with me, too, why didn't she say it? And if she wasn't, then why was she so upset? I had no answers.

"Emma's risking our relationship, yet she is playing that card," Alexandra went on. "And that's a big card to play. If she loses me, and then you – I know she'll go back to drugs. Have you seen Emma on coke? No? Well, once she gets high, there's no stopping her."

I slid to the floor. *That's why sex with her is so great.*

"And when she's down, she gets suicidal. I'm her lifeline, the thread that keeps her clean," Alexandra screamed. "But this thread has been thinning out, so now she's holding on to you. Are you ready to be that for her? Do you have it in you? Or do you just want to have some fun, and then get out? What do you want?"

I wanted sex with Emma and the insurance of Alexandra. But at that moment, I just wanted to run. As far away as possible. I screamed inside, wondering what I was going to do.

"I want to be with both of you," I said. "Don't cross me out of your life. You're all I have." That was true. "And I don't believe you about Emma and drugs," I added, sobbing.

Alexandra pushed my hands away and walked out.

I sat on the floor and thought how naïve I had been, thinking that they'd save me from the misery of loneliness, giving me the push I needed to start living my life. Instead, they had buried me. Or, rather, I had dug my own grave. In Moscow. We were going back in two days. I wanted to run, but felt chained to a fence. The chain was too thick to break.

III. RUSSIA

· 24 ·

I came to the window of my new Moscow apartment, a one-bedroom rental on the second floor of a four-story panel-block walk-up, a hideous example of Soviet-era architecture. Despite the drab exterior, low ceilings, and a kitchen the size of a closet, the rooms were light and airy. Maple trees touched the windows with their hand-like leaves in the setting sun. I reached out and brought them to my face. Dusty and tired, the leaves smelled of the summer past, of rains and sunsets, their green slowly turning into orangey yellow, settling for the fall's arrival.

We had planned a dinner at my apartment to celebrate the signing of our first client – which had officially inaugurated our enterprise, IQ Consulting. I had invested the last of my money in it. How I was going to repay my student loans remained an open question.

Alexandra had arranged all the formalities. I felt relieved, guilty, and left out all at once. I came to the office every day, yet couldn't make the business mine. And I had questions. Emma and I had been cheating on Alexandra since our return from Miami, and, in my view, getting rid of me would have been Alexandra's natural next step. Yet we plowed ahead as if nothing had happened. On top of my own uselessness, I couldn't define Emma's purpose at the firm. I didn't know if she was Alexandra's necessary ballast or her charity case? Or perhaps Emma had a greater role, the significance of which I couldn't grasp.

All the previous week, I'd sat around procrastinating, staring at the list of the U.S. firms recently opened in Moscow, checking my email, or going downstairs to a depressing Soviet-style cafeteria to get a cup of truly awful coffee. I felt like an observer, a faint shadow of Alexandra's, walking in the wrong direction.

I also discovered the depth of chauvinism ruling my native Russia.

"Our men usually don't believe a woman can run a business on her own without having to sleep with someone first," Alexandra had said the week before. "So, this makes them wonder – did we really do it on our own? That's a threat. And if we indeed did sleep with someone, then with whom? One another? Well, that's an even greater threat, as it cancels out men altogether. Bottom line, you should behave like a man in meetings if you want to get any business. Remember that, Belova."

I didn't want to behave like a man, at work or anywhere else. I was tired of the constant bending of my personality. I should have gotten out of this mess back in Miami. But I couldn't: I was addicted to Emma and couldn't get enough of her. I loved the dimples on her cheeks when she smiled, and the way she tilted her head when looking at me, and how she twirled in excitement at seeing new things. No way was she a drug addict. She was a kid, constantly surprised by the world around her, and a master seducer at the same time, a seducer whose power I couldn't shake off. I wanted Emma to make love to me. And even though I knew we shouldn't without Alexandra, I couldn't resist Emma's hands, lips, and whispers, and kept coming back for more, unable to pull away.

I was bored with her otherwise.

The doorbell rang. I let go of the leaves. At the entrance Emma stood, panting, bags of groceries in her hands.

"We have half an hour before Alexandra gets here," she said.

"Do you want to start cooking?" I asked.

"It can wait."

She took my hand and led me to the small bedroom.

We sat down on the bed, the maple tree still waving its hands at us. As Emma kissed me, the doorbell rang again. I went to open the door.

On the landing stood Alexandra – radiant, with two bottles of wine in her hands, and a laptop hanging over her shoulder. I wiped my lips and kissed her on the check.

"Open this," she said. "I want to finish writing our mission statement. I'll help with the cooking in a minute."

She went into the room without greeting Emma, who had gone into the kitchen. I followed Alexandra.

"Don't you want us to help you with the mission statement?" I asked.

"You? Of course. Not Emma. She doesn't think on this level," Alexandra said without looking up from the laptop set on the coffee table.

"What level?" I was offended for Emma and stunned by Alexandra's words.

"Statements level. She's good with concepts, but she is useless with expressing her thoughts in a comprehensive manner."

"She can hear you," I warned.

"I want her to hear me. Do you hear me, Emma? You're not good with statements."

Emma walked into the room and approached Alexandra's chair. With no smile on her pale face, she wiped her hands on her pants and sat down on the couch.

"Do you not want me to take part in any of this?" she asked meekly.

"I want you to stop fucking around behind my back and get your act together," fired Alexandra, looking directly in front of her. "I'm sick and tired of your girlish ways, of your games where you don't have to make decisions, of your pretense of innocence."

"What are you talking about?" I asked.

"I'm talking about her being irresponsible: with you and me, with our new company, with things you'd better not know about," Alexandra said.

"That's enough!" Emma got up. "Inga doesn't need to hear this. It's all nonsense anyway."

"Nonsense? Taking money out of the company account and putting down a deposit for a summerhouse in Sochi is nonsense? 'Inga doesn't need to hear this?'" Alexandra's face reddened, and I felt crushed. How much I still didn't know about those two. I felt as if my life in Moscow had turned into a swamp, sucking me down, instead of being a trampoline for my career.

I looked at Emma in disbelief. I didn't feel angry; instead, I was in awe that she could have so little sense, to proceed with a transaction of such magnitude and think it would go unnoticed.

"Did you really put down money on a house in Sochi?" I asked Emma, almost stuttering. "Company money?"

Emma lit a cigarette – as if she could be saved by the dim red flicker. She took a long hit and looked me straight in the eye.

"I did. It was meant to be a surprise for all of us. Remember? In Miami, we talked of having a house of our own? And I meant to pay back your two-thirds once our next deal came in."

"Shut up!" Alexandra flew off the handle. "Surprise? As in – I'll spend all of our money now, and Alexandra will somehow figure it out later? As in – this is a getaway for me and Inga?"

"Please don't make me an accomplice," I said. "This is the first time I've heard of it."

"Fine, sorry." Alexandra looked up from her laptop screen, first at me, then at Emma. "Here is what we'll do. Emma cancels the deal, recovers the down payment on the house, and apologizes to both of us. Once she's done, she can be part of the company again. For now – she is off the payroll, and I don't want any input from her on any deals."

Alexandra got up and went into the kitchen. I couldn't feel the tips of my fingers. My legs below the knees went numb, as they always did when I was frightened. It had first started when I was six and had gotten lost in the woods. I thought I'd never see my parents again, would die of hunger, or that the wolves would eat me. An old man found me after I'd been shouting non-stop for an hour, which to me seemed like a lifetime of despair.

"Inga, I'm ready to help with the cooking," Alexandra shouted from the kitchen. "Our slogan is done: *IQ Consulting – Your Turnaround Agents.*"

I felt like a squeezed lemon. I left Emma in the room and followed Alexandra.

"Are you serious about what you just said?" I asked.

"You bet I am, and Emma damn well knows it."

"How can you be so harsh with her?"

"Darling, in the old days, I'd deny her sex and she'd come to her senses in no time. These days, she gets plenty of it from you, as far as I can guess. So my only weapon is money. And money means a lot to Emma, in case you haven't noticed."

I started making a salad. There was nothing else to say or do. My hands picked out the cucumbers, then tomatoes, and started cutting them, as if I were on autopilot. More than anything, I wanted to rewind the time and reappear in New York, in the moment before I'd announced I was going to Moscow. But I was still broke. And our firm needed to make money.

I watched Alexandra as she prepared chicken and rice in a light cream sauce. She was in good spirits again, as if she'd turned the page on a horror story in her book of life and proceeded to the next chapter – dinner at a friend's house. But I was stuck on the horror page. Emma set the table and brought out the wine.

We sat down and ate in silence, not looking up from our plates. If I could have, I would have left. Since it was my place, I stayed put, picking at the chicken, unable to taste the food.

"I'll do as I'm told," Emma said, looking at Alexandra. "I'm sorry. I thought it would be a nice surprise."

Nobody responded. Alexandra took a remote and turned on the TV, the old Panasonic I'd inherited along with the rest of the furniture in the apartment. *Moscow Doesn't Believe in Tears* was on, part two. We watched in silence the scenes we knew by heart: the main character runs into the old boyfriend who'd left her pregnant seventeen years before. They meet by chance: she – a successful executive and the mother of their grown-up daughter, he a cameraman for a TV program on which she is to appear. We watched for another hour, sipping wine and not talking, until the titles rolled on the screen.

"I'll see you tomorrow in the office," Alexandra said to me, getting up. "We have a couple of interesting meetings. And Emma will deal with her real estate issues. Thanks for dinner." She brought her plate to the kitchen, gathered her laptop bag, and headed for the hallway.

"Thank *you* for dinner," I whispered.

Emma hurried after Alexandra, giving me a quick kiss

on the cheek before closing the door.

· 25 ·

Being in the office without Emma was strange and liberating at once. Alexandra had made it clear the night before that from then on she and I would be strictly business. What remained of sex, and with whom, was to be sorted out with Emma, for each of us individually.

As I stared at the laptop screen, traffic humming below on Zubovsky Boulevard and heat waves rushing in from the window, my mind worked feverishly. I had to get out. Broke or not, I had to run for my life. My gut told me Alexandra would only welcome it. She'd had enough of me. Emma was another story. I called and asked her to lunch.

We met at Stella on Pushkarskaya, a lovely Italian restaurant the three of us had frequented in the summer. Emma was late, as always, and I waited with a glass of white wine in my hand, taking in the soothing peach décor, framed by heavy off-white curtains and black-and-white photos, oversized portraits, on the walls. One face reminded me of someone, but I couldn't place him.

I didn't know if I was really going to break up with Emma. I still loved her. I didn't know if she would become a drug addict again, and if it would be my responsibility.

She arrived in a hurry – impeccably dressed in a Yamamoto pinstripe suit and a crisp white shirt with oversized collar and cuffs – looking fresh and sexy, possibly after a morning spent at a spa. I was certain she hadn't tortured herself with thoughts of what to do when banned from the office. She sat down, and I stared at her for a moment.

"Have you recovered the deposit on the house?" I asked.

"No." Emma waived to a waiter and pointed at my wine glass. "I borrowed the money from a friend to return to the company's stash, but I'm going through with the house transaction." She smiled and touched my hand. "It will be our house, baby. For you and me." She emanated so much love and joy that I could only shake my head, unable to talk about the end of us.

"First of all, Alexandra will kill you when she finds out," I said. "Second of all, I'm not dealing with this until you and she make up. What's happening between you two?"

Emma lit a cigarette and gave me a look.

"What do you think?" She paused. "We're finished. She doesn't want me any more because I betrayed her. I don't want her any more because I love you. So we'll just work together and I'll move out to my apartment in a month. The renovation is almost done."

I recalled that Emma and Alexandra had purchased separate apartments, Emma's on the top floor of a new twelve-story building, overlooking the horserace tracks, with sunsets staring at the bedroom windows.

She took a sip of wine. "I hope you'll move in with me."

I put down my glass, my hands reaching for the napkin on my lap, as if trying to hide.

"Thank you, but I can't. I love you, too, but I'm suffocating." I paused. "Sorry. I can't do this anymore."

My lips started trembling and I stared at the portrait of my unknown person, as if asking for his help. Emma regarded me with a heavy look of disbelief.

"Do what?"

"Us."

"You are not serious! Did something happen?" She took my hand. "We're great together, baby. Just remember Miami..."

"I'm sorry. I just can't anymore."

I looked down, my hands tearing at the napkin, wanting to duck under the table as I had done three months earlier at Starlight Diner, when Alexandra asked me whether I had ever considered the option of finding a great woman instead of a man. I could feel Emma's stare drilling through my skin. I lifted my head, and wrapped my hands around the edges of the table but couldn't feel my fingertips.

Emma got up, her expression stern and icy. "What a bitch!" she said. "First you get into our business. Then you break us up. And now you're running away. You're a sorry loser who used us, and now that you're done, you're just leaving us hanging!"

Emma almost threw a glass of wine at me but chugged it instead, put out her cigarette, and left without looking at me. I thought I saw tears.

I turned to the portrait again and remembered. The face resembled Vlad's. I sat very still, holding back the tears ready to flood my face, my thoughts, my life. "I can't cry," I said to the portrait quietly, hyperventilating.

I opened my eyes, an excruciating pain in the back of my head. A waiter stood over me, panic on his face. I looked around. I was still in the restaurant, but I was lying on the floor. Thank God the place was half empty.

"What happened?" I mouthed to him.

"You fell down. And hit your head on the table. Are you all right?" He put a wet towel on my forehead. It hurt.

"Fainted!? How Victorian of me! This hasn't happened since the time I watched blood being drawn from my vein when I was twelve," I muttered under my nose. "I'll be fine."

I reminded myself of a character from a famous Russian film, *Sluzhebnyj Roman (A Workplace Affair)*. The man lands on the floor holding a statue of a bronze horse, pretending it had outweighed him, so that his boss, whose love he'd tried to win, would come to his rescue. Their affair took off from there. I, too, liked being on the floor with someone worrying over me: the same feeling as when you'd gotten sick as a kid and could stay in bed, surrendering all responsibilities, and your parents brought you tea with honey and read you books because your eyes hurt from fever and you couldn't read yourself, and no homework was asked of you. Anything to get you better.

I propped myself up on one elbow and got up, pressing the wet towel to my right temple. I touched my forehead – there was a bump brewing. My whole body hurt, yet I was glad it had happened. Somehow, it had made us even – me and Emma, who was still wearing dark glasses after Alexandra's punch in Miami. I asked for the check. The waiter shook his head not to worry. *Maybe I should have fainted more often – after a full dinner and not just drinks.*

I thanked the waiter, handed him the towel, and walked

out to the street, the Indian summer in full swing. I didn't return to the office, not with the bruise and the pain, and the anguish of being misunderstood and insulted.

I walked out onto the empty wide Lubyanka square, no longer crowned by the statue of Dzerzhinsky, the Iron Felix, father of the KGB. My knees almost gave in again, and I hailed a cab, a Volga.

As we headed towards Dinamo, my head throbbing and ready to explode at every bump in the road, I couldn't help reliving the nightmare at lunch. I wanted out of the business, of Moscow, of my life. But where could I go? I knew only Igor and Sanjay.

The cab languished in traffic, and my helplessness became tangible. I felt lonelier than I had in New York, yet willed myself not to cry. So much for the Motherland empowering me.

I called Alexandra and left a message that I was sick.

I spent the following week in bed. I couldn't tell anyone about this – neither my father nor my friends. I cried into the pillow, watched TV, and didn't leave the apartment. I stopped taking showers and hardly ate. I scribbled notes to myself, just to have a conversation with someone, to try to understand how I had ended up where I was and how I could get out of it. I tore them all up and burnt them in an ashtray. I started smoking. I felt as helpless as I had back in New York, when an endless job search would prove futile despite months of trying or when yet another guy would disappear soon after spending a night in my bed. I didn't return Alexandra's calls: I had nothing to tell her. Someone else called but left no messages – probably Emma.

On Saturday I got out of my pajamas and looked at the desk calendar. I flipped to the current date: a whole week had passed, and all I'd done was watch three films a day, picking at bits of bread or canned peas, or seeds. I ate the two eggs that had been sitting in the refrigerator. I couldn't even order in, as delivery was a concept that hadn't arrived in Moscow yet.

I went to the bathroom to take the first shower of the week. The mirror showed a rail-thin girl, eyes opaque and glossy, with almost transparent, gray skin. I felt hungry and lonely. I sat down on the toilet and cried, feeling really sorry for myself. I cried until I got tired of it, until my face hurt, until my mouth could no longer be stretched into the crying position. I needed to wipe my tears, but there was no toilet paper left. And there were no friends in Moscow who could feel sorry for me the way I did. I knew it was much better to feel sorry for oneself when someone else was doing it too. *I could die alone in this apartment, and nobody would care.* I started sobbing, smearing the tears over my face. I could imagine what

Alexandra would say to me, her pathetic ex-girlfriend, had she seen me wallowing in my uselessness.

"Shut up!" I said to myself in the mirror.

I felt disgusted.

Emma was right to call me a bitch.

I dragged my feet over to the bathtub, smelling the stink of old sweat, and almost threw up. The first water ran down my limbs, bubbling on my skin, disappearing into the metal circle below. I stood motionless for what must have been fifteen minutes, my skin burning from scalding water, and stepped out on the wet floor when the burn became unbearable, almost falling down. Once I'd dried off and put cream on my bony cheeks, I felt human again. I shuffled to the desk and lowered myself into the chair.

The calendar showed September 25, the day of Vlad's exhibit opening at The Manezh. I stared at his name as if seeing it for the first time, and then it hit me: I could go to the exhibit. What for, I didn't know. I knew I'd be out of place there, jobless and sad, surrounded by oligarchs and their wives or lovers (or both). Yet I craved human contact. I dialed Vlad's number.

"*Privet!* Can I get a ticket to your opening tonight?" I whispered without introducing myself.

"Inga?" He paused. "How long have you been in Moscow? I didn't know how to find you."

"You wanted to find me?"

"Well, I thought we could stay in touch," he said, and I could picture him smiling though his thin-rimmed glasses. "Just one ticket?" I heard hesitation and hope in his voice.

"Yes, just me. It would be great to see you."

"I'll meet you by the entrance at 6:30," he said.

I hung up and smiled for the first time in a week. I could confide in Vlad. And maybe even hold his hand.

· 26 ·

The invitation-only gathering for the opening of Vlad Lepkin's personal exhibit moved like a giant, sparkling snake. Men clad in tuxedos and women shimmering like Christmas ornaments stepped out of shiny BMWs and Mercedes-Benz. I straightened my black overcoat, certain that I was the only person there who'd taken the subway that night.

I noticed a Rolls Royce parked at the steps and wondered which oligarch had decided to grace Vlad's opening with his presence. I'd recently read in some paper that Russia imported more Rolls-Royces than all of Europe combined. I believed it: flashy was in style in Moscow. And I could no longer stand it.

As I turned around to flee, I spotted Vlad talking to

someone at the entrance, a few feet away. Alexandra. I buried my face in the collar, my lipstick catching on fibers, and hid behind someone's shoulder, moving sideways, until my elbow bumped into something soft.

"What the... ?", said a female voice impatiently. I lifted my face.

"Inga? Long time no see!"

Almond eyes under arched eyebrows. Lips pouting. Head tilted.

"What's with the lipstick all over your face? New trend in make-up?"

Alexandra's small hand reaching out to my cheek, her palm cold and soft. Quick fingers gliding over my skin. *You're not together anymore*, I reminded myself.

"Where the hell have you been all this time?" She spoke as if no wrong had passed between us.

"Home," I said, then turned to Vlad. "Congratulations – quite a crowd."

Alexandra looked at us and wrinkled her nose.

"Before you nearly knocked me over, I was telling Vlad about our company and how you disappeared right at the start," she said, looking at me as if appraising my worth to her business. "The guys I met on Wednesday would have loved you, and it would have been much easier to close the deal, you know, if your lovely smile had accompanied our conversation." She paused. "Well, I signed them anyway, of course. Our first automotive account – Audi, no less – and a possible buyer of Vlad's art. I brought them over here. Congratulations to all of us."

I was glad and embarrassed at the same time. I felt idiotic and out of place, my smile stuck in the corners of my mouth, as if someone had applied glue too strong for me to undo. How did Alexandra do it? Why was everything so easy for her? Or perhaps I just thought it was easy, when in fact it had been her hard work I hadn't noticed. How did she manage to float above obstacles and make everything work while having fun and infecting others with her tireless energy? I looked at Vlad to make sure he couldn't hear my thoughts.

"Congratulations to all of us indeed! It truly is great," I said.

Vlad suggested we step inside. He exuded the pleasant vibes of achievement and good fortune and probably wanted to talk about his art, not Alexandra's business. I was taken by his elegant attire and soft manner. Male attention was nice, I thought, inhaling a whiff of his eau de cologne – fresh yet warm, not too masculine.

Vlad touched my elbow. "Everything okay?"

"Yes, sorry." I inhaled deeply one more time before taking a look around.

Alexandra disappeared in the buzzing crowd, and I felt the mental claw that had been crippling me release its grip.

I followed Vlad through the gallery, awash in soft yellow light, with his giant canvases hung at different heights, creating a colorful landscape of hues. His paintings had texture. They were tangible and warm, the abstract scenes inviting one to get lost in the fantastic world of the imagination. Some images screamed depression (*Did he paint those in New York?*), while others were soothing and soft. I couldn't call myself a specialist in art then, yet I knew when something spoke to me. Vlad's paintings did. The crowd grew quickly, with television cameras popping up here and there.

"I'll have to deal with them at some point," he said, "but let's have a drink first, before it gets crazy." He picked up two champagne flutes and led me into a quiet, dimly lit corner.

"It's nice to see so many people attend," I said, taking a sip of champagne. "Is Lisa coming?"

"No, she's staying in New York. Some new project she can't get out of."

I concentrated on the bubbles in my glass. What else could we talk about? Our kiss in New York? What for? IQ Consulting? No. Whether he could help me figure out the rut I was in? Whether he could be my friend?

"How long are you in Moscow this time?" he asked instead.

"As long as it takes to straighten out my life." I looked

him straight in the eye. He returned my stare, with a tired and kind look of understanding.

"Can I help?"

"Maybe. Do you know how to break up with someone and stay friends?"

"Never worked for me, if I remember correctly, except with Alexandra ages ago." He paused. "Who is the unfortunate fellow, if you don't mind me asking?"

"Not at all. It's a woman. Two, actually," I said, finishing my drink.

"Is Alexandra one of them?" he said without surprise, as if he'd known all along.

"Sort of."

He took my hand and kissed it.

"Just be honest with her, and…" He didn't finish.

"*Monsieur Artiste?*" A silhouette behind Vlad. The man was tall, bald and well-built, yet I couldn't see his face against the brightly-lit hall. "Are you hiding from us?"

He entered the dark corner, and after my eyes had adjusted I saw the man's tan face, strong jaws, dark eyes behind rimless spectacles, and an impeccably-pressed white shirt, its collar open. A bright red tie hung loosely around his neck, and the glass of champagne in his hand was untouched.

"Oh, sorry to interrupt, I didn't see the lady," he said, turning to me. "I'm Justin. And a huge fan of Vlad's art."

He stretched out a hand the size of a frying pan. I shook it, noticing the muscles and the tan under the rolled sleeve. He was an American in his forties, and his Russian was flawless. "Again, excuse my intrusion. I'll come back later," he added and turned around.

"Inga. Also a fan of Vlad's art." I said to his back. "You didn't interrupt anything."

"Fantastic." He turned around. "Vlad – I'm buying two pieces, let me show you which. Inga – would you like to accompany us?"

Vlad shook Justin's hand and went towards the center of the exhibit hall, inviting me to follow. We passed gorgeous women, some in smart suits, some in see-through dresses, conversing with polished-looking men. A few faces looked familiar, but I didn't acknowledge anyone: I felt safe with these two, and didn't want to lose them in the crowd. We approached two large canvases in the middle of the room, with a reporter in front of them talking to a camera.

Justin stopped at a respectful distance, waiting for the reporter to finish. He then approached the paintings, around nine by six feet each, variations on the same abstract theme – one in orange, another in yellow – and pointed at them with both hands. I held my breath. One reminded me of a stormy sea, the other of a field of dandelions. I saw individual brushstrokes applied heavily, sticking out like little seashells on the momentous canvas resembling the ocean. I could picture Vlad laboring on those individual inches of orange and yellow, beads of sweat on his forehead as he painted. Apparently Justin had good taste, and a very large apartment.

"They're beautiful," I breathed out.

"I call them 'Before' and 'After', but decided to leave 'Untitled' in the catalogue. It's only for close friends to know," Vlad said, smiling.

"I assume the orange is 'Before'?" Justin asked, looking at me, even though the question was for Vlad.

"Of course. It's actually a series of three. But I haven't finished the third one yet. It has a bit of both in them," answered Vlad, also looking at me.

"Can I buy that one?" I blurted out. Where would I hang it, and how would I pay for it?

"That one is not for sale yet, but we can talk about it later."

I noticed Justin studying me with interest. I was certain he would have loved to buy the third piece, too. Or maybe he was wondering what a woman with gray skin and hollow eyes was doing at this vanity fair. I turned to him.

"You have great taste in art," I said. "These are the centerpieces of the show."

"I have no taste in art," answered Justin, who still seemed to be studying me. "I just love orange; it's the color of joy for me. And there is too much sadness in the world, so I buy joy to make life manageable."

I wondered if I could buy some joy, too, so that the back of my head would stop hurting and the Moscow nightmare would have a happy ending.

"I love orange, too," I said. "Would you excuse me for a second, please?"

Justin handed me a business card.

"I'd love to stay in touch," he said.

"Sure," I said, taking the card. "I'll be right back."

I went into the crowd. After a few moments, I spotted Alexandra and Emma on the other side of the room. I tripped over someone's shoe and almost fell, then recomposed myself, hoping Vlad and Justin hadn't seen me. Hidden by the crowd, I watched the two women talking, their voices energetic but civil, Alexandra's eyes attentive and even soft, as if she were ready to forgive Emma. They were sorting things out, I thought, with no help from me. How naïve I had been to have thought they would wait to speak with me first before reaching any conclusions. I sipped my champagne and watched, eager for them to finish and part. I still wanted Alexandra to hear my side of things.

I turned and, seeing Vlad speaking to a reporter on camera, felt quiet warmth spread inside me. I felt connected to him by a strange bridge that spanned Moscow and New York, connecting their inhabitants, yet not letting them settle, leaving them forever walking in between. I was happy to see him successful, with people not just admiring his art but opening their wallets to buy it. When the reporter switched off his camera light, Vlad stepped toward me but then stopped. As I wondered why, Alexandra touched my shoulder.

"Emma tells me you broke up with her. Interesting. Oh, yes, and, by the way, she thinks you're a bitch." She raised her eyebrows and scratched her nose.

"She's right on both counts," I said. "If it's any consolation, I fell down and hit my head on the table at that lunch," I said, and wiped the back of my neck which had become sweaty.

"That explains everything. And where have you been for the past week? Are you ditching the business, too?" Alexandra wasted no time.

"I spent the week in bed, if it's anything to you. And I'm not ditching anything. I just want out."

"And what's the difference between ditching and wanting out, exactly?"

"It means I won't take any money from the clients you'd already signed," I said, feeling a drop of sweat run down my temple. "And I'll bring you at least one client before I leave."

"How noble! What about the money we've already

invested in setting up the business? I suppose you'll want yours back?"

"Actually, I do. But I understand that's probably not possible. Unless you don't mind." I felt my insolence gathering in me like an autoimmune response. I knew that to win with Alexandra, I'd have to play the game by her rules.

"We'll see. If Emma returns the money she 'borrowed' for her summerhouse, we'll talk about returning your part of the total. Even though, legally speaking, we don't owe you shit. As to bringing in a client – that works for me." With an impatient air, she brushed back a loose lock that had fallen over her forehead. "Anyway, I didn't offer it; you did. Just make sure it's at least a fifty-grand deal, okay?"

Alexandra smiled, high-fived me, and turned back into the crowd.

As I watched her go, my stomach went hollow. As much as I'd wanted it to end, I hadn't bargained for such an anti-climax. Hadn't there been more to what we'd had? Or had I been delusional about the whole affair from the start?

I stood in the middle of the humming crowd of oligarchs and bankers, TV producers and boutique owners, feeling myself at a dead end. I wondered how it was possible that I had once wanted to be one of them. Instead, I'd become my own version of an old lady with a broken pail from the old Russian tale. Had there ever *been* a goldfish that granted wishes?

Russia no longer made sense. I longed for New York. From there, Moscow's displays of wealth – the heavy jewelry on every body part, the fur coats in the summer – were seen for what they were: grotesque. But nobody seemed to notice it here. I picked up another glass from a waiter and stepped up to the paintings that Justin had bought.

As I looked at the bits of orange and yellow struggling for space on the canvas, I saw myself as one of them, a speck of human dust lost in its desire to belong and to make sense, to flee from nowhere to somewhere. As I kept looking, the orange expanded and the yellow dimmed, the canvas becoming a magnetic landing pad for lost elements that had found their home. I wondered if Vlad saw himself as one of those traveling bits. I knew I was one of them. Maybe Justin was, too.

Thinking about him calmed me. I hardly knew him, and that made him interesting in my imagination. I could think of him as a well-adjusted, not-New-York-neurotic, kind, and stylish man of forty, which would make him a rarity in both metropolises. In New York, men like him were still hunting for their perfect match; in Moscow, they were probably divorced and had taken up drinking.

I kept standing in front of the centerpieces, imagining I was in Justin's sprawling apartment, in the middle of a high-ceilinged room, with these painting on the walls and white flowers on glass coffee tables. I was certain he'd made a few million on his investments in Russia. I didn't even know if he was single. Or maybe he had one of those Russian trophy girlfriends in her early twenties who spoke no English, whose jaw-dropping looks and long legs absolved her of that or any other flaw. *None of my business either way*, I thought, turning to see if he was still around. He was standing right there next to me, admiring his new purchases. I kept quiet, waiting for him to initiate a conversation. He didn't wait long.

"If you buy the third painting, would it mean that I have an incomplete collection or that we have a complete one between the two of us?" he asked.

"Depends on how you look at it."

"I look at it as a complete collection. Unless Vlad sells it to someone else."

"Supposedly, you and me are the only people who know about the third," I said.

"Shall we request a private viewing?"

I smiled. "That would be positively Victorian."

We stood silently side-by-side.

"Vlad told me you started a company in Moscow. That's very brave," he said.

I winced. I wished my meeting Justin hadn't had to start with rehashing the path that I had traveled with Emma and Alexandra, but I didn't want to lie or to pretend.

"I joined someone's business but will be leaving it soon," I said. "Too many tensions outside of the office."

"Oh, I know about those." Justin nodded. "In fact, I took a new position a month ago. The previous business I built here has finally pushed me out. They no longer needed the American who taught them the ropes." He looked as if he wanted to say something else but cut himself short. There was no bitterness in his words, only acceptance that this was how things worked. Soft wrinkles appeared on his cleanly-shaven face as he smiled, shaking his bald head.

"What business pushed you out?"

He named one of the better-known banks. I'd read about it in the papers – the first Russian bank with a transparent investment strategy, founded by a Russian and an American.

"And you are staying in Moscow? Haven't you had enough?" I asked.

"Oh, I love it here." He gave me a huge grin. "I've been here for a decade. It's still so much fun, and there's so much business to be done, and the people are great. True, it's not always a fair game, but who says it's different anywhere else?"

"But aren't you tired of the Moscow pathos? It seems you can't do anything here unless you wear Prada or Rolex and spend summers in Spain or Sardinia. You're not even taken seriously unless you first prove you are loaded or connected. It's like they're trying to be Palm Beach but don't know how to manage it. It gets old so quickly."

"Well, that comes with the territory. New money always does this to people – doesn't matter if you are in Moscow, Prague or Cape Town. You can just choose to ignore it," he said.

"Can you really? You'd be the first person I've met who can do it in Moscow."

"It's a matter of lifestyle, I guess." Justin put the champagne glass to his lips, savoring the drink, and motioned to the waiter for more.

"Moscow isn't your home, is it?" he asked.

"Definitely not. I don't even know where home is anymore. St. Petersburg or New York, or somewhere in between."

"So, did you come to Moscow to find a new home?"

"Good question."

And then I felt like I could tell him everything. There was nobody else who could hear me out and understand and not judge. And even if he did, I didn't have to see him again.

"I wanted to have my own company, built from scratch,

an overnight success type of thing, to be read about in the papers. I wanted to live life on my own terms, without being chained to a desk, and without feeling like a second-class citizen, as I did in New York. So I packed up and came to Russia. And when Alexandra offered to start a company together, I agreed. I thought it would be an obstacle-free highway to my dream, much easier than doing everything myself. But I totally miscalculated. I forgot there is no such thing as a free lunch. All I want now is to get back to New York."

"You give up that easily?"

Did I? But what was I giving up? I had nothing in Moscow. And I had nothing in New York. My head started to hurt, and the most dreaded of feelings, helplessness, took hold of me. Again I was a scared little girl who'd lost her parents in the crowd, unsure which way to go at an intersection.

"So, what's the ultimate goal?" Justin squinted.

"At this point, to find a way out of the rut I'm in."

"Well, why don't you do it differently? Do you have to start from scratch? You could be hugely successful if you joined one of the U.S. consultancies here. They're scrambling for good people. You wouldn't be the CEO, but the opportunities are amazing."

He sounded like a mentor now, yet without being patronizing. I also felt I could trust him because he had tasted the life of my people and didn't condescend to them, as was often the case with expats. Nor was he arrogant, like most first-time tourists with no clue about the country. Having read Tolstoy, Dostoyevsky, and Chekhov, they knew all about the Russian soul – or thought they did.

"You're right. I did propose to McLadley to open an office in Russia but never heard back from them. So I first took a job with Obundy here – which I quit after two months… Long story. After that I became part of someone's business in Moscow."

"Why don't you talk to McLadley Europe directly? They're much closer to Russia than New York," Justin said simply. I looked at him, stunned. I also felt relief, even though nothing had changed.

I was about to respond when I saw Emma and Alexandra coming. There was no time to get lost in the crowd, or to step aside from Justin. I stared at them. Moscow was a tightly-layered city indeed.

"Justin, good to see you," Alexandra said, all smiles.

Justin nodded, looking at Emma. The two hadn't met before, yet Alexandra didn't introduce Emma. So they hadn't settled their arguments, after all.

"May I steal Inga from you for a moment?" Alexandra asked.

"Only for a moment." Justin gave me a long look and

bowed his head slightly.

When we had walked far enough, Emma exploded.

"So? Already found your new lay?"

I looked at her and whispered, "Emma, please don't make a scene! You still want these people to respect you, even if I go back to New York."

"Bitch! Now you are running away, too?" Emma almost danced with anger.

"Shut up, baby," Alexandra said to her. "Just shut up. And go wait for me outside."

Emma turned around and headed for the door. Alexandra was the only one who could bring Emma back to her senses. I waited until Emma had disappeared into the crowd before turning to Alexandra, who said, "Listen. This whole thing between us is a total mess. None of us wants to be together or work together. I'm letting Emma go, too. She actually wanted to have a business with you, but now that's out the window." She took a sip of champagne. "Don't worry. She'll be fine. And you know what? Don't worry about bringing any clients, either. Perhaps New York is where you should be… with a nice American dude making enough money for you not to work." She looked up from her glass.

"Thanks. I'll think about it," I said, choking back the tears. "You've become so mean. Didn't take long, did it? And how do you know Emma will be fine? I thought she was a drug addict and you were her lifeline."

"Not for you to worry. She's been through worse and came out unscathed."

I didn't believe her. I wanted to ask what else Emma had been through.

"So, if you want to stay friends," Alexandra added, "the less we see of each other, the better. Say, for a year or two. Then we'll see what transpires."

"I'll make sure of that," I said curtly and went back into the gallery, my heart pounding.

I could read between the lines: *Get out of Moscow.* Yet I had my own plan.

I sped up, almost running towards the exit, and waved goodbye to Justin, who looked puzzled at my departure. I'd explain everything later: that meeting him triggered the left side of my brain; that in place of the emotions that had been dominating my life for the last few months, I had at last resorted to some logic; that the fear that had been stifling me – of failing, of being alone and a perpetual immigrant no matter where I lived – had finally lifted. I felt as if a pair of windshield wipers had cleared the view ahead, exposing the real threat – relying on other people to make decisions, of seeking out and succumbing to easy solutions, of going around instead of through. As I ran through the exhibit hall, I was determined to act on my own again, and that required losing my inhibitions.

Before I reached the exit, I repeated to myself, "The umbilical cord with Emma and Alexandra has been cut. You have no money left and nothing in Moscow or New York." I expected to feel scared again. But instead, I felt free. "Think," I said to myself. "You need inside contacts at McLadley Europe....Who? Who?"

I practically fell out of the cab and ran upstairs to my apartment. Without taking off my coat, I headed for the phone and did the unthinkable: I dialed the cell-phone number of the McLadley partner for whom I'd done a project before grad school. What were the chances he'd remember me? That he still had the same phone number? My heart was pounding as I considered whether email might be more suitable. But no, I'd never write what I wanted to say in an email, and even if I did, he'd never answer. "Spill it out," I whispered to myself. "Now or never."

"Chuck Briggs," said the familiar, crisp voice.

"Chuck, sorry to interrupt your Sunday." It was 11 AM in New York. "This is Inga Belova. I hope you remember me. I'm calling from Moscow."

"Yes?" He sounded neither welcoming nor put off.

"Quick question: McLadley still hasn't entered Russia, right?" My fingers tapped a staccato rhythm on the desk's surface.

"Do we have to discuss this now?"

"I want to help launch it. The timing is perfect. I wrote it all down in my proposal to the corporate board but never heard back. But now I'm onsite and have more real data, and even several prospects who have voiced their needs." This last statement was a bit of a stretch, but Chuck had no way of checking. "Will you help me?"

"Do what?"

"Convince McLadley London?" I said, listening to my heart in my ears.

"Shoot me a proposal before Monday AM," Chuck said. "I'll take a look. If it's solid, I'll forward it to Europe to discuss internally." I waited for some more *ifs* or *buts*, but none came. "Didn't know you wanted to go back to Russia. Interesting times," he said. "Have a good one." He hung up.

My heart's beating deafened me. I was intoxicated with the possibilities. Dad would be proud, I thought. I went to my desk and started typing.

As the lines ran across the screen of my monitor, I laughed, reminding myself of Jerry Maguire and his memo, only I hoped to have different results. I didn't sleep. With familiar scenes from *Pretty Woman* playing on my TV on mute, I finished three cups of coffee and a half-stale baguette. By five that morning, the proposal was ready. When I emailed Chuck, the sky was soft pink. I wanted a miracle. Too exhausted to move to the bed, I closed the laptop and crashed on the couch.

My dreams were entangled and colorful that night, like a kaleidoscope of images observed from the Ferris Wheel at Coney Island or a golden web of lights above JFK at night.

· 27 ·

I woke up late, feeling liberated yet slightly off-balance, as if I were walking on the parapet of the Eiffel Tower with no safety net below. I sat on the edge of the bed thinking, *No office to go to, no fights to fight, no money.* I poured myself a cup of coffee and had just sat down by the kitchen window when the phone rang.

"Baby, it's me," said Emma.

"Yes?"

"I'm so sorry about last night, and I'm sorry about what I said at that lunch," she whispered. "Please forgive me. Can we meet and talk? You shouldn't leave our company; I already talked to Alexandra. I miss you."

I looked at my hands, in need of a manicure, then at the mess on the kitchen counter – old bread and stale cheese. My heart ached for Emma, but I wouldn't be wooed again.

"Emma, I'm sorry. It's too late. Someone is here right now."

She hung up.

I pushed back the thought that if McLadley didn't work out, I'd have to go back to New York with nothing. I could picture Lisa's "I told you so" grin. I could see Kristina telling me that everything was for the best, that New York would welcome me back no matter what. I dismissed these thoughts. I needed neither pity nor judgment. I wanted to fight. Something deep inside me had crystallized and shone through, like a newly-planted tree that had the right amount of water and sun and couldn't wither but only grew and became stronger as its branches aimed for the sky. Maybe I had to go through the rollercoaster with Emma and Alexandra to arrive at that point in my life. I didn't know how long this upbeat version of me would last, so I willed myself to stay focused on this new feeling while it did.

I opened the laptop and wrote to Kristina in New York to get things off my chest, not expecting an answer, since it was six in the morning there. A moment later, an incoming message chimed. From the screen, the glaring letters came together to form the message that Kristina and Nick had separated, all having been finalized the previous week in New York. *Must be a full moon.* Why hadn't she told me right away? I dialed her number, and heard a hushed "Hello."

"Kristina, sweetie, come visit me," I pleaded, "for a week or so. Get your thoughts together. It will be nice to get away."

"Maybe," Kristina said, crying. "I just feel so useless. I was so proud of my marriage, and my parents will be devastated."

"Don't worry about your parents. Come, will you?"

"I have to go now," Kristina whispered and hung up, her sobs having become uncontrollable.

I took a shower to clean up my thoughts. I rubbed my skin red, as if trying to erase all the problems, mine and Kristina's. I stopped when it hurt. As the water trickled down, I realized I *had* hot water. It hadn't been turned off, an oversight or a lucky exception, since no matter where you lived in Russia the pipes had to be fixed between June and September. Not having water in the summer was as common as having a cold in the fall. The warm water tickled my face as I tried to remember how much money I had left. I hadn't checked my balance in a month.

I wrapped a towel around my waist and went into the room, water dripping down my legs, forming puddles under my feet as I sat at the desk and logged into my bank account. As I looked at the screen, I wished I hadn't:

my savings were at zero, with an overdraft in checking. The new me began to wilt. As I tried to think what to do next, a new email chimed in. From Nick, Kristina's newly ex-husband.

"Inga, I have good news," his email read. "I signed your friends from the Airplanes. They should be coming to New York to record an album in a month or so. Hope you are well. Nick."

That was all. I stared at the screen, surprised he had written to me at all. After he'd left Kristina? Didn't he remember we were best friends? And I no longer cared for Anton's band anyway. Let them go to the moon if they wanted to.

I wandered around the apartment. I didn't know where I would get the money to pay rent. I no longer had an income. And would Emma really slide back into drugs because of me? The sum of all the components in need of resolving added to the grotesque picture of my life. However you added them up or looked at it, I was in deep trouble. Would Alexandra force me to leave Moscow if I didn't on my own? I knew she could orchestrate anything, like turning Laura Paulson from a demanding boss into the sweetest little thing once Alexandra had "talked to her." Maybe she had threatened her. And I didn't know how I would get back to New York. I didn't even have enough for a return ticket. I could, of course, pay with the only credit card that hadn't been maxed out, but how would I pay rent in New York? I circled around, half-naked and restless. I might have to borrow money. From whom? Sanjay? Igor? I prayed for McLadley to accept my proposal.

The email chimed again with a new message, this time from Lisa. She never wrote emails.

"Inga, dear. I thought I'd write to you because I can't talk to anyone around me about this. And you are far enough, so even if you're going to judge me, there is still distance between us."

I sat down on the couch.

"I met a new guy. He worked on one of my projects. We fell in love. But he has a family back in Russia, and I know he won't leave his wife. Tomorrow is our last day together.

"Why are the good guys so good that they have to go back to their families? Why can't I meet a guy who'll be all mine, who won't make me wonder whether he still loves me or is ever coming back – like Vlad? I've had the best two weeks of my life, and now I feel like tomorrow is my funeral…

"Did you see Vlad in Moscow? Do you know if he's seeing someone else? I can't wait for him forever."

I kept looking at the screen, biting my nails, willing the text to disappear. Then I got up and put a T-shirt on.

"I saw him at the opening," I typed and stopped. Then added, "I know nothing of another woman. I have to run, will write later. Please stay strong." I hit Send.

Red circles danced in the backs of my eyes. I put on my gray coat, an orange scarf over it, boots without socks, and ran out the door. My apartment had become stuffy, crowded with problems. I yearned to be among regular people, doing their weekend chores, living normal lives. I went grocery shopping with the last cash I had.

The store across the street was a mix of an old Soviet "supermarket" and a new Western store, with displays old and untidy, yet a remarkable variety of goods, local and foreign. I'd treat myself to a nice dinner at home. Feast in the time of cholera: two bottles of cheap red wine, Viola cheese, mineral water "with gas," and meat dumplings, *pelmeni*, with sour cream – my favorite.

I paid at the *kassa* with the shortest line and went back to the counter to hand the receipt to the lady behind it, who dispensed the items accordingly. There were only a few other shoppers in the store, older women with worn-out tote bags shopping for bread, cabbage, and meat, and men of unidentifiable age, buying cheap vodka to start the evening early.

"Hey, you!" one of them gurgled at me, shoving a crooked finger with a black nail in my face. The alcohol in his breath choked me. "Your underwear is showing. Cover your *pizda* in a public place!"

I pulled my coat tighter and ran out of the store.

Back in the apartment, my coat and boots still on, I opened one of the bottles of wine and drank half of it in one gulp. It tasted of grapes and sugar. Then I got on the phone and, just to hear someone's voice, dialed Sanjay.

"Where the hell have you been?" he asked. "Veil was telling me the most interesting stories about your company."

"Like what?"

"Like how you can't make up your mind about what the hell you're doing in Moscow and how you're driving people crazy with your half-baked steps. That's what she said – 'half-baked.'" He paused. "I thought you'd become friends. You definitely don't want Alexandra for an enemy."

"Definitely not," I said. "I think she's trying to push me out of Moscow."

"But you just started a business together!"

"I'm no longer part of it. Something is very wrong there, and I can't figure out what. And I don't want to anymore." I sighed. "But I can't go back to New York right now. Do you think she'll do something nasty to me?"

"Like what?"

"Make sure I couldn't work in this town? She knows everyone."

"Are you so important that she'd spend time on that?"

"I'm not important at all. It's just that she's the type

who, if she gets something in her head, won't stop till it's done."

"You sound paranoid. Have a drink," Sanjay said.

"I've already had several."

"Want to go out tonight? Good party at Justo."

"Some other time."

I hung up, put water on the stove for *pelmeni*, and poured more wine. *Maybe I* should *get out of Moscow before it's too late.*

I finished the bottle as I ate the *pelmeni*, then licked the plate clean. I went to bed, my head spinning, my stomach happy with the weight of meat dumplings.

In the morning, I discovered I'd missed a record number of messages on my machine. Vlad had called to confirm Tuesday and announce a trip to New York the week after: a well-known curator had decided to represent him in the States. Anton called, drunk, telling me that Nick had signed his band. Lisa called, asking me to erase her email to me. And finally, Justin called, inviting me out to dinner after our visit to Vlad's studio.

· 28 ·

On Tuesday evening, I stood before a large, panel-block building, looking up at the giant windows on the top floor, remnants of the artists' studios from the 1970s. The studios had been dispensed by the government to the "official artists" working in the style of "social realism" – painting overachieving steel workers and peasants. Artists who had dared not follow the Party guidelines had remained unacknowledged and often persecuted, yet Vlad had evolved long after social realism had been forgotten. I wondered how he had gotten one of those lofts. Under my short gray coat the wind hugged my knees. I walked in.

I entered a fenced cage of an elevator and hit the button displaying 10, with a "0" scratched out. As it slowly climbed up, I stared at the old buttons and the inner wooden doors, which – once you pulled the outer metal door open – folded onto themselves, and I remembered that an identical elevator had been installed in our old apartment building. For a split second, I wanted to halt the lift, run to the train station, and board a train to St. Petersburg, to the coziness of my father's apartment, the safe place where I didn't have to make big decisions. I shuddered, knowing full well that wasn't an option. And knowing that it had been somehow changed since Emma and Alexandra's visit there. I counted floors, forcing myself to think. Chuck from McLadley had written that my offer was being considered, yet he hadn't said it was accepted. I untied my scarf as I needed more air.

Dressed in a white linen shirt and dark brown slacks, a smiling Vlad waited for me at the landing, a glass of red wine in his hands. Soft music streamed from the dim space behind him.

"Welcome to heaven," he said, handing me the glass.

I kissed him on the cheek. "How did you get this space?"

"It's a long story. Friends of friends of friends. Let's just say I didn't have to prostitute my art for it," he said, leading me into the studio.

We entered a narrow corridor that stretched as long as the eye could see and ended in complete darkness. A row of rooms branched to the right. I heard someone shuffling in the first room and followed Vlad into the next one, enormous, with floor-to-ceiling windows lined up on the right. All of Moscow lay before us, as if in the palm of my hand. *This is why pilots become pilots*, I thought.

The wall on the left was covered with Vlad's paintings. Several canvases were stacked together, crowded on the floor. I noticed my "number three" and came closer. It had elements of both of the paintings Justin had bought, yet there was more intensity to it. I concentrated, wanting to know the reason for the effect. Then I noticed it – the orange/yellow canvas was pierced with small drops of maroon, as if the painting were bleeding. I came closer and saw miniscule maple leaves in dense maroon, some blurry, some contoured, some refined. From afar, the painting seemed dramatic and tense, yet when you came closer, it became inviting and romantic, nothing dangerous about it. Almost like life. The unfamiliar was often scary, but once you got to know it, it became a part of life.

I turned to Vlad, who'd been standing at a distance behind me all that time.

"I love it. That's the third one, right? What is it called?"

"'During,'" Vlad said. "It's not finished."

The elevator door slammed and Justin walked in, interrupting the conversation as he'd done the first time I had met him.

"*Dobryj vecher!* The front door was open, so I walked in. Good to see you," he said, smiling at me. He handed Vlad two bottles of Merlot. He was again dressed in a crisp white shirt, dark gray slacks, and super-shiny shoes, a clear sign that he didn't walk around much in Moscow. To Vlad he said, "I heard about the New York curator taking an interest in you. Congratulations!"

"Oh, yes!" I said. How could I have forgotten? "*Pozdravlyaju!* It seems everyone I know is heading to New York."

"Thanks!" Vlad was all smiles but didn't ask who else was going to New York.

"Well, I'm staying right here," Justin said. "And I'm very excited about it. We might be getting involved with a couple of fantastic projects. Some friends are about to launch a Moscow office. And I sure need to get things going for my new bank."

Almost involuntarily, I took two steps back and tripped, hitting the wall. I practically slid to the floor but managed to prop myself at the last moment, the wine spilling onto one of the paintings and over my favorite maroon dress. I stared at Justin embarrassed, afraid I'd ruined the painting. Did Justin know Chuck at McLadley? Would I have to buy the ruined painting? I held the half-empty glass high above my head, my shoulders against the wall, my body an oversized question mark.

Justin rushed towards me and unglued me from the wall. "Are you okay?"

"Fine." I straightened up, handing him the glass. "Vlad, I'm so sorry. I've ruined your painting. I really am sorry." I was stammering like a kid who just broken her mother's favorite china, and forgot to ask Justin about Chuck.

Vlad looked at the artwork and smiled.

"Interesting," he said. "I told you it wasn't finished before, but now it might be. A touch of Pollock, if you will. By way of Inga Belova. What do you think?"

I was speechless and tried to wipe off my dress. It had become soaked with wine right around my crotch.

"I like it that way, too," Justin said. "Can I buy it now?"

"It's not for sale," said Vlad, handing me a towel and another glass of wine.

I went to the bathroom, Justin accompanying me through the dark corridor.

"Do you know Chuck Briggs?" I whispered to him on the way.

"Do I know Chuck? He was my college roommate! We were at LSE together." Justin raised his glass as if greeting someone.

I gulped the wine and handed him the empty glass. "I'll be fine from here, thanks. Let's talk about Chuck at dinner, please."

When I returned, tipsy, Vlad was at a makeshift bar opening another bottle of wine. As he struggled with the corkscrew, the door behind me opened, and silence enveloped the room. I turned to see a young woman in the doorway. I figured she had been the one making the shuffling noises in the anteroom. It was Tanya, the young creature I'd met at Sanjay's a couple of months earlier, looking to marry "a financially-secure American." I couldn't suppress a smile, but Tanya shook her head ever so slightly, as if asking me not to reveal we'd met before. I turned to look at Vlad, as did Justin.

Vlad turned around, and an enormous smile spread on his face. "Tanya!" he exclaimed, before rushing towards the girl, who towered on immensely high heels, dressed in a strapless black cocktail dress barely covering her slim thighs. Her skin shimmered, her whole being emanating youth and freshness. She could hardly walk in those stilettos, so Vlad was just in time to escort her to the bar. "Wine?" He handed her a full glass of red, then held her elbow as she sat down in a plush chair by the window, crossing her legs à la Sharon Stone in *Basic Instinct*.

"Tanya is my apprentice," Vlad said. Justin bowed.

"Apprentice! How fabulous. What does it mean exactly?" I couldn't resist the question.

"I'm helping Vlad with his work," Tanya said, a little too seriously. "I won a competition at my art school, and they let me intern with one of the artists interested in mentoring students."

I remembered Tanya telling me she was a journalism student. "How fabulous," I said. "Does it mean you will accompany Vlad to New York for his show at the new gallery?"

Tanya looked at Vlad inquisitively while I wondered how Lisa, his New York girlfriend, would react to his arrival with a young long-legged addition from Moscow. As I remembered, Vlad and Lisa were still a couple in Lisa's mind, despite the distance and the affairs they suspected one another of having.

"That would depend on my deal," Vlad said, smiling at Tanya, and I felt a pang of sorrow. I was sorry for Lisa, who'd been waiting for Vlad to come to New York for over five years, fighting her miserable single existence via one-night stands with Latino drummers and married Russian visitors. I was sorry for Vlad, enamored of a young girl obviously using him to get to New York to find a "better deal" once she was there. And I was sorry for Tanya, who, despite looking vibrant and fresh at the age of 18, was so pragmatic that there was no innocence left in her. I looked at Justin. I wasn't sorry for him. He was riding the waves of expat highlife in Moscow, with plenty of attention from beautiful women, executive compensation, and great career prospects anywhere he wished to settle:

Moscow, London, New York. And I no longer felt sorry for myself, either. I was sick of feeling sorry for myself.

· 29 ·

Justin and I sat in the back of his Mercedes as his driver maneuvered through the evening traffic of Moscow, dark and unpleasant in September rain. I watched the blinking streetlights, thinking of the happiness I'd felt riding through the rain with the girls after our first night together. It seemed as if a year had passed since then, yet it had hardly been three months.

I sat close enough to Justin to smell his cologne, yet far enough for our hands not to touch. I thought of him as my mentor or an old friend: his stability and good humor were the things I yearned for, a person without dirty secrets (that I knew of) or money problems or raging insecurities. The everyday drama in the lives of my friends, on top of my own rollercoasters, had started to take a toll: I knew I looked tired and disoriented. I wondered why Justin had asked me out, with so many other options available to him in Moscow. His quiet presence, sharp observations, and down-to-earth manners made him so refreshing that I was afraid I'd fall for him. Yes, against all odds, I found him attractive: his bald head, his large face, the deep-set eyes framed with glasses, the half-smile on his full lips. He was a man, calm and smart. I was attracted to the promise of normal life, whatever that meant, but didn't allow myself to like him too much. I'd learned my lesson not to mix work and love. And I hoped the dinner invitation was not a date but a meeting of friends, with maybe just a little bit of a date in it, because – let's be honest – women crave attention, be it from a mentor or a delivery guy.

The car stopped at a black metal door. Justo had been my usual hangout with Emma and Alexandra, the most coveted restaurant in the capital, which served fantastic Japanese fusion cuisine at obscene prices to the sounds of the latest Hotel Costes tunes, in a setting of white curtains, brick walls, and low-set bamboo tables and leather couches.

I looked out of the car window and asked Justin if we could go somewhere else. He motioned to the driver to keep going.

"Any preferences?" he asked, looking at me attentively,

yellow light dancing in his glasses.

"Just somewhere quiet, if possible," I murmured. "Sorry, I can't handle running into any more people tonight," I said in Russian, hugging my elbows inside my tired gray coat, my wet, rusty-orange shawl over my shoulders.

"I'd love to invite you to dinner at my place, but I'm not sure it's appropriate," he said, leaning closer. I wanted to throw myself into his arms and thank him for being so proper. "Why don't we go to Castle? I invested in the restaurant, and we haven't announced the opening yet. It'll be nice and quiet, almost no people, only those who wandered in by chance. And I bet you there won't be many on such a night."

"Great." I turned back to the window, watching strings of rain hitting the matted glass, spreading into thin slices of blurry gray, and wondering when Justin planned to tell me about Chuck Briggs and McLadley's plans for Moscow.

The restaurant exuded quiet coziness: white linen and candlelit silverware, the dimness all-encompassing and reassuring. A dark-wood gothic ceiling floated above the yellow walls, with a massive chandelier gracing the center. The only other wanderers of the evening – a couple at a corner table – sat as if praying over their meals. A maître d' in tailored black slacks and expensive light blue shirt shook Justin's hand and led us to an alcove by the fireplace.

"Moscow needed a place like this for a long time," I said, looking around. "Now I see why you love it here. You mold the reality to serve your comforts."

"Don't we all?"

"Apparently not," I said as we sat down at the table, my back to the window where the rain had turned into a storm.

While I looked trough the thick, cream-colored pages of the menu in a heavy leather binding, Justin ordered a bottle of Burgundy. I wished the prices hadn't been so exorbitant, not because I would have to pay, but because this place was bound to become another restaurant for a chosen, filthy-rich few. My father would never have ventured out to a place like this.

"But how come the prices are so high? Don't you want to see normal people sitting around you?"

"There are plenty of normal people with plenty of money," Justin said, smiling. "You know it, don't you?"

"Maybe I just haven't met them," I said. "Which brings me to the subject of those I *have* met: Did you talk to Chuck recently? He was the one I worked for before grad school." I waved to the waiter to fill my wine glass.

Justin looked up from the menu. "He called the other day to see what I thought of them opening an office in Moscow and whether I'd be interested in talking to them as a client once they did. I told him it was long overdue."

"And?"

"And he mentioned your name." Justin lifted his glass.

"He did? Why?"

"Because I called him the night we met and told him that I'd met a fantastic person."

I stared at him. "I don't believe you."

"He said they've been thinking about opening an office in Russia for a while, so your proposal landed on the right soil. And he couldn't believe it had come from the same person I'd met the night before, who also happened to be his former employee. How was working for Chuck, by the way?"

"So, is it a yes or a no?"

"Well, he actually wasn't supposed to discuss it with me, so I won't discuss it, either. Maybe you should call him." He took out his slim black cell phone, dialed a number, and handed it to me. I pressed the End button and pushed it back to him.

"Are you trying to push my buttons, or do you really think I'd be stupid enough to call Chuck from your cell phone?" I said. I knew I was being rude, but I had no time to tiptoe. Regardless of Justin's and Chuck's friendship, I wanted my own damn deal, clean and straight, without innuendo.

"Sorry – my bad," Justin said. "I've known Chuck for

ages. Remember, I told you we were roommates at LSE. I wanted to play a joke on him. Sorry." He sipped his wine. "I think they're going to go for your proposal."

"Because you told him you liked me?" I was insulted, as if I was no good by myself unless someone else – Alexandra, Justin, or whoever – endorsed me.

"No. Because it was a comprehensive and timely proposal. That's what Chuck said." Justin smiled so widely I could see his wisdom teeth.

"I can't believe it," I said, fanning myself with my serviette. "I just can't believe it." I didn't elaborate as to what, exactly, I couldn't believe. "Excuse me." I got up, ruining a stocking on the chair, and went to the bathroom to think.

I entered a dim spacious restroom, tiled in white and brown marble. Moscow bathrooms were more impressive than the restaurants they belonged to. They deserved a place in travel guides. I approached a large mirror and stared at my reflection, ready to burst from the good news from London, not quite believing it, wondering how this affected my relationship with Justin. He liked me; there was no doubt about it. Why else would he have talked about me to one of his closest friends?

"First things first: no more mixing of business and pleasure," I said aloud to the mirror, drawing a stare from a woman who had entered the bathroom behind me. I smiled at her and went to a stall.

Justin got up when I returned to the table. "I'm sorry if I was blunt just now about calling Chuck," he said. "Must be all that wine at Vlad's. Apologies."

"That's fine," I said. "I'm all business." Justin kept smiling, though disappointment showed in his eyes.

"Let's order?" he asked as he helped me into my plush chair. The rain had subsided, but the drops were still hitting the windows in even staccato beats. We both ordered pasta. I wondered if I should explain about my ordeal in Moscow. I felt that Justin could understand it all and not judge me. And this would be a good test of how much I could trust him. I started from the beginning.

"On the subject of business, remember I told you about the company I'd joined? It was Alexandra's. And now things have gotten pretty convoluted. In fact, I'm a bit scared," I confessed.

"Of Alexandra?"

"It's a long story. Are you sure you want to know?"

"I'm listening."

And I let go. *Clean slate, clean slate,* I kept repeating to myself. My father could never know, and my friends would never know, but I needed to tell someone. The wine in my bloodstream made it easier.

"Well, I told you I'd been wanting to open my own company in Russia ever since I started grad school. So I came to Moscow. And fell in love. With Alexandra and Emma. They offered me the business, and I joined. But that was wrong. Not the love part – that was great." I took another sip of wine and watched the tall cream candle flicker between us. "Choosing the easy path and piggybacking on their idea was wrong. So I ruined everything. And the reason I'm telling you this is because I wrote the proposal to Chuck after I talked to you. Meeting you made me think straight." I looked at him, embarrassed and hopeful that he would understand and laughing inside at the unintended play on words.

"I suspected there was something between you and them," Justin said, making it unnecessary to continue that part of the story. "There's nothing wrong with piggybacking on other people's ideas as long as you contribute fairly, which I'm sure you did. And I'm also sure you haven't ruined everything." He, too, sipped his wine and looked at the candle. "Things like that happen left and right – the business part, I mean. From what Chuck told me, you were a great addition to his team at McLadley, and I have a hunch you'll be indispensable to them this time, too, once you find your footing."

"I think I've already found my footing. Mostly thanks to you – however strange that sounds."

"Nothing strange about it," Justin said.

I couldn't remember the last time I'd felt so content. Maybe watching movies in bed with Emma and Alexandra.

An hour later, the car pulled up in front of my building. We sat in silence for a minute. Then I gave Justin a quick peck on his cheek and stepped out. "Thank you for tonight," I whispered before disappearing through the doorway.

What Justin had offered was too good to be true and still depended on Chuck Briggs & Co.'s final decision: Justin wanted to help. When I'd asked him why, he said, "It's a rarity to see a woman in Russia striving to establish herself not through a marriage but through business."

I wanted to prove I could do it – as if I were back in my teens, competing to win the approval of teachers or parents. Maybe the little girl inside had never grown up. Maybe we, women, always needed a pat on the shoulder from our fathers or a nod from our bosses – to be justified by someone else.

The email from Chuck had been sitting in my inbox for a while, precisely for the hours I'd spent at Vlad's studio and at dinner with Justin. I was to travel to London on Monday for meetings with the partners, to present my proposal. Chuck would be there, too. There would be some questions to answer and additional projections to be made, but overall, I had a green light to go ahead!

"Tee-teree-tere-te-teee!" I sang my Russian song of joy, running around the apartment in stockings and a bra, throwing my dress and shoes in the air. "Yeehaw!" I jumped on my left leg, then on the right, twisted in the air and landed on the bed, hopping with my whole body, bouncing like an Easter bunny. I wanted to call Alexandra and shout, "I can do it!" And then tell my dad and Igor and Sanjay and…

I stopped myself – too soon again. Nothing was finalized. But *someone* had to be happy for me. Kristina! Lisa! Anyone… I turned up the radio and danced to the latest Yazz streaming from *Europa Plus* FM until I fell down on the bed, breathless and sweaty.

· 30 ·

London was the usual mix of drizzling rain and cars on the wrong side of the street. I took the tube from Heathrow to the hotel booked by McLadley. There were meetings scheduled for Tuesday and a return flight the next day. Kristina would be joining me in London on her way to Moscow. She had decided to get away after all.

As I sat on the tube, I thought how lucky I was to have met Justin. When Chuck had asked for additional data on market growth and foreign investment into Russia, Justin had provided both, and I had dutifully included the slides in my revised presentation.

I noticed that a tall black man across the aisle was eyeing me, trying to catch my glance. In New York, I'd have thought him obnoxious and asked what his problem was. But being a Londoner, he meant only to evoke a smile, and he succeeded. At Earl's Court, I could no longer avert my eyes, and looked at him. *Only a couple more stops,* I thought. He moved to the seat next to mine.

"Quite a trip, innit?" he sang in his proper British accent.

"Indeed," I answered, trying to use "British" words, so as not to be taken for an American.

"Mind if I ask what brings you to London?"

"What makes you think I don't live here?"

"The look in your eyes, mostly," he said, smiling at me again, his wild braids falling over his chiseled high cheeks and sparkling dark eyes.

"And what's that look?"

"Sadness and happiness at the same time," he said.

"That's because I'm from New York and from St. Petersburg before and after that."

"Complicated." He paused. "No – exciting, right?" He leaned a bit closer, and I smelled lush eucalyptus mixed with something warm, completely indefinable.

I looked at his torn jeans, black leather jacket, large hands with rough nails and dry skin. He must have been a musician.

"'Exciting' is more like it," I said. "This week, that is. Last week was miserable." I smiled. Once more, I was sharing intimate secrets with a complete stranger.

"I'm getting off at Knightsbridge," I added.

"Too bad. Would have loved to hear more. If you want to have a drink or listen to some tunes before you head back to New York or St. Petersburg, give me a ring." He handed me his card. I got off at the next stop.

The hotel room, immaculately clean, warm and inviting, overlooking a small square backyard, was an example of Western good living. It reminded me of the Marriott Tverskaya in Moscow, where I'd often had lunch with potential clients – and once, in a penthouse suite, sex with Emma and Alexandra.

I went to the bathroom to check out the amenities, as I believed those were the real measures of a hotel's level. This one was indeed a five-star: the towels – too many, plush and whiter than snow, embroidered with the hotel's logo – with rows of shampoos and shower gels displayed as if they were works of art. And the bidet – how European of them. I should try it one day, even though I couldn't imagine women actually doing such a thing. Why would you squat – or, better yet – sit on it and put the stream of water up your crotch? More than anything, it would have aroused me, and I remembered the moments in a Jacuzzi with Emma and Alexandra when they would make the stream touch me right there. Pure pleasure.

I decided to try it later.

The McLadley offices occupied an entire five-story building on Piccadilly, impressive in its royal standing. I produced my biggest smile at the security desk downstairs, as if to win their support for my proposal, to win over the people upstairs. The combination of my Russian passport and New York driver's license raised a few eyebrows, but I was let through with a visitor's badge that properly displayed, "*INGA BELOVA, McLadley.*" I liked seeing those words together.

The receptionist asked me to wait. Racks of magazines, from *Time* to *Red Herring*, made me hungry for my New York lifestyle: Sunday brunches on the Upper West Side, reading *The New Yorker*, and pavements free of slush and mud – a constant in Moscow from September till May, destroying fine shoes within days.

I had just set up my laptop when the glass door opened and Chuck Briggs appeared. He hadn't changed since I'd seen him two years before. Still fit and tan, a dark blue, pinstripe suit clinging perfectly to his tall body and the same clean haircut on his full head of dark hair. He opened his arms and smiled at me, soft wrinkles reassuring me I was doing the right thing.

"Inga, good to see you, kiddo." He hugged me.

"Chuck, thank you so much for making this happen so fast."

"I didn't make anything happen. You helped them with

a missing piece in their puzzle for Russia, and I just forwarded it to them. Now it's show-time." He led me to the window, as the receptionist's curious gaze followed us. The morning bustle on Piccadilly was dying out, with office workers already consumed by their cubicles, the mass of tourists not yet at its peak.

"Couple things you should know," Chuck said. "There are six people in there. Bob Gordon is your guy. He runs the show for Eastern Europe, so his opinion is ultimately the one you want on your side. He will ask questions, so don't be shy to let him know you know the market. Then there is Patty Richards. She is above Bob, runs McLadley Europe, knows less about Russia, but everything about the European Division. She won't ask questions, but she will be listening to your every word." I stood with my head bowed, as if writing down his words on my internal blackboard. "The rest you don't have to worry about. Good luck in there."

He led me into an airy conference room. I took a couple of deep breaths, shook my hands, then made them into fists, and entered the room with my head high, a half-smile on my bloodless lips.

The people around the table got up, stretching their hands for introductions. All were smiling, with the exception of Patty Richards, the only woman in the room. The men were dressed almost identically, in white shirts and dark blue suits, only their colorful ties setting them apart. I didn't notice anything else. I introduced myself to each, with an extra diction effort, saving my biggest smile for Bob Gordon.

Patty Richards spoke first.

"Inga, Chuck has told us good things about you and was impressed with your proposal. I didn't have time to look through it, but Bob Gordon, in charge of Eastern Europe, did and told me it's in line with our plans for Russia. Please proceed."

With that, she sat down, slid her thin rectangular glasses on the tip of her nose, and opened her laptop – either to take notes from my presentation or to check her private email. Her right foot stuck out from under the desk, and I noticed the spiky toes of her stylish, expensive-looking leather shoes.

I opened my laptop without sitting down while an office assistant appeared out of nowhere to hook up the projector. I thanked him, cleared my throat, and started on the first slide, "Patty, gentlemen – thank you for letting me present to such a distinguished group. I strongly believe, and hope to convince you, that now's the right time for McLadley to enter Russia. And not only Moscow. My proposal outlines a long-term plan, with future expansion to St. Petersburg and Novosibirsk, so that McLadley becomes as dominant a player in Russia, and in all of

Eastern Europe, as it already is in the rest of the world."

Through a corner of my eye, I saw Bob Gordon nod. I flipped through slides, presenting each with conviction. I felt I was being transformed from an immigrant girl unsure of her plans to an executive in charge of her destiny. Like a chameleon, I was shedding the old doubts and mistakes and taking on a new calm and assurance. Even if they didn't approve my plan, I'd passed the test for me, Inga Belova. And that was worth more than any job offer.

"Inga, thank you. Gentlemen – I have to go. I believe you know what's next." Patty gathered her laptop and the papers and left the room. I didn't know what her leaving meant and looked at Chuck, feeling my head floating above my shoulders like a blimp. He nodded and blinked for me not to worry.

The rest went by in a daze, and I only recalled the view from the window, sophisticated buildings in brick and dark brown, with large windows framed by beige window-panes.

An hour later, I was given a final green light.

It took me a moment to comprehend. These things usually took months to approve. I wondered what had happened to the proposal I'd sent to them in May, before Chuck had forwarded this modified one to Patty and Bob's personal attention. Had it been sitting on some secretary's desk unopened, or had Bob neglected it because nobody higher up the chain had told him to pay attention?

"Inga, welcome aboard," Bob said. "Let's go over the details after lunch – HR, your package, office needs, and so on."

He got up, shook my hand, and left the room. Others followed, congratulating me on the way out. A thought entered my mind. Did they see a competitor in me? Would they accept me, an outsider, a Russian-American transplant, into their intricate web of shared responsibilities and performance metrics?

"Welcome back," Chuck said, once we'd returned to the reception. "Well done. Let's grab lunch before my flight to New York."

I sat in a daze. I knew that the hard work would only begin at that moment: I'd have to implement everything I'd just talked about, which was a thousand times more difficult than having my proposal accepted – almost like giving birth and then raising a child. Was it really what I had wanted all that time? I closed my laptop, shook Chuck's hand and went for fresh air. And then it hit me. I still needed to deal with Alexandra. But I'd think about that later.

· 31 ·

Kristina had arrived on a late morning flight. By the time I returned to the hotel, she was already unpacking in my room. I ran to her, dropped my laptop on the bed, and pulled her into a waltz.

"We did it!" I screamed and hugged her to my chest. "So good you're here! Time to celebrate!"

Kristina looked at me, puzzled. Of course she knew nothing of my business presentations and acceptances. Then I remembered her divorce. Oh, why couldn't I be completely happy just for one moment, yearning for someone's support? Yet I knew she was in London for my compassion, so I came back to Earth.

"How are you?" I asked. "Feeling better?"

"A thousand times better than last week," said Kristina

with a weak smile. I noticed that the dark circles had almost taken over her entire face, and the hollow eyes lacked any sign of light. She had aged, too. Her posture was that of an old woman, with drooping shoulders and hands hanging limply.

"We'll make you feel better, I promise," I said, wondering who the "we" were. Me and London? Me and Moscow? I told her of my success at the presentation and of the bright future for both of us, because "when one door closes, another opens." I wanted both of us to believe it.

Kristina smiled and surprised me with a question.

"I didn't realize you'd closed any doors. You're still with Emma and Alexandra, right?"

I'd never told her that we'd broken up. Had I really carried it all inside, except for Justin? I recapped the story, telling her that this trip to London signified a new beginning of me, running my own show. Kristina still looked puzzled.

"So when did this breakup happen?"

Happy though I was to take her mind off her divorce, I had no desire to dwell on my heartaches.

"Two weeks ago." I paused. Only two weeks had passed. Time had once again accelerated with this trip. And had it not happened, I'd probably have been lying in my bed in Moscow, cursing myself for being a failure, wallowing in what I thought had once been so beautiful between me and them – my two girls, lovers and friends. Now there was Emma the drug addict and Alexandra the blackmailer who could ruin my McLadley deal in Moscow.

"Things have really become complicated in Moscow. To tell you the truth, I'm a bit afraid to go back. But that's my only chance to finally make something of myself – and, more importantly, to make any kind of living. I only hope Alexandra doesn't rain on my plans."

"What do you mean?"

"I heard she can do nasty things to people if she chooses to." I looked at my watch. "I personally haven't witnessed anything like that, but she did change the mind of my boss at Obundy. And that's no small matter."

"How do you think she did it?"

"Must be something about that black man Laura was dating."

"Is it illegal to date a black man in Moscow?"

"Of course not. But I think there was something else to it. Maybe Laura is pregnant and will be leaving soon but doesn't want anyone to know, and Alexandra could ruin the secret?"

"Well, you can't keep pregnancy a secret for too long."

"True. But still."

"Are you pregnant?" Kristina asked.

"My God. Where did that come from? I've been a

lesbian for the last three months, remember?"

"So you think she can ruin your new job by announcing to the whole wide world that you're a lesbian?"

"That I don't care about." I went to the mini-bar and took a half-bottle of red wine. I did care about that but hoped with all my might that Alexandra would never go there. Another worry overshadowed that one. "I'm afraid she'll tell people that I'm a fraud and that they shouldn't work with me. All ideas and no action. A sissy."

"But you're not."

"Sometimes I am. But not today. And we won't talk of it now. Not on the most important day in my life. Here is what we'll do: we're going to hit all the new gallery shows in town, and then we'll go clubbing with the musician I met on the subway."

Kristina nodded, hugged me, and went to take a shower. I took off my suit and spread out on the bed in a thong and a bra. I dialed the number on the card and asked to be put on the guest list for his show. I thought of calling Justin but decided to do it later.

I sat and listened. It was awfully quiet in the bathroom for someone taking a shower, no water running, no clothes being shuffled. I came to the door and knocked, feeling a knot tightening in my stomach. No answer.

"Kristina? Are you okay?"

I heard muffled cries and knocked louder. She needed

me, even if she didn't want to need me.

"Kristina – open up. Let's talk."

"It's open," she wailed, and I stormed in. She was sitting on the toilet with her hands pressed to her face, the same position Alexandra had assumed while crying over my betrayal in Miami. Memories of that night came rushing over me. I knelt in front of Kristina, just as I had with Alexandra, and took her hands into mine. My mind was empty, but my heart was so heavy that I felt as if my chest were about to cave in.

"It's okay to cry," I said for lack of better advice. "You need to get it out of your system. Don't hide. Let it go." I stroked her hair. This undid Kristina. Her feet slid apart. She leaned forward onto her hands, fell on her knees, and sprawled on the floor. I'd never seen anyone weep on the floor before (except for my own reflection in the mirror). I lay down beside her on the thick, white rug and hugged her shaking shoulders, which were covered with goose bumps. It was the saddest that I'd seen my friend in the years we'd known each other. She was a little girl, just like me, whose big life project hadn't worked out, and she didn't know where to start picking up the pieces. "Maybe we should stay in, order a bottle of red, and watch old movies all day," I suggested. She kept crying, tears falling onto the carpet and dotting it with gray spots.

"Sweetie, you're strong. You'll be fine; I know it. Do you

want me to draw you a bath?"

She stopped sobbing for a second and let out a quiet "yes," which turned into crying again. I propped her up against the bathtub, started the water, and went to the minibar. When I returned to the bathroom several minutes later, she was still on the floor but had quieted down, her hand under the faucet, watching the water travel through her fingers. There was something calming about the scene. I sat down next to her on the floor, and we sipped decent red wine from mini-bottles. At that moment, I knew Kristina was the closest friend I had, and she probably thought the same about me. Our sadness grew into calmness, and we kept drinking in silence.

It was dark when we walked out of the hotel. With all the galleries already closed, we found ourselves at Piccadilly Circus, sitting at the Eros monument and listening to a rugged middle-aged man play guitar. A guy next to me with dreads and silver rings on his dark fingers offered me a joint, but I refused. Kristina and I sat there, in the middle of London, two homeless birds, and I felt as if we were back in our early twenties exploring a grand new metropolis.

I wanted to say something that would sound British.

"That bloke just offered me a joint in full daylight," I said.

"Really?" She perked up. "I'd love a hit."

Surprise. I couldn't recall the good girl Kristina ever smoking pot or wanting to. And what about her asthma? I turned to the guy on my right and told him I'd changed my mind. He nodded and passed me the short stub. I tried not to think of germs and sexually transmitted diseases. As I watched Kristina inhale with gusto, and then again, I thought of the asthma attack she'd had on our trip to Cuba last Christmas.

During our six-hour drive from Havana to Trinidad in an old Cadillac we had breathed in enough fumes to make a horse ill. Later that night, Kristina had collapsed in my arms, crumbling to the ground like a sandcastle hit by the ocean wave, her skin ghostly pale and lips blue. Despite my panic, I dragged her to a hospital, screaming *"Ayuda! Ayuda! Ella tiene asthma attack!"*

A tall doctor, young and lanky, led us to a room that looked like a hospital ward from the 1950s, with a lonely naked bulb in the ceiling casting a bluish light onto scraped green walls. He placed a rugged rubber cord from a dark green oxygen tank (perhaps an artifact from World War II) into Kristina's mouth and unveiled a giant, rusted needle, which had probably never been sterilized in its lifetime, to give her a shot. Kristina started crying. I begged him to reconsider. He produced a disposable needle from some secret drawer. Half an hour later, still holding a prescription written on what looked like Soviet-style salami-wrapping paper, we left the clinic, Kristina's breathing restored, my hands still shaking. I couldn't sleep that night.

Back in London, Kristina didn't exhale for several seconds, and I motioned her to let go. She released a massive cloud of smoke, and a smile took over her face.

"I think London is already working wonders on me," she said, giggling and pulling me up. She mouthed a thank you to the smoke-dispensing guy, who nodded, his eyes sparkling, and we dove into our night.

We walked past the boutiques and jewelry stores, already closed for the day. Brightly-lit night windows exposed lifeless mannequins dressed in slick outfits, projecting the false notion that any sad person or circumstance could be cured by the right dress. Had the shops been open, I knew Kristina would have maxed out her credit cards on the spot. But we continued strolling to SoHo towards La Floridita, a restaurant suggested by *Time Out London* as having the best Cuban food in town.

We arrived before our dinner reservation and found the place abuzz. The hostess led us to the bar next to the spiral staircase in the center of the room. Everything sparkled: mirrors, lights, people's eyes and smiles, jewelry on women, and the words *La Floridita* in neon red above rows of bottles on the wall. A tall bartender, Cuban and handsome, was making five Mojitos when we approached, and waved for us to wait. The band played samba. Moscow didn't have this, even though in ten years the restaurant would probably have a franchise there. I wanted to dance and to flirt and saw that Kristina had also revived from being a wreck. Maybe we all needed a little bit of Cuba to make us alive again.

We ordered mojitos, and when they arrived, I noticed as an older man landed next to Kristina. Having shed her sadness and inhibitions somewhere near the statue of Eros, she started talking to him. I could only shake my head. He was what Lisa called *"sostificated"* – well-ironed expensive suit, heavily starched white shirt, golden cufflinks, a noble profile. Answering Kristina with short measured answers, he carefully studied her short red dress and matching shoes. She looked like Red Riding Hood, but I was no Grace Kelly, either, in my black miniskirt with a strapless silver top.

I observed the older guy from the corner of my eye, his cufflinks, Rolex, and shiny shoes, and thought that he might be a CEO of some multinational – a good match for Kristina.

He stretched his hand towards me and introduced himself as Willard. I did my best not to burst into laughter. I composed myself and told him my name, then poked Kristina to find out what she wanted with the guy. She leaned close and whispered that maybe we should invite him to join us for dinner.

Willard ordered appetizers and suggested that we try a certain main course, after which we learned that he was an investor in the restaurant. Then he told us he had Russian roots. I didn't believe him until he named every member of the Russian Transitional Government after the 1917 Revolution. His grandfather had been one of them. I still wasn't convinced he wasn't putting on a show for Kristina. He didn't speak a word of Russian and had never been to the country. Kristina hung on every word.

Part of me separated from my body and floated above the table, admiring the view and the conversation. We were all immigrants in this world. The nobility or post-Soviet youth; we always came and went and moved between. Countries. Lovers. Marriages and jobs. Our mothers' wombs.

I descended back to the table and asked Willard what he thought of president Yeltsin, sounding like one of those American men who always wondered how I liked living in the States. Willard explained that he never discussed politics or religion over dinner, the true nobleman that he was.

"I'd certainly go to Russia if I had some reliable individual to show me around – one who knows it from the inside," he said.

"Why now?" I asked.

"Why not? We only live once."

"Would you go if I showed you around?" Kristina asked him, her eyes glazed from multiple mojitos.

"I'd be most delighted," Willard answered, chewing a piece of fried plantain.

I thought he could be Kristina's perfect match, a man who'd finally appreciate her, with her Russian soul and insecurities, and make her into a perfect bouquet to treasure. More than anything, Kristina wanted to be treasured. On the other hand, he could be just another fraud in her collection of men. I whispered to her to join me in the bathroom.

"Listen," I harped the moment we slid into a stall and closed the door. "If you're seriously thinking of taking him to Russia now, you are mad. It's too quick. He'll just be your rebound – trust me. That's why Mark and I didn't work out. I only realize it now. He was my rebound! If you like Willard, take your time. Make him come to New York first. Make sure he's not a fraud."

Kristina, speechless, looked at me. She was propped against the wall, her eyes glazed and unsteady.

"Do you like him?" I asked.

"Definitely. But I'm too drunk and stoned to decide anything now."

"Don't. I'll do the talking."

She smiled and dismissed me with a half-wave of her right hand, all the while holding onto the wall with her left. We returned to the table as our main course appeared. Sounds of salsa filled the room, and several couples went to its center, hips swaying to the music, hands holding tightly. Willard nodded to Kristina. She got up, chewing on her piece of fish, delight on her face: she had mastered the steps on our trip to Cuba. Willard led her to the dance floor. He was a good dancer, and Kristina had imbibed enough to loosen her limbs and properly follow her partner. They glided across the floor, and I felt happy.

After a few moments, I saw Kristina's limp body hanging on Willard's hands. He dragged her back to the table.

"We have a situation," he said in a rushed whisper. "I think she's had too much to drink."

I noticed her troubled breathing, her scared eyes and her blue lips mouthing something to me.

"She's having an asthma attack," I said, getting up and rummaging through her purse. There was no inhaler. I froze. She must have left it in the hotel, and pot smoking, topped by Willard's cigar, had triggered the attack. What had she been thinking? My hands were shaking. Willard made a call and asked me to accompany him and Kristina to his house: his personal doctor lived next door.

· 32 ·

When we entered Willard's townhouse, with spiral stair-
cases, beige rugs, and yellow lights revealing original
works of art on the walls, I felt like fainting, too. I sat
down in a chair by the door. There were turtles everywhere –
made of marble and silver and wood and precious stones.
Some were dog-sized, resting on the marble floors, some
tiny, nestled on the bookshelves. I had hardly managed
to take it all in when four dogs came running towards us,
all Rhodesian ridgebacks. I gasped at their beauty – and
then at the fact that they were Kristina's worst allergens.

Before I had uttered a word, Willard screamed, "Ashley,
put the dogs away immediately! Didn't you get my
message?" A housekeeper in a dark blue dress with a
white apron appeared, made a curtsy, and shooed the

dogs away.

After half an hour of anxious waiting, the doctor came downstairs and nodded reassuringly at our inquiring stares, as if putting out a fire. A minute later, Kristina appeared at the top of the stairs, pale and uncertain on her feet, and Willard rushed to help her with surprising velocity for a man of sixty. I kept thanking the doctor and Willard until the doctor left.

My adrenaline was still at the height of the Empire State Building. I was convinced that meeting Willard, a single, White Russian millionaire, was a definite harbinger of good things to come. But then I thought about Alexandra's threat. I was genuinely scared to go back to Moscow. Maybe I never really wanted to run my own business. Maybe all I'd ever needed was for someone to believe I could do it, and now that I'd gained that trust, I no longer yearned for the actual work.

Willard asked us to stay for dinner. I moved to a wide beige couch and took in the artwork. Kuindzhi and Filonov hung on one wall, Chagall on another. I decided that Willard must have been a true nobleman, White Russian, after all, and his family had used to collect art. Had the Bolshevik Revolution not happened, he'd probably have had a mansion on the Fontanka embankment – in the golden center of St. Petersburg – instead of London. And I understood how he might like Kristina, a

Russian woman who could be devoted and loyal, yet with enough Western-ism to be presentable in London's high society. Most importantly, she could be his last chance at great sex.

I settled deeper into the soft couch. Tchaikovsky's Concerto #1 was pouring from the ceiling as the maid poured Pinotage Reserve into wine glasses, which could have been mistaken for vases. I no longer wanted to return to Moscow, and not because of Alexandra. I wanted the normalcy of unpretentious life. Which New York offered. As did London. But I was still broke. The doorbell rang.

The maid left and returned with an announcement of "Bob Gordon's arrival." I stared at Willard as Bob entered, and then looked at my new boss, whose eyes held an enormous question mark. Willard waved at the newcomer.

"Inga, Kristina – this is the nephew I mentioned earlier, the one who often travels to Russia. Please meet Robert, everybody."

"It's Bob, uncle."

"Of course, dear."

"Nice to see you again," I said, getting up from the couch, my feet unsteady.

"You know Uncle?" inquired Bob.

"'Know' is too strong a word," I said. "We met at La Floridita tonight."

"Of course. Will's restaurant. Did you enjoy it?"

"Greatly – to a certain point." I looked at Kristina. I didn't have a chance to continue before Willard ushered us into the dining room. The large rectangular table was covered with embroidered white cloth, silver goblets – three per setting – and silverware. Long peach candles, in sets of six, glittered evenly in antique silver holders, imparting a soft lazy glow to the room. The chandelier was half-dimmed, as if not to interfere with Kristina's recovery. We were to sit boy-girl, Bob at my side, with Kristina and Willard across from us. Suddenly, I felt like a schoolgirl who had run into the wrong backyard and gotten lost. Bob pulled my chair out for me, as did Willard for Kristina. I detected a certain resemblance in their noble features, with high foreheads and large eyes, and made a note to myself that being a relative of Willard's made Bob a White Russian as well. I wanted to talk about it, about the Russia of the 1920s, to drown my jitters about returning to the Moscow of the 1990s.

Was Bob's reason for wanting to open an office there the same as mine, to find out where he belonged? He hadn't mentioned a thing about it during our lunch earlier, limiting his discussion strictly to my compensation package (six-figure salary plus bonus), the corporate apartment, and the length of my vacation. The news that Bob would also be relocating to Moscow, which had weighed on my jubilant mood at lunch, had become a cause for celebration by dinnertime.

I turned to Bob. "You must speak Russian, correct?"

"Yes, after a lifetime of taking it in college and frequent trips to Moscow."

But he changed the subject.

"Tell me again how you met Uncle?"

"He joined us at the bar, and my friend Kristina asked him to stay for dinner. Then she had an asthma attack, and we ended up here."

He paused, as if calculating whether to verbalize his thoughts, and then whispered, almost to himself, "He's still chasing his perfect Russian woman, even though he despises the country and doesn't speak the language."

"He's never been married?"

"He has, but that fell apart a long time ago."

I slumped in my seat, wondering whether Willard was such a good match for Kristina after all. I looked at her, busily eating baked cod with fava beans, couscous, and mango chutney. I had tasted a similar dish at one of Kristina's dinner parties in New York, for which she was somewhat famous in certain closely-knit circles.

"So how do you two know each other?" Willard chimed in.

"Bob is my new boss," I answered. Without a pause Bob added, "In a new McLadley office in Moscow."

Willard took a long sip of his wine, as if pondering the news and looked at Bob.

"So, you're going to live in Russia, after all. Our family history hasn't taught you a thing." He then changed his tone and turned to me. "And would this be the new job you mentioned earlier?"

"Yes."

The addition of my new boss to our night out in London had left me uncertain of how to behave. I retreated to observation once again, deciding not to speak unless spoken to – a major achievement for me.

Bob was studying Kristina across the table when Willard took her hand.

"Still not feeling well? Would you like to lie down?"

I darted a look at Kristina. She shook her head.

"You've been very kind," she said. "I'm just slightly overwhelmed, considering that I arrived this afternoon, was divorced as of last week, and just had an attack."

Bob glanced at Willard as if to say, "Now you're the one who hasn't learned anything from our family history," which Willard ignored. He seemed genuinely worried about Kristina, and I was comforted to see that a stranger could be so involved.

"Sorry to hear that. Let me know if you need any help. I have a great lawyer," Willard said, turning to his fish, making it known that he'd been there, done that, and wouldn't dwell on the particulars.

"Ashley, the fish is delicious. Thank you!" he raised his voice, to be heard in the back room. The maid came in to pour more wine and collect the plates. We spent the rest of dinner in a solemn mood, not least because the next morning Kristina and I would be going back to Moscow.

· 33 ·

McLadley gave me two weeks to wrap up my current job while I helped their Operations find a new office. I assured them that two weeks was plenty of time to achieve both goals. They thought that I was still with Obundy, which I had quit even before Laura had gone on maternity leave (I had guessed right), giving me the best recommendations. I was smart enough not to mention IQ Consulting at all.

I took Kristina on the hunt for office space by day, and we went clubbing at night. She paid. Memories of Emma and Alexandra haunted me at every step, as McLadley's office search repeated the track we had taken when looking for IQ's space: decent business centers in Moscow could be counted on one hand. After several days of looking on

Tverskaya Street and along the Garden Ring, I wrote to Bob that my preference was Ostozhenka; I had found a perfect townhouse there. Bob was scheduled to arrive the following week to sign the documents for the launch of the Russian office and to confirm (or not) my choice of location.

At clubs, Kristina and I kept running into the same people I'd seen when out with Emma and Alexandra. It felt as if Moscow's social circle had frozen along its seams, and whoever had managed to slip into it during the summer had remained, their faces masks of boredom and condescension, with a few variations in between. I didn't know those people's names, but they always recognized me and looked surprised at seeing me with a different entourage. I felt like my threesome had been imprinted on me wherever I went, and I couldn't shed its residue despite trying to forget. I felt used and slightly scared, but I couldn't discuss it with Kristina just yet. I missed Emma, too. Suddenly, London seemed like a figment of my imagination, and I almost had to pinch myself to believe I had indeed traveled there and gotten the job. Moscow was swallowing me again.

Then the Saturday before Kristina's departure arrived. We sat in the small kitchen of my apartment and were drinking coffee when I realized that once she'd left, I'd be alone to battle the Moscow phantoms – that, despite the fact that I'd been hired by the Brits, I'd still have to see the same faces, play the games of Moscow's "inner circle."

Except I had never been a part of it. I'd been the trophy girlfriend of two lesbians who had a lot of power in this city. My aspirations "to build my own company" suddenly seemed laughable. *They don't take a Russian woman seriously when she's on her own.* American – maybe. But not Russian. And I no longer cut it as an American, my eight years in New York tainted by my four months in Moscow. I'd become a local with a bad break-up history with those in power, and the stain was permanent. Or so I imagined as I sat across Kristina, who sipped black coffee and enjoyed a croissant.

I wanted to leave. This time for good. I couldn't stay in Moscow by myself. It would eat away at me, little by little, and eventually, I'd become one of those empty faces in a trendy bar. And even McLadley wouldn't shield me: Moscow was cruel in a way that even New York could never be. It worked on you slowly and irreversibly, like rust. And eventually, it left you hollow inside, with the last traces of goodness erased by its cynicism.

"Are you all right?" Kristina asked.

"Why?"

"Your lips are twitching."

"I think I'm scared."

"Of what? You finally have your dream come true! You'll be running your own show in Russia, Miss America!"

"You don't know the half of it."

"Oh?"

"I probably don't know the half of it myself," I said, getting up to look for something sweet in the fridge and finding half-empty jam jars and a piece of stale chocolate.

"I feel like Moscow is a huge mirror from *The Picture of Dorian Gray*. It makes everything and everyone ugly," I told her. "Even you said I'd become different after living here."

"Why didn't you think of that before you went to London – or to Moscow, for that matter?" Kristina asked.

"Because I needed to prove to myself that I could get a real job with a real company and stop feeling second-class," I said, sitting back down.

Kristina pulled her white robe tighter and went to the counter to refill her coffee cup.

"Sometimes your emails did sound like you'd become a total self-absorbed brat," she said, her back to me. "But I guess we all do that when we're in love or happy about our success."

"Well, I'm back to Earth now. No longer in love and still wondering what the hell success is."

"I think success is when you conquer your own demons. And you've definitely done that."

I looked at Kristina. Was it that simple? Did I have demons?

"What was my demon?"

"Always wanting better or more, always looking for where the grass was greener," she said.

"Really? I thought I just wanted to end the misery of being an immigrant."

"We're all immigrants, wherever we are, and you know it. If you're talking about New York, it fits you like a glove," Kristina said, lifting her coffee cup.

"You really think so?"

"Absolutely. All that stuff about 'conquering Russia' is so overrated. You just caught the bug, and now that it stung you properly, you've probably had enough."

She was right.

"Perfect. Just when I get my dream job, I've had enough of Russia."

"Your dream job doesn't have to be in Russia, does it?"

"True. But I've invested so much of myself in this place already."

"You invested even more of yourself in New York, yet you left without thinking twice."

If she only knew how much I had thought about it, driving myself to the point of desperation and self-loathing, asking myself the same questions that Alexandra had asked: *Why couldn't you have done it all in New York? What are you afraid of?*

I looked at Kristina, as if trying to find the answers on her face. Yes, I had always been afraid. Afraid of being invisible, unappreciated, of wasting my time on something not intended for me, not fulfilling my purpose. Of being too small to matter. But what a bunch of crap! Purpose. What purpose? I hadn't made anyone happier by going to Moscow. Nor had I made anyone happy by getting a McLadley job. Well, that wasn't true. My father had been ecstatic when I'd told him. His golden girl had finally gotten her gold. Except she didn't think of it as gold anymore.

"Do you think you matter?" I asked Kristina.

"Depends for whom."

"In general, do you think your life matters?"

"To my parents – yes. No longer to my ex-husband, that's for sure."

"Do we only matter when we're children, or when we have children of our own?"

"Are we in the fifties now?"

"No, but I know that kids and parents are the only people to whom you'll ever really matter." As I said it, I couldn't believe I had spoken the words, yet I'd known it all along. Then why all the anguish, meandering from country to country, from lover to lover?

Kristina looked at me curiously.

"I think I get it," I said.

"What?"

"It's ambition. We have to lose our ambitions to find ourselves," I declared.

"I'll drink to that," Kristina said, moving to open the fridge. "Do you think you and I both lost our ambitions?"

"I certainly did," I said, feeling relieved.

"Now that I'm divorced, I've lost my ambition, too."

"Okay, let's drink to losing ambition and inhibition!"

We both laughed as Kristina opened a bottle of white wine and poured it into our empty coffee cups. It felt like we had found freedom. From ourselves. And that was a success.

· 34 ·

The next morning, I saw Kristina off at Sheremetyevo – jealous about her going back to New York. We kissed at customs and promised to see each other soon, neither of us certain when or where that would be.

On the way back, I took a *marshrutka*, an airport-city shuttle, which had the magical powers of bringing one back to reality, away from expats and executive compensations to simple local folk, those who saved enough for a vacation but couldn't afford either a cab or a car. Like my father.

I sat in the crumbling yellow minivan across from a middle-aged couple, who looked content and relaxed, possibly after a vacation on the Black Sea. I thought of Dmitry Vernik picking me up from New York at this same airport four months earlier, now in Paris on vacation with his wife. He could work for McLadley. He was well versed in the lingo of Western brands entering Russia, and I could bring him onboard. The thought lifted my mood.

I opened a copy of *The eXile*, a recently-launched, trashy English-language weekly for expats – the *National Enquirer* of Moscow. I never read it, its gossip and language too offensive, yet needed to busy my mind with something on the way back to my lonely apartment. I flipped through a few pages and saw a photo of myself. I gasped, then regained composure. *The eXile* never ran regular news stories; it was known for bashing everything and everyone. The title over the photo read, "Lesbian-turned-whore goes for big guys (and bucks)."

"Fuck..," I said out loud. The couple in front of me sized me up and exchanged looks. How the hell had this happened? My hands were shaking. I didn't know anyone at the paper and had never talked to anyone about my life in Moscow except for Kristina in New York. But it seemed like someone had done quite a bit of talking about me. Alexandra? I didn't think she'd sink so low. That left Emma. Was she really so full of venom? Could she have used Alexandra's connections to sell them a story? Only what story was it? I started reading.

"Why do we love Moscow? Because it never ceases to surprise us....

Nah, not really.

What we love about Moscow is its endless supply of gorgeous women. And when those babes go wild – we love it even more! We learned of a 30-year-old recent transplant from St. Petersburg-turned-New Yorker who came to conquer Moscow, and boy, did she ever. First she got into bed with two lesbians, rather well-known socialites, and milked them dry of their money! She got hold of their connections – the idea was to become a businesswoman (she supposedly has an MBA) in Moscow. But who are we kidding? We know there are no businesswomen in Russia. (They still can't get their heads around it!) But Moscow's glamour, so tantalizing and appealing to our senses, was so hard to resist! The lesbian threesome turned out to be a VIP pass to the best Moscow has to offer. Then – you guessed it – she decided she was no lesbian, after all, and poof! The threesome falls apart, the girlfriends are no longer such, and our opportunist is now seen around town with one of the top bankers in Moscow. Of course Amerikanskij! *They do look awfully cute together, as seen at a recent art opening at Manezh, but the ex-girlfriends are fuming. And here's our gift to you: enter a contest to identify the woman and win $100!"*

I wanted to wake up, as if from a bad dream. It felt as if someone had poured a bucket of vomit over me, and I sat on that bus, soaked in slimy filth, wondering if I'd ever be clean again.

Who'd see this? Justin, for sure. He could probably sue the paper, I thought, but he hadn't been mentioned by name, and there were no laws in Russia. Who else? Most of the expats. But no McLadley people. Everyone who went to Hungry Duck, Rosy O'Grady's, City Grill, and Kodak Kinomir. Pretty much everyone who spoke English in Moscow, including Obundy employees.

My jacket had become too tight, and I unbuttoned it and the shirt underneath. I couldn't tell if I was more offended by the unfairness of it all or afraid that it might mean the end of my business aspirations in Moscow. Maybe Alexandra had been behind it, after all. Emma wasn't smart enough to orchestrate a 'black' PR campaign. So what was I to do?

Demand a retraction? As if they'd bother.

Sue my former girlfriends? On what basis, and with what money?

I had to stop the paper from revealing my name and stop anyone at McLadley from seeing the paper. I twisted a lock of my hair until I almost pulled it out. Sanjay! He must have known someone at *The eXile*. I fidgeted in my seat, cursing myself for being an idiot and the minivan for being so slow, wishing I'd gotten a local cell phone for Moscow.

I dialed Sanjay the moment I walked into the apartment. "Did you see *The eXile*?"

"This week's?"

I flipped to the first page. "Last."

"I don't think so. Anything interesting? And since when do you read *The eXile*?"

"I don't. I just picked it up at the airport. They ran my picture, called me a lesbian-turned-whore, and now they're holding a contest to identify me."

"Fuck. Amessin does go overboard, that asshole," Sanjay said. "Any truth in it?"

"Don't be an asshole yourself," I said, almost crying. "What's it to you?"

"Just curious."

"Oh, stop it," I said, twisting the cord around my hand. "I need your help. Can you ask him to not publish my name? Please?"

"I can ask him, but I doubt he'll listen."

"But this is slander! It's illegal!"

"His whole paper is based on slander, and you know there are no laws in Russia anyway."

"So can you help me or not? I'm about to represent McLadley in Moscow, and this fucking paper can ruin everything."

"Really? I thought everyone knew it was full of bullshit. You think your boss at McLadley would care if he read this?"

I thought for a moment.

"How am I supposed to know? But this ruins whatever business reputation I might have had in Moscow."

"Oh, forget it," said Sanjay, laughing. "Business reputation. First of all, you didn't have much of a reputation – let's face it. And second, you know what reputation Stebleva or Litsker has? It's all the same: if you're a businesswoman who's making money, you're definitely a whore. So join the club and relax."

I hung up. Sanjay had a point. But I also knew that stupid article would soon be available online. If I was identified, it would be a definite personal disaster, albeit one of small proportions. And I was really mad. I looked at the back of the paper for the number and dialed, my shaking hands hitting the wrong numbers. I hung up and dialed again, asking to speak with the Editor-in-Chief. To my surprise, I was put through.

"I'm calling about the photo in the last issue – the contest," I said, squeezing my temples.

"I need your name and proof that you know the girl in the picture," a man's voice answered.

"I *am* the girl, and you'd better stop this nonsense. Who put you up to this?"

"Ah, what different does it make?" he said, laughing. I heard him cover the receiver and whisper to someone next to him. "We had a good story and ran it. I had a few people call to identify you, but none were right."

"So, you know my name?"

"Of course, Miss Belova. I'm in the business of gathering facts, gossip, and everything in between. I'm surprised you didn't call sooner. It's been out for a few days."

Do you know that you're an asshole? I wanted to scream at him. But I had to win him over.

"So, what would it take to stop this contest?"

"Money works well."

"But you know that this is slander, and I can sue you!"

"Honey, we're a tabloid." He paused. "In Russia. No chance, and you know it."

I hung up. Yes, I knew. My only chance would be to scare him off, to send some mean guys with guns to threaten him, *krysha*, the roof. But I didn't have a *krysha* anymore, the necessary protection by powerful people with serious connections, as it had all disappeared, together with Alexandra. Maybe someone could threaten to close the paper. He must have had investors. If they threatened to pull the plug, he'd have no choice but obey. *My God*, I thought, *I'm turning into one of those characters I'd seen on TV about the Moscow mob of the early nineties.* I only needed a gun, a sports suit, and an inch-thick golden chain around my neck to complete the picture. As I thought about that, I knew nothing of the sort could have happened in St. Petersburg.

But at the same time, this felt inevitable. We always

have to pay for our weaknesses, sooner or later. Now it was my turn. I'd thought I could spring ahead with being an important executive in my homeland, closing the page on everything before it. But it wasn't that simple. Alexandra was smarter by degrees, and I was a little puppy trying to save its tail. If I cleared out of Moscow, I was certain she'd stop the contest. And if I stayed?

I called Justin.

"Justin, I need your help."

"Good to hear from you, Inga," he said.

I hadn't called him about my trip to London.

"I got the job with McLadley. Sorry I didn't call right away."

"Congratulations! How can I be of help?"

How could I tell him this?

"*The eXile* called me a lesbian and a whore and is running a contest to identify my picture." I started crying. No, I was wailing, like a toddler forgotten by his mother on a playground, scared and utterly alone. "It is so unfair…"

"I'm sorry," he said. " But please don't believe everything you read in the yellow press. He'll never publish a name of the person in that photo – trust me. He knows there'd be consequences if he did. So, while I know it hurts to be offended so badly, you don't have to worry about people finding out your name."

"How do you know?"

"Because it's not the first time he's done it. He just wants to make sure his paper is being read, and when folks start calling, he knows they do. That's all there's to it."

"But those who know me will know it's *me*."

"Those who know you will know it's *not* you." I could hear him smile through his last words. How had he managed to turn the ugliest of situations into a trivial matter not worth sweating over?

"But Bob Gordon, my new boss at McLadley, might see it," I said.

"So what if he does? I'm sure he'll be smart enough to ignore it. It's not *The Moscow Times* we're talking about."

Still, I didn't deserve this! And yet was I utterly helpless to change a thing. It was the same exact feeling I'd had growing up in the Soviet Union: when you knew you didn't matter, when any waiter or store clerk could insult or expose you and make you feel the need to apologize – for asking a question or demanding proper change. Once you'd been taught to feel irrelevant, you'd graduated to being a professional cynic or become a character from Chekhov's stories – small, insignificant, and superfluous. And we had only figured it out much, much later. My epiphany had come in New York, when I realized that, had I not left Russia, I might have become a perfect product of the land of deception, an insignificant speck in the gray machinery of party slogans. And I certainly hadn't left Russia only to be treated like dirt once I was back – by an American expat on top of that! My fury was boiling over.

"Justin, what would you do if this happened to you?" I asked.

He didn't answer right away. Of course it could never happen to him, I thought.

"I'd ignore it – imagine it never happened, and go on with my life. You can be certain that worse things have been done to me, and I'm still around, doing fine."

Why would you stay in this God forsaken city if people had worse things done to you? I wondered. What kind of town was this?

"I'll try." I swallowed hard, knowing full well that I wouldn't be able to sleep or think about anything else besides the article with my photo. But if my mentor, as I thought of Justin, thought this was the approach to take, I'd follow his suggestion. I had no alternative.

"I'll come over if you want," Justin said.

"No, it's okay. Thank you." I hung up.

Indeed, I couldn't sleep that night. My mind itched with a question: Who? Who had orchestrated this? Who'd take the trouble to contact the paper and bother with the details of – if I was finally being honest with myself – my insignificant persona? I just couldn't believe that Alexandra would stoop that low or that Emma was clever enough to think it up. I once read somewhere that, when in doubt, one had to go in the direction of fear. And so I did. It said 2:30 AM on the light-green screen of my alarm clock when I got up and called Alexandra. I had to know. When she picked up, I almost went deaf from the noise coming out from the receiver. She was at a party, as always.

"Hold on," she screamed. After a minute of hurried shuffling, the noise died out, and I could hear her impatient voice.

"What? Can't sleep?" she asked.

"How did you guess?" I sat down on the low couch in my living room and turned the TV on mute: Clint Eastwood in a cowboy hat squinted under the blaring sun, mounted a horse, and rode off into the mountains, clouds of dust behind him.

"I need to know who did this," I said.

"Did what?"

"Oh, please. You know exactly what I'm talking about. The nasty story in *The eXile*."

"Belova, you're crazy. I don't read *The eXile*." She shouted to someone that she'd be right there. "What happened, anyway?"

Looking at the horses galloping on the TV screen, I wondered whether she was a masterful liar or indeed not in the loop.

"It's about our threesome. No names. But with a photo of me."

"Fuck!" she said, sounding as if she was chewing on a pen. I wondered why she would have a pen with her at a party. "I know who did this…"

"Who?"

"Remember the two guys you met at the penthouse dinner, from *Bulletin*? They've been waiting to get at me."

"At you? Then why the hell did they have to run *my* picture?"

"Oh, they know my weak points."

I hung up. No mystery. One more proof I'd made a mistake by coming to Moscow in the first place.

IV. LONDON

EIGHT YEARS LATER
2005

· 35 ·

The doorbell rings and I have to run downstairs myself, as the maid is out shopping. I'm not expecting any guests, and it's too late for the mail, so annoyance and fear rise in me simultaneously. Is it a stranger, or did something happen to Andrew or Justin? I trip over the rugs in the foyer and almost torpedo through the glass doors. When I open them, there's Justin with a basket of white roses, the same kind that he gave me for our wedding.

"Happy anniversary, *krasavitsa*," he says handing me the basket, smiling with his eyes. I put the flowers on the floor and lean into him with my whole body, his large hands lifting me off the ground. I love my husband. We've been married for five years, the best of my entire life.

"I can't believe I didn't look at the calendar today," I say, kissing him on the lips. "Is it really our day?" August 20th – the day at the end of summer.

He plants my feet back on the floor and announces, "Yes, but it's the beginning of summer for us this time. We're off to Spain next week – all three of us!"

I start hopping on my left foot and then remember: "But Andrew has to be in school September 1st! And what about my opening?"

I run a gallery of contemporary Russian art in London. Vlad Lepkin is my bestselling artist. Kristina and Willard were my first clients.

"I talked to the school; they're fine. Plus, it's not really a school, dear. He's only four. And you told me you're all set for the show."

"*Ya lublyu tebya.*" I tell him that I love him. The sacred words I've only said before to Anton, Alexandra, and Emma.

"Right back at you," he says, lifting me up with his hands, carrying me upstairs to the bedroom.

"What are you doing? Andrew will be back soon." I half-resist him, anticipating the magic as always. In the seven years we've been together, it's never been boring in bed. I wrap my arms around his neck, and he closes the door behind us.

We make love unhurriedly, basking in the familiar and

the comfortable. It is neither passionate nor routine. It's as if the ocean waves have carried us out to the wet sand and we don't need to rush to the higher ground, nor do we want to dive into the waves. We're basking in the soft warm foam, white bubbles caressing our bodies: the storms have passed, and new ones haven't formed yet.

My face is in the nook of Justin's shoulder, his large palm stroking my back. He reaches under the bed and pulls out a little package, wrapped in white. I sit up and look at him with a half-smile. We're not big on presents, or rather we give them just because, and rarely on certain dates, so this is a surprise. He hands me the little box without a word.

I know it's not jewelry because he's already given me all the required diamonds in platinum, for my fingers, ears, and neck. And I don't like any jewelry other than diamonds in platinum.

"What is it?" I ask dumbly, knowing that I should just open it.

He nods for me to go ahead. I unwrap the tissue, save the bow for future present-giving, and take out a slick flat box. It's a frame. I tear off the paper, assuming there'll be a picture of the three of us, and freeze. In black and white, there is my mother at the age of 30 or so, with a baby on her hands, both looking at the camera. The baby is me. I've never seen this photo before in my life. I look and look at it, before bursting into tears.

"Where did you get this?"

He holds me in his arms, and we rock from side to side, something we do with Andrew when he needs consolation.

"Your father. He digitized all of your family photos – it took him two years – and asked me to give it to you on the next special occasion." He draws my face toward his and kisses me softly. "So, this is from him, really. I just printed and framed the shot I liked best."

With this photo, my Dad has given me my mother back, a part of her I've never seen. She's back in my life, tangible and real: not a grave to visit, but a young woman with a baby – me, her Inga. And I know I loved her, even if I hadn't told her that as often as she'd hoped.

"I've never seen this before," I explain to him, and now it's his time to be quiet. We both look at the photo, holding hands, and I know at this moment we've reached a higher level of two people who are one.

"Do you have other photos?" I ask Justin. "Did you see them all?"

"Two CDs' worth! I only looked through a few shots before picking one to print. They're yours to discover."

"Thank you."

I can't wait to get the disk and look at the rest of the photos, some never before seen, but I want Justin to be part of it. And Andrew.

"Why don't we watch a slideshow together?" I suggest. "Tonight?"

"Sure," Justin whispers into my ear as he caresses me for the second of lovemaking.

I'm happy and content. But as a true child of St. Petersburg, I let sadness enter. Sadness about people lost and things not achieved. Today, I have found my Mom. But Emma is lost forever.

I'd left for London with Justin in August of 1998. By May, the McLadley Moscow office had been well-established. I'd managed to hire decent people, of whom London had approved, and had had Dmitry Vernik installed as head of accounts: he was the only person in Moscow I could trust unconditionally. He had also impressed the McLadley bosses with his suave ways and fat Rolodex of Western executives in Moscow. For a while, he and I had become a team again, as we had been back in school, sitting at the same wooden *parta,* devising the next adventure for the entire class.

Then Justin had gotten an offer in London. We'd been living together for six months by then, and I urged him to accept it. I'd requested a transfer to McLadley London, and we left two months later. Dmitry Vernik was named new head of operations for McLadley Moscow: he assured Bob that things would be "peachy keen." He'd learned that expression from me.

I'd kept in touch with Alexandra, but not with Emma, even though the nagging feeling inside had never gone away. The sticky mix of guilt and longing kept me attached to her in my mind and in my heart, but I'd had no news. When Alexandra had finally visited London, shortly after Black Tuesday, in the fall of 1998, she phoned me, and I took her to La Floridita. After two glasses of wine, I mustered the courage to ask about Emma. Alexandra looked at me and didn't answer. Assuming the subject was uncomfortable, I waved it off, but then she asked, "You really don't know, do you?"

"Know what?"

"She's dead."

I covered my mouth with both hands, staring at Alexandra, whose eyes had gone from steely to soft wet, then back to steely.

"What happened? When?" I braced myself for hearing it was a drug overdose.

"She was killed."

"I don't believe you," I stuttered, feeling the tears accumulating somewhere in my throat. "How?"

"Over a real estate deal."

I sat stiffly, staring at my glass of wine, rubbing my hands, unable to catch the liquid running out of my nose and eyes, as Alexandra told me what had happened. Apparently, I was the last one to find out, despite fast-traveling Moscow rumors.

Emma had gone through with her real estate transaction in Sochi, the city famous for the Communist Party's resorts on the Black Sea. "She bought that townhouse, the one for which she had embezzled money from IQ, and had it renovated. Real estate became her new business, and her new lover became her partner."

I flinched upon hearing that. Hadn't she learned her lesson?

"She borrowed money from a private bank and bought two more properties in Sochi: one was meant to become a bed and breakfast, another would be rented out. Then the city announced it might run for the 2014 Winter Olympics, and real estate prices went through the roof. Overnight." Alexandra's voice held steady.

"Emma was ecstatic. Then, one day, someone called and asked her to sell at a new price. She would have made a ton of money. I suggested she go through with it, but she never listened." Alexandra lit a cigarette. "Her partner bailed out because she was afraid of the people demanding the sale. Emma held on. And then one night her car was hit by a truck, which was never identified. She flew out through the front window and hit a tree. Instant death. Car burned. Case closed."

"Did you try to find out who did it? What about her sister?" I whispered, smearing the tears on my face.

"We both tried. They told us not to bother, as the people who did this had serious ties in the government. My connection wielded no power in those circles."

Emma was buried at Rublevskoe cemetery in Moscow. I visited her once, in 2000. Standing over her grave, motionless, I felt exhausted, as if I'd finished the marathon I'd been running for the last decade. I couldn't cry, and only stood there for an hour. I still loved her, but I didn't know what to do with it now that she was dead – as I hadn't known what to do with it when she was alive. I had brought her white roses, her favorite. If I hadn't left, she could still be alive.

Our wedding photo is lit by beams of the setting sun peeking through the window blinds, coloring the room in dense orange. We hear the entrance door open and rush to dress, picking up the clothes scattered on the floor and the chairs, kiss one more time, and go downstairs to greet our son. In his white shirt and maroon pants, shoes dusty and hair ruffled, our boy is glowing: the nanny procured a new fire truck for him on the way home from the park. Soon, there will be not one room in the house without several fire trucks resting on bookshelves, fireplaces, and coffee tables. I slide down the stairs and pick him up, burying my face in his hair, soft and curly.

"Look, look!" He lifts both of his arms in the air, holding the toy, his eyes glued to the shiny steel parts, without acknowledging my kisses.

"It has a real siren. Do you want to hear?" He smiles at me, quickly kissing me on the cheek, struggling to get down.

His little hands winding the key, he wrinkles his nose and sticks out his tongue, trying to turn it all the way. Then he looks up at me for a second and pushes the siren button. The noise is unexpectedly loud, and he jumps in delight, clapping his hands and stomping his feet, as the truck speeds towards me.

"Daddy, you like it?" he asks Justin, who high-fives him, a giant grin spreading across his face. I think of New York, with its never-ceasing sirens. This sound always brings me back to my single years in the city: when pacing the streets of the Village to the sounds of Anton's music in my headphones made my existence worthwhile and the desire to find someone to love again kept me going.

I look at little Andrew running after his truck, and Justin on the floor crawling after him, and remember our anniversary. Five years of happiness. Five years without Russia. I go to the side table in the hallway and flip through the mail. There is a letter from Moscow, hand-written, addressed to me.

"Could you please open it?" I ask Justin.

"Who is it from?"

"Doesn't say."

He opens the envelope and stares at the beautiful stationery without saying a word.

"What is it?" I ask him. *Had someone else died?*

"It's an invitation," he says, handing it to me.

I take the small rectangular piece of paper and my eyes run across the lines:

"*Alexandra Veil and Vlad Lepkin request the pleasure of your company at the christening of their daughter, Inga Veil, on September 21, 2005. The ceremony will take place at the Church of...*"

I don't finish reading. The irony of it makes me smile. I'm not surprised, only happy that, after traveling through the labyrinths of countries, intrigues, shady deals, and heartbreaks, two more people have found happiness. I look up at Justin.

"I'm going to Russia. Alexandra just gave birth to a daughter. Inga."

He puts his hand on my cheek. We're expecting a girl of our own. I already have the name.

ACKNOWLEDGEMENTS

My biggest thanks and eternal gratitude go to Natasha Nikitina, whose friendship, wit, and loyalty carried me through the decade it took to write this book.

I wouldn't have dared to write in English if not for the encouragement, and occasional wry scolding, from the late George Plimpton, and the late Eugene L. Scott – writer, publisher, tennis star, life-long friend and mentor, who had taught me perseverance and excellence. I miss him every day.

I'm forever grateful to Peter Selgin, the exquisite writer, dear friend and writing mentor, who has taught me the essence of "setup and payoff", who helped me structure this book, and whose "Don't state the implied," and "It has to be an *Aha!* ending," will stay with me, always.

I want to thank my friends and fellow writers Boris Fishman, Louis Venosta, Gary Shteyngart, Maureen Brady, Taye Selasi Claessen, Janet Goss, Laurie Silver, Debotri Dhar, Jenny Ladner-Brenner, Adjie Henderson, Miriam Polli, Pang-Mei Natasha Chang, and Gennady Pritsker for their advice, critique, honesty, sense of humor, and patience.

I'm grateful to my wonderful friends, Sergei Ilchenko, Bernie Sucher, Masha Zakharova, Maria Kostaki, Ilona Kolesnichenko, Fred Kahl, Olga Alfonsova, Alexander Makeyenkov, Audra Tiner, Dina Kim, and Eugene Goland, for their generosity and moral support.

And I thank Alexei Miller for everything. You are my rock, and none of it would have been possible without you in my life.

ABOUT THE AUTHOR

Vica Miller is a native of St. Petersburg (Russia) and a New Yorker for over two decades. George Plimpton called her a writer and she believed him. She is the founder (2009) and host of the Vica Miller Literary Salons, a chamber reading series held at select NYC art galleries, featuring both published and unpublished authors.

Vica has written for *Vogue Russia, Internet, Matador* and *Tennis Week* magazines. Her short stories have appeared in *The Jet Fuel Review, Asymptote, The Linnet's Wings* and *Thrice Fiction* literary journals. She has published a book of poems, and is currently at work on her second novel, *The Shadow of a Blue Doll*.

When not writing fiction, Vica runs communications for DataArt, a global technology company. Previously, she was a magazine editor, sports marketing director, multimedia producer, TV reporter, art publicist, and CEO of her own multimedia firm. She launched a New Media course at Hunter College (CUNY), now Integrated Media Arts MFA program, and later taught Public Relations there. Vica holds a Master's degree from the Interactive Telecommunications Program (ITP) at NYU's Tisch School of the Arts. She is an excellent swimmer, a beginner paraglider, and has synesthesia (as Nabokov did).

Vica lives on the Upper West Side with her husband and two daughters.

CPSIA information can be obtained at www.ICGtesting.com
Printed in the USA
LVOW07s1338191014

409484LV00001B/114/P